THE
LAST DAY
FOR
ROB RHINO

KATHLEEN O'DONNELL

 **ITALICS**

ITALICS PUBLISHING

$\prod$ **ITALICS**

Italics Publishing Inc.
Cover and interior design by Sam Roman
Editor: Joni Wilson
ISBN: 1-945302-29-1
ISBN-13: 978-1-945302-29-9

For my husband, Ed—my one reader.
Our kids, and sons-in-law, whom I love—Daniel,
Kayla, Che Sr., Kristen, Paul and Kenneth.
And, my mom, Pat Edwards—who
made sure I loved to read.

ACKNOWLEDGMENTS

Thank you to all the good people at Italics Publishing. Particularly Alex Roman for giving this novel new life. My undying gratitude to Marsha Bailey, who thought I could do it. Robin Winter, who taught me to move the furniture. Doctor Elizabeth Downing for all the medical instruction. Those early readers who cheered me along—Marybeth Carty, Lisa Rivas, and Angel Cottrell, and my friend Ray Barnds, who I miss, and who would have loved this book.

"I bought you the hat because you're scary bald."

Claire held the phone away from her ear, nostrils flaring. "I wouldn't wear a hat if Philip Treacy sailed it over himself on the *QE2*." She strolled the gateway to watch the planes take off through the windows. Her reflection in the glass mirrored back, her head shiny, embryonic.

Her stepdaughter let out a puff of breath. "Claire, you know how much his hats cost. It's just lying here on the floor."

"I don't give a flying—" Claire caught herself, counted to five. Annabelle meant well. "I don't do hats. I do bald. It is what it is."

"Listen, why don't you take a vacation?" The wheedling commenced. "Instead of going wherever, to do whatever, you could go to that place I told you about in Hawaii." Annabelle spoke in run-ons. "They have a state-of-the-art meditation center."

A woman wearing sweats gawked going by, smiling, nodding. Claire's condition elicited the sympathy of strangers. Maybe it was terminal. Whatever it was it looked bad.

"That place where I can sit around all day touching myself?"

"You can get *in touch* with yourself, Claire."

"I'm halfway to Pennsylvania where I want to go." Claire's free hand pushed against the window. "Me and my bald head." Airport foot traffic hurried behind her in both directions.

"Well, you look like crap. Please reconsider Hawaii. It's a luxurious place, the—"

"The ashram?"

"It's not an ashram. It's a—"

"Loony bin?" A harried traveler knocked her purse sitting by her feet. The pill bottles at the bottom rolled and shook, cha, cha, cha, a druggist's maraca.

"It's a retreat center. Andrew sent Meg there for her birthday. He said she loved it."

"Um-hum."

"Are you listening?"

Claire suffered in silence as loud as she could.

Annabelle tried a different way. "I'm worried about you. Jordan is too. Dad—"

Claire's sudden tears annoyed her. She stabbed her phone off with one rigid finger, rammed it into her purse. Enough of that nonsense. You can cry yourself a river, but you can't cry your hair back, or your life the way you wanted it.

****

Claire stared at the homeless looking guy sleeping on the airport floor and brushed the tears from her lashless eyes.

She looked around. There were serious looking men in expensive suits waiting for their flights. Most poking at their iPhones. Liam used to think every man who crossed her path wanted to sleep with her. Now if they saw her at all she repulsed them. Claire had been a beauty until she wasn't. An *emerald-eyed, fair-haired princess,* her dad used to say. *A long, tall, drink of water.* Before she'd been stared at, smiled on, envied. Now she was just stared at. Sometimes laughed or pointed at and almost always pitied.

The wreck on the floor moved. Propped up on his scaly elbows, nodding off, his mouth open, eyes closed. Even in his unwashed state he looked familiar. Like someone who used to be famous. Claire scanned the crowded O'Hare terminal but didn't notice anyone else looking at him. Maybe she was wrong. Maybe he was just another loser. She looked at her Rolex and wondered how late the flight was going to be. She couldn't remember now what the voice said on the announcement. Between the noise and the sedatives it was hard to keep up.

When she walked back to her gate the boarding had already started. She hadn't heard the announcement. Again. The man lying on the ground was gone. Maybe security'd shooed him away. She noted her seat number and got in line. Sweat broke out over her upper lip. Sweating was a problem with no hair. An added humiliation. She hoped they didn't dilly-dally too long with the drinks on the plane. Thank God for the three-hour jump in time going east.

She boarded then hunted for her seat—8B. She really needed to get some glasses. The plane was a small commuter with three seats across, a single on one side of the aisle, a double on the other. Claire found aisle 8 and was about to sit in her seat, one of the doubles, on the aisle, when she saw him.

The dirty hobo from the airport slumped in the window seat, 8C. Right next to her.

He sprawled out over both seats, looking fatter up close, and older, late sixties at least, despite the desperate dye job and combover. A bushy moustache like a squirrel's ass wasn't big enough to cover his pock-marked face. His gut hung over his thighs. He looked either asleep or passed out. He reeked.

"This is a mistake." Claire stopped, twisted around in search of a flight attendant. She couldn't see one. The teeming line of travelers behind her tried to keep her going. "This can't be right. I can't possibly sit here," she said like an Astor in steerage on the *Titanic*.

The Asian man behind her smiled, moved his head up and down.

She was about to indulge in a hurricane force panic attack when she heard, "This is a full flight. Please find your seats. Make sure your carry-ons are stored below your seat or in the upper bins."

Claire swung her Louis Vuitton bag into her seat hitting the filthy hobo's fat leg hard. He jiggled up with a snort and scooted over to his side. She heaved her matching carry-on into the overhead bin, sat down, dug a little blue pill out of her bag then swallowed it dry. She made a big show of settling into her seat so she could turn her head to see what he was doing without seeming obvious. He leaned against the window, eyes closed, mouth open. She could hear him snoring.

Claire stuffed her bag under the seat in front of her then fastened her seat belt with a click. When he opened his milky blue-gray eyes he looked at her with eyelids that appeared too heavy for him. All of a sudden he had the hearing of a dog. One side of his mouth lifted in a lopsided half smile. He leaned forward to make sure his ragged backpack was still there, fiddled with the seat-back pocket, readjusted his seatbelt. Satisfied that all was as it should be in his area, he gave Claire another look, one that seemed to urge her to give hers another check just to be safe. She did. In seconds he slept again.

It occurred to Claire her unwanted traveling companion hadn't noticed he sat next to a hairless woman. He didn't look her up and down and then quickly look away like most people. Nor did he insist on politically correct earnestness, meaningful, direct eye contact. Her grubby neighbor seemed to care only that seat trays were upright, all electronic devices were turned off, and appropriately stored until takeoff. Claire shook her bald head. Whatever drugs he was taking she had to get some.

The plane was almost full. Claire looked up to see a man about her age. One of the impatient ones in a pricey suit in the aisle next to her seat. Staring. *Oh no.* She could feel the color begin to climb up her neck.

"Hey, aren't you that guy?" the man in the suit said.

Claire exhaled. She turned to her right, startled.

"Yeah, you're the guy from that reality show, aren't you?" The suit wasn't budging without an answer.

"Uh-huh... yeah, I'm him." Claire's seatmate slurred, barely stringing the words together. His double chins fell forward on his chest.

"Rob," the suit said.

"Yeah, Rob."

The flight attendant came up behind the man prodding him forward. "I knew it," he muttered before moving toward his seat.

That's where she'd seen him. What'd he say his name was again? She turned toward him. Asleep again. "Hey," she elbowed him. "I thought you looked familiar. You were in a reality show. What else would I have seen you in?" She hardly ever watched reality television—at least not on purpose.

He eyed her Rolex and ten-carat diamond ring. "Nothing."

"I thought you were someone famous when I saw you in the airport." She knew she was right. She almost always was. "What else are you famous for?"

His head swiveled toward her, jowls sagging.

"My cock," he said. "I have a thirteen-inch cock."

CHAPTER

TWO

They stared at each other. She lifted her nonexistent brows to meet her nonexistent hair line. For what seemed like an eternity visions of fat pasty men, hideously endowed, traumatized her. She cleared her throat and scratched her chin.

A grin split his face as if carved by a machete-wielding lunatic. He was missing a front tooth. He leaned toward her lisping, "Baby, I'm a porn star."

****

"Would you care for a cock—?"

"No." Claire recoiled, a vampire rejecting a cross.

"—a cocktail?" the flight attendant finished.

"Yes. Absolutely yes. A vodka tonic please." Claire wiped her sweating upper lip with a wadded tissue. The porn star snored lightly again mouth hanging open.

She swallowed a mouthful of vodka and sat back in her seat. How could he be asleep already? There'd been no more inflight confessions from her pornographic neighbor. Just minutes ago he'd been like a monkey diving for lice on the scalp of his mate. Now he pounced on his backpack, dug out his mail, a pair of glasses.

"SoCal Gas," he said to himself, peeling open the envelope. With one cloudy eye he snuck up on the innards, tried to see what it said without taking anything out. "Highway robbery." He set it aside. "Verizon." Same routine. Picked up another envelope. This one yellow, heavily scented, definitely feminine. "Ohhh... interesting." He kept talking to his pile of mail. He took that fragrant lucky winner out of the envelope, looked down the slope of his bulbous nose and read. Every few seconds he'd hoot, smack the tray. Loud.

"That's what I'm talkin' about." He'd picked at his remaining front teeth with the corner of the yellow envelope. "Tsssst, tsssst." Every few seconds he'd made weird gyrations with his mouth and tongue. Some kind of turbo teeth cleaning.

Claire moved to the opposite side of her seat as far as she could go without falling into the aisle. Every time he opened his mouth her butt sucked up more of the seat cushion. After he regaled her with his genital dimensions he paid no more attention. No further information was forthcoming. Nor had he peeked at her or her hairless head. He wasn't interested in her story. She was dying to know his. She'd tried to see the name on his mail, but between her bad eyes and the pill/cocktail combo, no dice. Not without getting into his lap. Not going there for God's sake.

Without moving her head she looked downward and sideways—at his crotch. She clamped her eyes shut. She'd read once that the Elephant Man had a huge penis. The final, cosmic cruelty. She wondered how many times he'd gotten laid. Like zero probably. The problem was he'd been poor. If the Elephant Man had been rich he'd have been called distinguished. A curved spine and a skull divided in triplicate would have been all the rage. No such thing as a rich man too ugly to get a woman.

She hadn't worried about Liam's looks or his money. There was truth in that old saying: you could just as easily marry a rich man as a poor one. Not that it mattered. She'd have married Liam even if he'd been poor. Of course she would have. Definitely.

Claire grabbed for her bag and started digging for her pills flinging whatever-the-hell out the top. Why was it so hard to find the damn pills? There was a whole bottle from Doctor Freidman, Doctor Edgemont, Doctor Zucker.

Plus the one she got online. Not to mention one from her gardener's roommate, Guillermo, from Mexico City. In case of an emergency. She unfastened her seatbelt, leaned too far out of her seat. She caught herself, felt her stomach rise to the top of her throat. Her hands and feet tingled, went numb. Her skin felt pinpricked, icy. The sweat dripped.

"You're cool, you're cool." The porn star steadied her with his dirty hand. "Your purse exploded." He held up a pen, her cell phone, a tampon with the wrapper torn half off.

"I'm... I'm not... I'm not feeling well." Claire swallowed the sourness in her mouth, yanked the loot out of his grimy hands.

"You need crackers. They help with the puking." He held up his hand to get the flight attendant's attention.

"I don't have cancer. No chemotherapy," Claire croaked out. Her breath came too fast, too shallow.

"Uh, yeah. I figured," he said. "Too bad."

The flight attendant came, rustled up some crackers and a barf bag. By the time she made the necessary inquiries about whether or not Claire needed assistance the porn star was passed out again. After several minutes of breathing in and out of the paper bag Claire stopped feeling like she'd die. She took a pill, bunched up the bag and the empty cracker wrapper in her hand, mopped her still sweating brow and leaned back in her seat.

I figured? Too bad? What did he mean *he figured?* How dare he? He couldn't figure the first thing about her. What's too bad? Too bad she didn't have cancer? Asshole.

He hadn't asked her a single question. There'd been no conversation. He was too stoned for one thing. Lowlife crackhead. This was a commuter flight or she'd be in first class and he... he wouldn't.

Claire poo-pooed the flight attendant's over-solicitous ministrations. "I'm fine, I said." Was the woman deaf? She kept hovering.

"I think these are yours?"

The flight attendant with too much makeup on held out a wrinkled stepped-on piece of paper and a lipstick. She peered at the Wikipedia printout.

"Your info on, um, *exhumation*? And a lipstick." She turned the sleek black tube over. "Chanel. You must've dropped them or something."

She frowned at Claire's bag, sticking out too far in the aisle, then pushed it back with her airline-approved navy pump.

Claire mumbled a snotty thank you to Nosy Nellie Stewardess while she pulled her bag back out again, returned her belongings to it, and closed its clasp with a firm clack. She shot another peek at the slumbering bad omen sitting next to her. Maybe he was a sign from the gods who'd already proved to have a piss poor sense of humor. Perhaps she should go back home. She pressed her palm to her sticky naked scalp. *Not a chance.*

The fasten seat belt overhead lights went on while they prepared to land. Claire refused to look to her right. Under normal circumstances she'd have thanked him for his chivalry. But he was *not* normal. He was a Neanderthal not worthy of even the minimal social graces. The plane hit the runway with a screech and a hop. He made no effort to speak to her.

Claire's hearing improved when a velvet voice from the front of the aircraft gave them permission to disembark. She grabbed her bag, tried to race out of her seat. But her Courtney Love slosh through the friendly skies made her exit less than dignified. *Shit.* She stopped, took a few wobbly steps back, then shoved the other passengers out of her way.

From the overhead she grabbed the carry-on she'd left behind in her haste.

The one with Liam in it.

CHAPTER

THREE

S he was such a bad solo traveler. Liam always got their luggage. Stop Claire. Liam wasn't getting the luggage. Liam is in the luggage.

After a staggered stop in the ladies' room where her crackers, vodka, and a pill or two made a violent comeback, she floated down the escalator to baggage claim pulling her carry-on behind her, then squinted to find her flight number above the carousels.

The bags dropped. Claire nosed around while she waited for her other bag to make its way out of the bowels of the plane. She searched for the porn star hoping not to find him. Maybe he'd overdosed between the plane and baggage claim. Doubtful he'd have bags. He'd been wearing the same clothes for weeks by the smell of him. He wouldn't need a suitcase since he never bathed or changed his clothes. She wouldn't see him again if there was any justice. She'd suffered enough.

Grateful to see her luggage come whooshing down the chute she chucked it off the carousel, pulled both Louis bags behind her, and went in search of the rental car dealer. She took one more glance around. No sign of him.

Things were looking up.

****

The clerk at E-Z 4U Luxury Rentals (where had her travel agent found this place?) looked up, saw her, looked down again and said to the counter, "Can I help you?"

Claire stood in front of him for a few seconds, waited for him to come back up. From the top of his platinum head with its pitch-black roots she guessed he was young. She tapped him on the shoulder.

"I'm up here. You won't turn to stone."

He looked up beet faced. "I'm sorry. Really. I'm... I'm new."

Claire cocked her bare head to one side sizing him up. "It's fine. You're not the first. I'm not exactly Halle Berry."

"Oh God lady. I'm sorry. Really. I—" he squirmed, his eyes met hers.

"I know you are. You and everybody else. Most people want to look away," Claire said. "I feel the same way when I see that ring in your lip. Can we get on with it?"

His hand went to his pierced mouth. "Yes," he said his voice a cross between a croak and a squeak.

Claire chuckled to herself while she filled out the necessary paperwork. He fished out a set of keys.

"Will anyone else drive the car?" He cleared his throat.

"No. I do know how to drive," Claire said. Whatever high she'd had before left after her purge had worn off. It did that quicker now anyway. A lot quicker.

"Standard question. Sorry." Rental car boy started sweating too.

He made her tense. Between his unintentional condescension, and the map she was trying to read, it was touch and go. She wanted to take another pill. She spread the map out on the counter.

"The damn thing might as well be upside down." Claire poked at the map, pushing it away from her.

"It is." Boy turned it right side up.

Claire stared. "What's the difference?"

Reading maps was another thing Liam had always done. Claire cut to the chase and asked the clerk how to get to the highway she needed. He wrote it out for her on the back of her receipt trying to make up for his earlier lapse with superior customer service.

He insisted on carrying her bags to her car, made like he'd take her arm but changed his mind. His young brow caved in. He looked worried she was ill, about to keel over. Or more likely that she'd complain about him to someone several rungs above him.

"Is there anything else you need?"

"No, really. I'm good. But thank you."

It was too complicated to explain. She'd been a little rough on him earlier so she tried to be gracious. He was only a kid. She knew she could have milked it, gotten something for nothing. Maybe an upgrade or a gift certificate. That got old. Plus she couldn't think of anything she wanted. A GPS would make things worse. She had one in her own car. Didn't know how to turn it on.

When they stopped in front of the nondescript sedan she'd been assigned the clerk put her bags in the trunk. It wasn't the Mercedes she was used to, but it would do. She had a two-hour drive ahead of her. Small towns were always two hours from anywhere.

After one U-turn, a stop for directions at one rest area, and two gas stations, Claire made it to the correct route. Twenty or so miles farther, another little blue booster, she felt less anxious, able to take notice of the Pennsylvania scenery. Beautiful in its own quaint way. So different than the cosmopolitan West Coast beach town that she was used to. Soon she was in the middle of nowhere—wet rocky terrain that looked straight out of *Deliverance*. She hoped to Christ she didn't have car trouble. All she'd need was to get strapped to a tree and forced to squeal like a pig while some inbred hillbilly plucked the banjo in the background.

Alarm gripped her until houses and buildings appeared on the landscape again. She was halfway through the drive, the sky a melting sherbet of pinks and oranges. She'd hoped to beat sundown to her hotel, but it'd be close. She passed a sign that read Fasten Your Seat Belt for the Next Million Miles. She'd been so distracted calculating just how many states that would cover she almost missed the eight-foot tall chicken. She whipped her head around for a better look. Was that papier-mâché? She turned back around just in time to see the two, six-foot dinosaurs. Definitely papier-mâché. She whizzed passed a sign imploring her to Let Jesus Save Your Soul, posted next to Minnie's—Best Strippers in Town conveniently located next to the Son-shine Assembly of God, to the left of Paula's Porn Palace, adjacent to Ma and Pa Kettle's Kristian Kiddie Day Care—"We don't spare the rod or spoil the child."

For the next thirty miles Claire drove the pathway to porn or the highway to heaven—depending on your point of view. She could get massaged at Hal's Asian Hussy's or prayed over by Susannah's Saints. Buy a bucket of wings and a lap dance at Mustang Sally's or join the We Pray for Prisoners prayer group. New Testament Studies or Blow Jobs. Name your perversion or your parish. It was hers for the picking. Claire thought her head would spin off her neck from trying to look at both sides of the road at once. She drove much slower than the rest of the traffic, almost got rear-ended. Twice she about ran into the guard rail.

Her head was mid-spin when she saw him.

She saw the bright green rubber clogs first. He hitchhiked—thumb out. Between the pill, her eyes, the sun, her astonishment, she almost hit him. She slammed on the brakes with both feet. With agility surprising for a fat man he leapt out of the way. Her tires pummeled the gravel shoulder, left a tornado of dust and rock in their wake. Claire came to a violent sloppy stop. Her bald head jerked forward and back with a snap. It took a full ten seconds for her to remember where she was or what she was doing. The dirt settled around her car like volcanic ash.

Had she hit him? Was he dead? She threw open the car door and got out. Cars were whipping past her like nothing happened. He still stood. She'd been rubber-necking not traveling anywhere near the speed limit.

"Are you all right?" I... I... the sun. I couldn't... are you hurt?" Claire's chest felt tight.

The porn star ambled over like he didn't have a care in the world. They met halfway. He took both her arms in his hands. She towered at least a head taller. He gently moved her farther away from the busy highway.

"It's cool, it's cool. I'm okay. You missed me. No worries lady." He shrugged, pulled at his shaggy moustache.

Claire could feel the tears threaten. Her head pound. Why did she have to cry in front of this jackass? She was glad she hadn't run him over even though he was a pig. But now she wanted him to go away. What was he doing so close to a busy road anyway? If he wasn't so drugged up he'd probably have better judgment.

"What were you thinking?" Claire paced. "What idiot hitchhikes this day and age?"

"Do it all the time." Porn star stood his ground on the side of the road. "Never had a problem 'til you."

"I don't believe that for a second. You almost killed both of—"

"No, *you* almost killed both of us." He'd turned on his rubber heel and headed toward her still smoking rental. "But you can make it up to me."

Claire scrambled behind him. What'd he just say? Make it up to him? He should beg forgiveness.

"You can you give me a ride." He walked over, opened the passenger side door. "I've been thumbin' it the whole way. I'm almost there. About ten more miles up the road." He got in, shut the door behind him.

She jerked the driver's side door open, bellowed. "What are you doing?"

"Putting my seat belt on. It's the law."

"You think I'm taking you somewhere?"

"You did almost run me over. I think it's the least you can do."

Was he batting his eyelashes?

She slammed the door shut, took a few deep breaths outside as the traffic whizzed by. Now what? What were her options? She could say no and make him get out of the car. He was obviously a drug addict although he seemed more alert than on the plane. Probably near-death experiences did that to a person. Near death. Right. She'd almost killed him. Claire put her hand on her smooth head and rubbed it back and forth. She should loosen up and take the porn star where he needed to go.

What's the big deal?

She was driving anyway. It'd take all her good breeding. Well, she didn't have good breeding. But he didn't know that. She closed her eyes, thought of him carefully nudging her away from the oncoming cars, like he didn't want her to get hurt, and got back in the car.

"Where are you going?" She turned the key and started the engine.

"Alex's Adult World Gift Emporium and Warehouse. Keep going straight. Can't miss it." He leaned forward, adjusted his backpack, adjusted it some more. Still not satisfied he shifted it forward, then backward, then sideways. Claire hit the gas, pulled out onto the highway, and fantasized about shoving him out of the moving car.

Where was a banjo plucking inbred hillbilly when she needed one?

❖

C laire wasn't on the road five minutes when the snoring
started. His mouth hung open like a sea bass on a boat
deck, dead to the world. It was all she could do to not cram
whatever she could get her hands on down his throat to see
if he'd notice. Then she'd have to touch him. She'd almost
forgotten about his... appendage... and he stank. She cracked
her window and wondered why she'd decided to do the right
thing when the wrong thing was acceptable. Her purse sat in
the console between them. She glanced at it now and again,
daydreamed about the pills in it.

She should be afraid, driving alone in the middle of
Sodom and Gomorrah with some drugged-out sex fiend
she didn't know, but she wasn't afraid. Disgusted? Check.
Appalled? Check. Curious? Check. But afraid? No. She thought
of Annabelle who'd just turned twenty. If she'd embarked on
something this reckless it'd terrify Claire. Yet there Claire was
barreling down the highway with... good God... she knew
his dick size but didn't know his name. No clue. Couldn't
remember what she'd heard the suit say on the plane.

"Hey, wake up. Wake up."

Claire waited a few seconds for him to respond. Nothing.
She'd have to shake him. She reached over and shoved him.
None too gently.

"Wake up."

"Wha... huh... whassup?" he grunted and sat up.

"Don't you talk?" Claire said. "I assume you can stay
awake long enough for a five-minute conversation. If I have

to drive you, you have to talk. What are you doing in the middle of nowhere?"

"Oh. Yeah, well, that's cool. A conversation." He sat up straighter, smoothed his straggly hair. "Shit. Well, I'm here for a signing. I do those all over. My DVDs, old videos and stuff," he opened his eyes wide, stretched out his squat legs.

"Really? All over? All over where?" Claire said.

"The world," he yawned.

Claire veered to the left then jerked the wheel back to the right, hard. "The world? Plus the reality show? Are you kidding?"

"Um, no. And some other stuff."

"But that must be quite lucrative. I mean—"

"Yeah. Quite." He whistled through the hole where his missing tooth should've been. "Are you hot for my money?"

Claire flushed. "You're disgusting, you know that? As if I'd be interested in—"

"Whoa. There's my stop." He gestured to the right.

Claire let up on the gas and went farther up the road where she could flip a U. In her rearview mirror she saw the giant, flashing neon sign for *Alex's*. In the dusk, the sky's pinks and oranges dripped and faded to grays. Claire stopped in front. Seemed like quite the place. A warehouse full of blow-up dolls and movies starring men like *him* with their clothes off. The parking lot was half full, cars toward the front, semis lined up in the rear.

He grabbed his backpack and opened the passenger door. "Thanks for the ride lady."

"Wait—" Claire was about to ask his name when she noticed a church across the highway. "What a freaky place," she pointed. "The strip joints, massage parlors, next to all the churches."

The porn star laughed. "Yeah, it's a quirky town."

"Guess it comes in handy."

"Handy?"

"The churches."

"For what?"

"You can commit all the sins you want then confess."

The porn star's face rearranged itself, his mouth grim. "I'm not much for confession," he said.

"Just the sinning," she shot back.

He unlatched his seatbelt, let it snap into its slot up near the window.

I didn't catch your name," she said switching gears, filling silence.

He pointed up at the marquee with a short fat finger. "There it is. In lights."

Claire peered out the window. In bright red flashing lights, she read—The Last Day for Rob Rhino—her lashless lids keeping time with the blinking bulbs. "Didn't you just get here? Are you only here for one day?"

"Yes and no. If people think it's my last day then Alex does better business. Plus it's a truck route. Most guys are just passing through so they don't know any better. It's an old trick."

"Oh. Clever." Claire laughed out loud. "I think you're late. Day's over."

"It starts tomorrow. I like to get the lay of the land first. Guess I don't really need to. I've been here lots of times before. I'll be here for the next few weekends." He looked out over the giant, tin building with the sun setting behind it. "Alex is cool. We go way back."

"Rob Rhino huh? Did you make that up?"

"Of course." He laughed too, his features softened. "What about you? What are you doing here? You don't blend, if you know what I mean."

She wanted to say *what's it to you* but couldn't. He'd been amenable to her questions. Her eyes skittered across the highway, taking in the eight-foot cross.

"Getting rid of some deadweight."

Rob tilted his head to the side, pondering her. "You're a weird one." His fat jowls wobbled.

A stinging insult nearly flew off her tongue when he got out of the car shaking his big head with a chuckle. "Well, thanks again. Drive careful."

"I am careful. It's the brainless pedestrians." He shut the car door. She started to pull away when he knocked on the window. She rolled her eyes up and the glass down. He leaned into the car.

"Hey, I didn't catch *your* name," he said.

"It's Claire. Claire Corrigan."

"Ah. Well," he nodded, his heavy jowls wagging. "Claire Corrigan, why are you bald?"

No one ever came right out, asked her directly. She answered, "My husband died unexpectedly. Then my hair fell out. It hasn't grown back, probably won't. It's been a year." She ran her hand over the top of her scalp. "Not even stubble."

His already hazy eyes darkened, his bushy too-black brows knit together. He pursed and unpursed his lips. "Bummer. No wonder." He shook his head.

"No wonder? No wonder what?"

"You're an addict."

C laire drove so fast she made the bat out of hell look like the little old lady from Pasadena. Rob Rhino. Of course he'd think everyone lived like him—an addict. Those types always did. A deviant scumbag of the lowest order. Her breath came so quick she felt lightheaded.

Claire'd had a full body blowout. She'd rolled up the window so fast the porn pig had to jump backward, snatch his hands away. Her Gucci loafer hammered the gas pedal and peeled out onto the highway, leaving him standing in the gravel, in front of his name in sparkly neon, like when they'd started, lapping up her dirt on the side of the road.

Where the hell was the hotel for Chrissake? She'd been in town for several minutes. The hotel was supposed to be right where she couldn't miss it. It was dark. Claire was screwed. The Days Inn... the Days Inn... where was it for the love of God? Shit. Finally. The bright yellow sign welcomed her like a beacon at the entrance to the pearly gates. She'd never been so glad to see such a crap hotel.

She was going too fast when she turned into the hotel's driveway then bottomed out with a thump and a scrape. Perfect. That's all she needed, damage to the rental car. She idled by the lobby door in a huff. What was the hold up? Then she laughed—a loud crackle from the back of her throat— what an idiot. There's no valet. Where did she think she was? The Ritz? She grabbed her purse, turned off the car, and headed for the front desk.

****

Still fuming Claire flopped backward on the king-size bed covered with a loud Hawaiian floral bedspread. She landed on her back and kept going sideways, the surface was so slippery. She stopped herself at the edge before she pitched off the side. The room reeked of stale cigarette smoke and French fries. She'd have a word with the travel agent when she got home. She couldn't believe this fleabag. The nicest place in town? *He* must be an addict. Then she remembered the eight-foot papier mâché chicken and Paula's Porn Palace.

Claire leaned over the side of the bed and groped for her purse on the floor. With one arm she dug around 'til she came up with a pill bottle, twisted off the cap, and knocked it back 'til a couple hit her tongue. Thank God. She pulled her out cell phone. Dead like dirt. It was still turned off. She pressed it on, no good. Still dead. She'd forgotten to charge it—again. She sat up, reached for the phone on the nightstand, dialed out.

"Hello? Jordan? It's Mom." Jordan, on the back end of twenty-nine and still single. He lived in San Francisco and wrote screenplays no one bought. The child of her youth. They'd almost grown up together.

"No, it's Steven." Steven was one of Jordan's roommates. He had two: Steven and Maura.

"Isn't this Jordan's cell phone?" Steven bugged the shit out of Claire. He rubbed her the wrong way. For one thing, he always answered Jordan's cell phone.

"Umm... yes. Nice talking to you. I'll get Jordan."

Claire wondered why Maura hadn't answered. Maura and Jordan made such a great couple. The last thing they needed was Steven—my middle name is third wheel—Steven. Claire waited. Her skin felt loose around the edges. She started to unwind. Thank you, Doctor Edgemont.

"Mom?" Finally, Jordan.

"Jordan? Do me a favor."

"Where are you?" Jordan said.

"Pennsylvania. Remember?"

"I thought you might've come to your senses."

"No, but thanks for your support."

"I'm just sayin'. Has Liam's mother rolled out the welcome mat for you?"

"All in due time."

"I thought so. Come home."

"I didn't call to get harassed. Google someone for me."

"Huh? Now?"

"Yes. I don't have access. And you're better at this stuff."

"Okay. Go."

"You're fast. Rob Rhino."

The cell went silent.

"Jordan, are you still there?" Claire thought the call dropped.

"Rob Rhino, the old porn star, Rob Rhino?" Jordan said.

"That's him. How do you know who he is?

"Because I don't live under a rock? What's going on? Never mind. Don't tell me. Whatever it is, it needs to stop." Jordan's voice went up three octaves.

"Don't be ridiculous. I sat by him on the plane. He's a disgusting crackhead asshole. I'm just curious."

"Well, he starred on that reality show, reality *shows*, I should say. He's had a revival of sorts. He's famous because of his... well... because of his—"

"His giant penis."

"Thank you for that. I'll make an appointment with my therapist as soon as we hang up."

"Are you going to look him up or not?"

"Wow. Lots of info. He's almost seventy. Eww. Born in Minneapolis. Real name: Raymond Horowitz. So he's probably Jewish. The mighty sword is circumsi—never mind. Tried to make it in legit film but couldn't. Big surprise. Started making porn well before disco died. There's lots of pictures of him at movie premieres—regular movies—not just skinflicks." Claire could hear Jordan clicking his tongue against the roof of his mouth.

"Here he is at the Mansion with Hef and some Playmates. Nice combover. He must dye it himself."

"He does," Claire said. "Moustache too. Hideous."

"Good to know," Jordan went on, "He hasn't made porn since the eighties, but he travels the world making personal appearances. The reality shows made him a hit. He's made several. There was that one with the evangelist's wife last year."

"He told me he made appearances all over the world, but I didn't believe it."

"You talked to him? What? Are you two dating?"

"Not funny. If he's so popular he must have money."

"I assume."

"He shouldn't need to hitchhike. He could wear better clothes. Not to mention take a bath once in a while. The man looks homeless."

"Hitchhike? How do you know about his hitchhiking? For Chrissake, Mother, don't tell me—"

"Oh, what's the big deal? I drove him a few miles. So what?"

"So what? *So what?* You're picking up porn star stoners in the middle of God knows where, alone, no telling—"

"I didn't *pick him up*. He just got in. I almost hit him and—"

"You almost hit him?" Jordan was close to yelling, "With the car?"

"That's what I drove, yes."

Claire imagined Jordan standing up behind his artsy-fartsy industrial desk, red in the face, pacing back and forth his black curls ping-ponging.

"You almost ran down a porn star, how fast were—"

"It's not as bad as it sounds, calm down. I was trying to get a better look at the chicken and the dinosaur and he—"

"Mother, what on earth? No, *where* on earth is this place?

"Yeah, well good question."

"You aren't hurt, are you?"

"No. No one was hurt." Claire yawned loud. "It's all good."

"Sounds like you're right on top of it."

"I usually am."

"Mother, come home. You're not going to find what you're looking for there."

"What do you think I'm looking for Jordan?"

"Liam. Alive." Jordan the know-it-all.

"You know I have—"

"Hey, he's got a wife."

"Huh? Who's got a wife?" Claire said relieved at the subject switch.

"Your new boyfriend, Rob Rhino."

"What? No way."

"Oh wait. He *had* a wife. Gloria. They were only married three years from what it says here, in the seventies."

"Three years of hell. I'm sure she came to her senses."

"Oh well, not exactly." Jordan clucked his tongue some more. "She died."

"Died?" Claire perked up as much as she could. "How'd she die?"

Jordan went silent while he scanned for information. "Doesn't say."

"That's odd."

Jordan sniffed. "He probably killed her."

****

She fell back on the bed, woozy. Jordan was Claire's son from her first marriage. Annabelle was Liam's daughter from his. She was only eight years old when Claire and Liam married. Jordan, nearly grown by then, was sauerkraut to Annabelle's cotton candy. When Claire went bald, Annabelle cried every time she saw her for the first six months.

"That's quite a cue ball you've got going on there, Mother," Jordan said when he saw her. Annabelle didn't speak to him for three months after that.

"Bald women can be beautiful," Steven said. He'd come with Jordan. To rub Claire the wrong way. Why Maura wasn't there, Claire couldn't remember.

Claire floated in and out of consciousness. She kicked off her suede driving loafers, unzipped her jeans. Her last thoughts before going under were of Rob Rhino, his dead wife. Imagine that dolt thought she was an addict. She should've told Jordan what he'd said. He would've laughed and laughed.

CHAPTER

SIX

Claire wolfed down a plate of eggs and bacon. The waitress refilled her coffee cup for the third time and stared. Claire concentrated on her breakfast, threw back some chemical comfort with a swallow of orange juice.

There'd been no point looking for a room service menu. Not in that dump of a hotel. No hotel coffee shop either. She'd walked two blocks down the street to the nearest greasy spoon that, by all accounts, did a brisk morning business. Most of the other diners looked her way. Some were subtle, some weren't. A few pointed. They had their nerve in this hellhole. Claire doubted they'd know normal if it bit 'em in their papier-mâchéd asses.

She felt the familiar lull. Her shoulders slumped a bit. She sipped her coffee while flipping through the *Penny Saver* someone left in her booth. She snickered when she saw a half-page ad for The Hair System—Guaranteed Results or Your Money Back. When Claire lost her hair she'd been desperate for a cure. She'd spent thousands of dollars those first few months. Nothing. Not even a five o'clock shadow. Her doctor tried to tell her, but she wouldn't, *couldn't,* believe him.

"It's rare," he'd said (the doctor's way of throwing up his hands and backing away from the examination table). "But sometimes it doesn't grow back. Most often though your immune system is just waiting for a signal from you to start growing again."

"Really? And what signal would that be? I'm bald. I guess I thought that might be signal enough for Chrissake."

"None of those creams or potions works. So don't fall for any of those ads. Try to relax and lower your stress level. In the meantime here's a little something to keep the edge off." Doctor Freidman wrote her a prescription for Xanax and kept one eye on the door.

She'd gone for a second opinion.

"It happened to Princess Caroline of Monaco when *her* husband died suddenly," Doctor Edgemont had said as if that was comforting. As if she should expect something much worse than *this*, since she wasn't someone like *that*.

"No one is sure what causes it. A weakened immune system is the guess du jour. The shock of your husband's sudden death didn't help. After things calm down and you've had some time to get used to your new situation it will grow right back. Try not to stress out about it. Your anxiety isn't useful." He'd written out a prescription for Xanax plus refills.

Doctor Zucker had nothing new to add other than another Xanax prescription with a lot more refills.

Claire emptied her coffee up. That was forever ago. Forever or yesterday. She couldn't recall.

****

Moustache Rides Five Cents, his cap read.

Claire hoped the offender would notice her, do the usual stare and glare so she could air her disgust at his loathsome chapeau. Her eyes trailed from his brim down.

It was him.

"Claire Corrigan. As I live and breathe." Rob Rhino rambled over.

He'd cleaned up. His jeans looked washed. His hula girl and palm tree covered shirt as unpleasant as his hat, but it might've been new. Still with the green clogs.

Claire tried to shrink down in the booth, but it was too late. He slid in.

"What are you doing here?" Claire bared her teeth like a snarling dog.

Rob smiled, not the least bit self-conscious about his third world dentistry.

"Getting coffee. Don't worry, it's to go," he said.

"That's not what I meant. What are you doing here? In this place? Are you following me?"

"Ooh la la." He wriggled his bushy dyed brows. "Do you want me to be?"

She half stood. "Stop it. Answer me, before I—"

"Get a grip on your girdle. I come in here all the time. I stop here on my way—"

"Hey, Doc, here's your coffees. Black." The waitress handed him two Styrofoam cups in a cup holder.

"Doc? What the—"

"I'm the doctor of love," he cackled.

"Of all the stupid—" The overattentive waitress bearing the bill interrupted Claire's tirade. Was she fawning over him?

Rob handed her his platinum card. "This nice lady's breakfast is on me, Molly."

Claire didn't protest, too dumbfounded. Was this his attempt at an apology for his deplorable behavior outside Alex's warehouse? Well, she couldn't be bought. Not for a ten-dollar breakfast. A nice piece of jewelry maybe. Simpering Molly took his card toward the register.

"What are you doing here?" Rob Rhino said.

"I have business here." Claire scowled at the good doctor.

"In the diner?"

"No, you moron. I'm staying—" No way she'd tell him where. "I'm staying near here. I have family business in this godforsaken town. Not that it's any of your concern."

"You have family here?" Rob Rhino seemed concerned anyway.

"My husband does."

"Huh, whaddya know. My wife does too." A horn honked. Rob Rhino peered out the window. "My chauffeur's getting antsy." He signed his credit card receipt with pudgy fingers.

Claire glanced out at the ruby colored Corvette revving its engine in the parking lot. The blacked-out windows kept her from seeing the driver. The midlife crisis car crept forward while it idled. She could make out the personalized plates— FLESHHH. A question about Rob Rhino's wife teetered on her lips when he ducked out the diner door.

"Grace? It's Claire. I'm in town."

Claire called out on the hotel phone again. She'd passed out before remembering to plug in her cell phone the night before.

"Oh. I... er... hello. I didn't expect you so soon." Grace's voice shook, sounded old.

So soon? She and Liam were married more than ten years and she'd never met Grace. "I told you I'd call as soon as I got in. I'm in. I brought Liam. His ashes," Claire said.

Grace started sniveling. "Oh... oh my, okay, I—"

"Grace? Stop crying. Should we talk in person?"

Grace sniffled and blew her nose. "It doesn't matter. Whatever you want."

"I want you to give a shit."

"How can you talk to me that way? Of course I—"

Claire heard loud nose blowing, then nothing, except the sound of her whole plan going south. She tried to remember Lamaze breathing. "We talked about this already, before I left California. I want to inter Liam's ashes in the cemetery with his father. I'd like to have a memorial."

"I just don't know, I just don't—"

"What do you mean—you don't know?" Claire said. "What's not to know?"

Grace started whimpering. "Oh now you don't understand. It's just, well, I just don't know."

"You're right. I don't. Why don't you explain it to me?"

More sniffles. "Well... I... you... this goes back years."

"Let me help you Grace. In the ten years Liam and I were married you never set foot in our home or invited us to yours."

"Liam wouldn't have come if I'd invited him. You don't—"

"You didn't come to his funeral or send flowers."

"Liam didn't come to his father's funeral either."

"You never bothered to let us know he'd died. He had to hear it from our attorney who heard it from *his* mother."

"Liam's death devastated me." Grace turned on the blubbering and her convenient hearing. "I would've come, but I can't travel alone—"

"His brother or sister could've brought you. But they didn't come either."

"They didn't feel welcome. None of us—"

"You couldn't be bothered to pick up the phone and call. Not once in Liam's adult life. When he died I had to leave you a voicemail. You never called back. I brought your dead son to *you* and you're going to tell me *you don't know?*"

"Maybe we should—"

"I'm coming over in an hour. I have your address."

Claire slammed down the phone, grabbed her pills. She went to the bathroom for water, caught her reflection. Her scalp was so red it looked like the tip of a match. The second pill of the day began its dance through her bloodstream. Her breathing slowed, deepened.

She pulled her carry-on out of the closet and opened it. The mother lode. The box that held Liam's ashes was bigger than she'd expected, heavier. She didn't know what she expected. Everything about Liam's death was heavier than she thought it'd be. It was the first day of March when she got *the call*. She knew as soon as she'd said *hello* that something happened. The phone, the air, the voice at the other end. It all had an unbearable heaviness. Then there was her pain, her rage, her heart in her chest. It was all too heavy.

She hadn't expected to carry his ashes on the plane with her either.

"I don't think you can check Mr. Corrigan's ashes with your baggage," Steven had said. Fingernails on a chalkboard.

"How would you possibly know that?" Claire said.

"Mother, as hard as it might be for you to believe, other people experience death too," Jordan had said. "Steven lost someone he loved a few years ago."

Momentarily chastened, but not interested, Claire said "Well, I'll certainly check that out. Perhaps Maura knows for certain."

Steven was right for once. Dead people couldn't get checked with baggage. They had to go on the plane in a carry-on for whatever reason. She wondered how many dead people she'd traveled with in blissful ignorance. How many times had she shoved someone's granny out of the way because she took up too much space in the overhead?

Aha.

Claire snatched up the bottle of Absolut Mandarin she'd packed for whenever she might need a nip. Got to put it in the freezer. Probably have to settle for a fridge. After an annoying search turned major tantrum and an agitated call to the front desk, she had to concede. No refrigerator in Hades. A quick run down the walkway in both directions didn't turn up an ice machine. She stayed on the second floor. Maybe she'd find one downstairs. What a pain in her puckered ass. Have to deal with it later.

She lifted the box of Liam's remains out of her carry-on and put it on the bed. The big manila envelope she'd crammed in at the last minute caught her eye. Her heart stopped midbeat for a second. She snatched the envelope out, clutched it to her chest, and sat on the bed. It too was heavier than she remembered. It wasn't sealed shut, only closed with the metal clasp. She could easily undo it. No need. She already knew what was in it.

Holloway, Howard, and Lennox, LLC, would have to wait.

Time to get the cortege on the road. It was after eleven. She picked up the phone.

CHAPTER

EIGHT

S he drove toward the outskirts of town wishing she hadn't
slammed down the phone before asking Grace to confirm
directions to the cemetery. Claire told her she'd be late, that
was that. She veered past the Antique Barnyard, past the
bridge on the Underground Railroad where she turned right
at Bessie's Curl Up and Dye salon. She made another hard
right, meandered alongside the rolling lawns and imposing
brick buildings of the private university. So far so good. At a
distance the cemetery (among the many oddities of the place)
where they'd buried Liam's father Emmet loomed. If Claire
got her way, Liam's ashes would be interred there too.

She drove along the road on the outer rim of the
campus. When rows of headstones and monuments appeared
she knew she was getting close. A few crypts and mausoleums
with names engraved over their forbidding, elaborate stone
doorways. Names like Pembroke, Wallace, and Wilkes.

Floral arrangements in brilliant colors sprang up in and
around headstones of varying shades of gray, some ancient,
crumbly yet immaculate. Some shiny and new. Like everything
she'd seen since she'd driven onto the grounds they had a faux
antique pallor. She wouldn't be surprised to see a group of
Civil War widows, straight out of central casting, march up
over the rise singing hymns in honor of their fallen.

She steered through the wrought iron gates and got a
headlong view of the chapel and cemetery from all sides. She
knew if she rolled down the window she'd hear birds chirping.

Its pulse quick, so vibrant and alive for a place filled with the dead.

She parked the rental in front of the gray stone chapel. Once inside it felt cool and hollow, empty but for a few wooden benches. Her feet echoed, the leather soles of her shoes moved over the uneven slate floors with a soft tap. The stained-glass window loomed large over a small altar covered in a red velvet cloth at the back, Jesus on the Cross, loinclothed and martyred, eyes half closed. Must be a Catholic chapel. Only the Catholics keep Christ on the Cross. Clacking footsteps on the stone floors interrupted Claire's musings.

"Can I help you?" a tidy roly-poly woman in a polyester blue dress with short hair dyed to match said. She seemed startled. She looked at Claire's bald head and then the floor.

"I'd like to speak to someone about interment and memorial services at the cemetery." Claire held out her hand to the woman, "I'm Claire. Claire Corrigan."

"Oh well, Mrs. Corrigan. Is it Mrs.?"

"Yes," Claire said.

The woman grasped her hand with a warm tight clasp. "I'm Evelyn Wallace." Evelyn stopped looking at the floor. Instead she looked into Claire's eyes. Dead on. Anywhere but her head.

"You can call me Claire."

"Claire, you'll have to speak with the cemetery director, Mr. Lansing, about all of that. Are you alone? You're making these arrangements, er, um, in advance?

Alone? What was the old blue hair talking about? In advance? Oh dear. Evelyn thought she was dying. Claire burst out laughing. Evelyn jumped.

"Is something funny?" Evelyn said.

"Well, no. I mean yes. The arrangements aren't for me. They're for my husband. He died. I... I have this rare condition. I'm not ill." Claire usually didn't explain but Evelyn seemed so concerned.

"Good heavens. That's a relief. Oh I mean... it's... well, you poor dear. I'm so sorry. And you're so young." Evelyn stroked both her chins. "Oh mercy. I don't have good news either. I hate to be the one to tell you but our cemetery's full. At capacity I'm afraid."

Claire hadn't entertained that possibility.

"Full? Oh no."

"Indeed. It was half full when it opened centuries ago."

Claire couldn't believe her bad luck. She knew she'd waited too long, but centuries?

"You see there *is* another cemetery in town that's been here since the late seventeenth century, Creekside Cemetery. After the Civil War the board of trustees dedicated part of the university land for honoring the town's glorious dead."

Evelyn closed her eyes in tribute to their *glorious*.

She went on. "After the war many prominent interred citizens were moved here from Creekside. Took up half the real estate right away. Over the years the university bought adjacent parcels of land. In the eighties the board decided only trustees, their families, or major donors could be buried here since space was at a premium. Despite their cautionary measures it's full."

Evelyn fingered the sapphire and diamond brooch on the rolled collar of her dress. Claire, who carried a jeweler's loupe in her purse (just in case), could tell the stones were of good quality.

Claire sat and took off her jacket. How had Liam's father made the cut? He died about five years earlier. Claire realized she knew nothing about him.

"Oh goodness, I didn't even offer you a seat. Let me call Mr. Lansing, see if he has a moment. I'll be right back." Evelyn scuttled off toward the back of the chapel and disappeared.

Liam always said his family was jealous of his money because they didn't have any. So Emmet and Grace weren't major donors. If Emmet hadn't been a major donor could he have been on the university board? Not likely. Claire had no idea what Emmet had done for a living. Liam'd never said and Claire'd never asked. That seemed odd in hindsight. She had better things to do than figure out who did what in Liam's estranged family.

Evelyn clattered back. "Mr. Lansing's—"

"My father-in-law's buried here," Claire said. "Emmet Corrigan. Would you know if he'd been a trustee? He died about five years ago."

"Well, I can tell you every trustee name going back two hundred years." Evelyn's already ample chest puffed up. "He wasn't a trustee. I can tell you that. Perhaps a donor? Mr. Lansing will—" Evelyn no more than said his name when the chapel doors opened and Pinocchio come to life, but going bald, came bustling in.

"That was fast," Evelyn smiled.

Mr. Lansing's marionette legs made quick work of the space between the back of the chapel and where Claire sat.

"Claire, this is Joseph Lansing. I'll leave you two to get acquainted." And she did.

Joseph Lansing stuck his bony hand out. "Luckily I was on my way over here when Evelyn called me. I'm Joe. She told me you'd hoped to buy a plot here? Have a memorial service? Is it Kay?" Joe stared at her face like his life depended on it. Evelyn must've given him the heads-up. The bald heads-up.

"It's Claire. And yes, I'd hoped to inter my husband's ashes here. I don't think it's a plot I'd need. Perhaps a crypt. My father-in-law is buried here. I'd hoped they could be together. Guess it doesn't matter now," Claire said.

"Please do accept my condolences. I'm so sorry. Such a terrible time. Evelyn mentioned we're out of space?" Joe looked mournful, like a good funeral director should.

"Yes, she did. It never dawned on me that could happen. I should've called first."

Claire sighed. She crossed one leg over the other and dangled her cream and black ballet flat with the intertwined Cs at the end of her foot. She was just about to pick up her Burberry trench and bid her farewells when Joe intervened.

"It's such a gorgeous day Claire. Could I interest you in a bit of a tour? It *is* a beautiful cemetery."

****

Joe knew his way around a cemetery and talked a blue streak.

They walked along the stone pathways, stopped here and again so Claire could admire an unusual headstone or floral arrangement. She peered into the small windows of one of the mausoleums and could see sumptuous flowers inside. Some plots had gardens planted on top. Not a gardener in sight. Maybe God mowed the grass. Joe spouted historical trivia while Claire grew bitter about her missed opportunity. They'd walked to what looked to Claire like the end of the line. No more graves. Only a few scattered trees. Some small stone buildings.

Joe stopped.

"This is where the existing cemetery ends," he said.

Claire twirled her engagement ring around her finger. The sweat trickled.

"We've tried for years to buy this piece of property." Joe waved his hand out toward the land and trees. "But given the economy donors aren't as generous as they once were. We've raised some of the money. The owner is impatient, wants to put the land back on the market. We need to go big or go home."

Claire felt hope spring eternal.

"But even if we had the property, as Evelyn explained, you must be a trustee, a trustee's family member, or a major donor to buy a plot or crypt." Joe's expression turned ominous in a way only Vincent Price could match. "I don't believe you are, or your husband was, a trustee family member, or major donor?" Hard emphasis on major.

"As far as I know we aren't. Let's say it's a pretty safe bet."

"Your father-in-law is buried here though?"

"Yes. Curious, no?"

"Indeed. That is curious to say the least. If he didn't meet the guidelines."

Both of Joe's eyes rolled skyward appealing to the heavens for an answer to *that* somewhat distasteful riddle. When none came he settled for a mere mortal one.

"Fortunately for all concerned, *you* could become a donor. Should you do so, well *immediately,* that would kill two birds with one—" Joe turned as red as the satin Rest in Peace banner on the crypt behind them. "Oh goodness, forgive my poor choice of—"

"I might not have a hair on my head but I do have a brain in it. Let's get down to it, Joe. If I pay, I play. Right?" She wiped her wet brow with the backs of her hands. "A donation could close the deal? If I make one my husband could be buried here?"

"Of course, it would definitely need to be significant."

Joe didn't bat a money hungry eye.

Claire digested her only option. Liam'd had strong feelings about charitable giving.

I didn't get rich by giving my money away, he'd always said. Countless times during their marriage their affluent friends and Liam's business associates hit them up for their charities and pet projects.

Liam always said no.

Claire heard him like he stood next to her, still alive. *No one ever gave me a handout. I'm sure as hell not going to give anyone else one. The only organization I'm giving money to is the Corrigan Family Trust.* He remained true to his word to his dying day and beyond.

Liam even refused to buy Girl Scout cookies.

Claire chewed her lip. She knew what Liam would have wanted. Given his distaste for making charitable donations the decision was simple.

"Is five million dollars significant enough?"

L iam would roll over in his grave.

As soon as he got one.

Claire just unloaded a nice piece of her net worth to purchase a crypt with less thought than she put into buying last season's Manolo Blahniks. On the way back to the church she watched the ground beneath her disappear with every footstep, distracted. Joe sauntered ahead of her like a different man, almost giddy. A disconcerting trait in a funeral director. He bobbed along, weightless, as if the surf brought him in.

"How much time do you have today?" Joe said over his shoulder.

"None really. I'm late for an appointment," Claire said. And past pill time.

Joe stopped mid-bob to let Claire catch up. The chapel was in their sightline. "We have much to discuss. You're now one of our most esteemed donors. The dean will want to clear his schedule to thank you. In person."

Claire's anxiety imposed. "Not necessary. He can call me or send a note."

The imaginary needles under her flesh pricked.

"There's details, a lot of, well..." Joe pulled the bottom of his chin like taffy. "... a lot of things to consider."

"I just spent a boatload of cash. What else is there to consider?"

Her skin felt like she'd sat too close to the sun.

Cool as a corpse Joe said, "Why don't you get some rest and we'll reconvene tomorrow about ten? We can discuss all the details and opportunities then." He patted her arm.

"Opportunities? Oh I guess so, okay. Ten. Whatever." Claire would've given another million just to get out of there. Her fingers brushed the bottom of her purse, hit the jackpot of loose pills. "There's my car."

Joe's light friendly hold on her arm turned rigor-like clamp.

"Just one quick detail before you run. Are you familiar with a pledge form?"

****

Joe had shoved some form under her dripping nose, which she'd signed without reading to hurry along her exit. He'd yammered on about standard language and just like that officially hooked her for five million bucks.

Claire careened back around the rim of the campus after making her escape. Was it lack of sedation or had traffic doubled? She slowed to a stop at an intersection in front of some bronzed soldier atop his enthusiastic bronzed horse pawing the air on two legs, squinted to read the plaque but couldn't make it out. War hero probably. Must be the university library or some such. Her gaze wandered to the dark stone building behind the horse and rider. From the periphery she caught a zip of Valentino red.

It was that car. The red Corvette Rob Rhino had gotten into at the diner. Claire glimpsed the license plate dwindling in the distance—FLESHHH.

The driver must've come up behind her.

She'd been ogling the statue so he'd whipped past her. Claire gunned her gas pedal nearly ramming the second car that pulled out around her. She hit the brake. A few more cars went around her while she steamed. No use. The Corvette disappeared.

Claire eased forward, drove toward the gates, muscles tight, knuckles popped. Had they followed her? They'd left the diner at least half an hour before she did. Rob Rhino had no idea she was coming to the university, to the cemetery. He did know her car. Had he recognized her just now? She thought of the porn perv squeaking over in his ugly clogs as soon as he recognized her at the greasy spoon. He'd have honked, rolled down the window, waved, if he'd seen her. Obnoxious fool.

Get over yourself. That's what Jordan would say. But what in the name of Deep Throat was Rob Rhino doing here?

****

Claire knew she'd need her wits to find her way to her mother-in law's house but wanted pharmaceutical respite, needed it after the Corvette sighting. The right side of her head ached, she felt nauseous, cramped, slick with sweat and dread. Her tiny blue pal hadn't been much help. After a quick drive through the Dairy Queen for a burger/fry combo Claire couldn't put off her visit to Grace any longer. Joe'd given her detailed directions from the university. The town wasn't big enough to get too turned around in. She ate her burger with one hand

and drove with the other 'til she found the right street. She slowed to a near stop to squint at Joe's precise handwriting on the back of the old bank statement she'd used as a notepad.

The small green and white Victorian house, like the rest on the street, sat inches from the curb and the neighbors on both sides. No landscaping or adornment of any kind, the place looked stark, empty. No plants, pots, statues, or welcoming kitschy bric-a-brac. Grace's neighbors filled their narrow steps with geraniums, ferns, garden gnomes, pink flamingos. Flags with embroidered rainbows and unicorns stuck out from their window frames. Grace's house claimed a front door, shuttered windows, a single concrete step. Claire'd bet the farm she could eat off it.

She parked, stashed the burger wrapper and dirty napkin into the bag, backed it under the seat with her heel. Claire examined her reflection in the rearview mirror. Like an amputee whose missing limb still itches, she put her hand to her head to smooth back her phantom hair.

Claire made it from the car to the front door in two strides. Her balled-up fist drew back in the standard knock-knock position when it opened before her knuckles made contact. A fortyish looking, scruffy, pale-faced figure stood behind the door opened a few inches. She'd either come to the wrong place or Grace needed to rethink her stance on upper-lip hair removal and buffalo plaid. Scruffy pale face looked like Liam in a way Claire couldn't name.

"Yes?" He looked her up and down, eyes darting left to right. She could tell he wanted to shut the door. "Can I help you?"

"I'm Claire." Claire stuck out her hand. "I'm here to see Grace Corrigan—I'm her son's widow."

"Oh no, my heavens." He grasped her hand with both his and pulled her inside. "I'm sorry... I... well. I... you... don't have any—" He stumbled for sensible words.

Claire touched her scalp. "No. I don't have any hair and you aren't Grace."

"Oh no. I'm not." He moved aside and shut the door. "I'm Connor. Liam's brother. Finally we meet."

Connor inspected her like he'd been searching for her species his whole life. He skimmed over her baldness, registered it, moved on. She scanned his face, saw no contempt, only an edgy fervor. Her eyes closed in self-defense. His eagerness an unwelcome antidote to her sedative.

"You must need to sit down, what with your illness," Connor said.

"Oh no. I'm not ill. It's not as bad as it looks."

Ballsy bastard. Who said anything about illness?

"I'm bald. No big deal. My hair fell out right after Liam died. It's never grown back."

He nodded. His thin lips all but disappeared. "I—"

"Is she here?"

Claire's lids snapped up like vinyl shades at the sound of another female voice. Grace.

"Yes, Mom. She's here." Connor touched Claire's arm. "Please come sit down."

He held himself taut, like he was afraid a sudden move would spook her.

Claire sat on the plastic-covered floral sofa. It objected when her bottom made contact with a loud squeak and a *phhooot*. She jumped, dropped her purse on the floor.

"Mom and her plastic. This couch is older than I am and it still looks new. Well, it would if she'd take the plastic off." Connor's eyes darted to Claire's purse, stayed put.

Grace entered the room like a woman half her age, her perfect posture enough to make a debutante's mother cry. When she walked her limbs moved but the air didn't—a geriatric stealth bomber. She sat in the plastic-covered wingback chair across from Claire. No noise when she lowered herself into it. Connor maneuvered next to Claire.

Grace settled in, looked up at Claire, back at Connor, "Lord have mercy, she's bald." Grace took off her glasses and pressed a Kleenex to her forehead. Claire looked at Connor.

"Mom, yes, she's... she's—"

"I'm bald. It's okay to say it."

"Her hair fell out when Liam died. From the—" Connor looked at Claire, his face a question mark.

"No one knows what causes it. Could be an immune system thing. The shock probably didn't help."

Grace's face crumpled. She started to cry.

"Mom, don't cry. Come on now. Would you like something to drink? Some tea maybe?" Connor mouthed, *She'll be okay,* to Claire.

Of course she will. Claire was the bald one for Chrissake.

"No, don't mind me. I'll be all right." Grace dried her eyes and put her glasses back on. "I see you've met Connor."

"Yes. This is upsetting to you. I'm sure. I'm afraid we didn't get off to a very good start this morning on the phone."

Claire had a plan. She intended to get her way. Indulging her temper again wouldn't do. If she needed to grease the skids, so be it.

"I apologize for my ill manners. As you can see, I'm not myself. I've lost a great deal. I've lost my husband and—" She pointed to her scalp. The bald card was dealt. She intended to play it.

Grace sniffled. "We all have. I've lost my husband *and* my son."

The old lady trumps with the dead son.

"Indeed. Maybe there's a way to make some sense of all this loss." Claire cleared her throat. "To bring some comfort to each other."

"Maybe. I don't know." Grace dabbed her eyes.

There she went with the *I don't knows* again.

Claire searched Grace's face to find a resemblance to Liam. Perhaps around the eyes. She couldn't see much facial similarity but the way she carried herself was all Liam. Proud, dignified, formidable. Claire wouldn't have pegged Grace as much of a crier, not that she knew much about her. But with her advanced age, the death of her son, things change. Her short gray hair curled tightly around her ears like the rods just came out and she didn't brush it. Probably got a bad perm at the Curl Up and Dye once every three months whether she needed it or not.

Connor broke through Claire's reverie. "Mom said you hoped to bury Liam at the university near Dad?" He looked anxious to please. Who couldn't get along with him?

"Yes. I made some of the arrangements today. It's complicated but I'll know more of the particulars tomorrow. I'd like to buy a family crypt for everyone. I don't know where Emmet is exactly, but he could be moved, exhumed. I'd handle all the expenses, of course."

Claire knew she talked too fast. But it all came out and she couldn't stop it.

Grace turned the faucets on again. "I'd be hard-pressed to tell you where Emmet is. I don't get out to the cemetery much at all anymore since I stopped driving. Connor and Deborah, that's his wife, live out at the farm. Elizabeth is here in town, but she won't take me unless I pay for gas. I'm on a fixed income. I don't have—"

"That's okay, Grace. You don't have to tell me exactly where he is. I can find that out later."

Just say yes so we can get on with it. We're not digging anybody up today. Her daughter makes her pay for gas? Did she hear that right?

"Claire did you say the crypt is for *all* of us?" Connor said.

"Yes. I thought since I was buying one, you know, I might as well buy one large enough for the whole family."

"Guess it'd have to be pretty big. Not that I'm up on crypt sizes. There's..." Connor looked up at the ceiling, his mouth a crooked kiss. "... let's see... well, there's at least seven of us. Not sure who'd go for cremation—"

"Heaven forbid." Grace pressed her tattered Kleenex to her mouth.

"No telling how much space they'd take up." He glanced down at Claire's purse on the floor, then at Claire. "And you. There's you. So eight. At least eight."

Was he going to engineer the whole thing now?

"Those are details we don't need to worry about right this second." Claire felt the room shrinking, her head expanding. "Can we first agree on the concept?"

"I'm for it," Connor said. "But I don't know why you'd want to do it. Considering."

Claire squirmed on the plastic with a pitiful squeak. Sweat broke out over her upper lip. Her pulse started its run for the border. She wished for another pill, cleared her throat again. "Because whatever differences you had in life can be set aside in death, can't they? It'd be wonderful for Liam to be with his father, right?"

Claire looked at Grace who sat in her chair in silence.

"Liam's father... God rest his soul..." Grace made the sign of the cross, soggy Kleenex in hand. "... a saint if ever I knew one. Liam could've been with him any day of the week while they were both living. When it mattered. He chose not to."

"That was before my time Grace. I can't do anything about that. I can only bring them together in the afterlife," Claire said. The religious nuts should be all over the afterlife, shouldn't they?

"Yes, all well before your time. Before Liam turned his back on his God, his church, his family, and his wife. Bonnie, that poor woman. Who'd have ever thought—" Grace shred the tissue in two.

Connor leaned forward. "Mom, Claire isn't here to dredge all that up. She's obviously trying to make peace."

Grace didn't respond.

"Yes, that's what I am, a peacemaker."

Whatever, blah, blah, blah. The sweat ran down her temples now. She wiped it away with the palms of her hands. The vice grip around her chest cranked tight.

Connor looked concerned for Claire. "I'll get you some cold water." He leaned down, picked up her purse, sat it next to her on the squeaky couch. "Be right back."

Claire felt her naked wet brow crinkle, she looked down where her purse used to be.

"I suppose you're both right. It's time to make peace. At least for us. Only the good Lord can forgive Liam for Bonnie. Connor thinks it's what Emmet would want. We're all getting old," Grace finally said looking down at the torn wet Kleenex in her lap. "I need to talk to Elizabeth, my daughter. She's got plenty of reservations. She came earlier but she's got a job you know. Most of us have to work."

That sounded like a yes to Claire. Elizabeth might be a hurdle but not an insurmountable one. A possible hitch in her get-along. Connor was in. He'd help bring Elizabeth around, tighten the screws on the mother.

"Here you go." Connor handed Claire a glass of ice water and a cool damp towel, his face contorted with concern. "Are you sure you're all right? Do you need anything else?"

"I'm fine."

Claire pressed the towel to the back of her neck, took a long drink and glanced around the living room away from Mr. Helpful. Religious symbols and pictures hung on every dark-paneled wall. Jesus nailed to the Cross, dying for the world's sins, pious and bleeding in a thorny crown. The Virgin Mary illuminated in purity and powerlessness. Hanging crooked over the fireplace, a cheap painted rendition of the Last Supper, Jesus in the center, disciples on both sides. One plots his doom, the others blissfully ignorant. On the coffee table sat a photo of the pope—who knew which one (the Lassie of the religious world) and a ceramic nativity scene even though Christmas was months away.

No wonder Liam got the hell out of Dodge.

A plastic runner striped down the center of the rug. She'd been there less than half an hour. Couldn't wait to leave. A lifetime? Crucifixion seemed like the easy way out.

"Like I said tomorrow I'll have more details. Why don't we talk again then?" Claire stood, legs tingling. She inhaled deep to slow her racing heart. After a moment she left the towel and glass on the table. "This isn't easy for any of us."

"I'll walk you out." Connor stood up too. "Mom, I'll be right back. We'll go over to the grocery store, okay?"

"Claire?" It was Grace. "Where is my son?"

"At the hotel," Claire said.

"I'd like to see him—his ashes—if you don't mind," Grace said leaking eyes downcast.

"Tomorrow. Of course, tomorrow. I'll call and let you know a good time."

Claire turned and walked back toward the front door with Connor behind her. On the wall near the door a faded color photograph hung framed in tacky cheap gold leaf. Even aged she could see it was Liam in a powder blue tux standing next to a virginal bride. A clichéd poof of white crinoline and lace. Liam and Bonnie—Bonnie the pure. Claire looked around. There were no other photos on the wall. Other than the pope there were no photos period. She wondered if Grace put it up for her benefit. She stepped closer for a better look. Bonnie was plain. The girl next door or the girl who sat on the bus next to the girl next door. With a full head of chestnut hair.

Tramp.

"Sorry. It's hard for old people to change I guess," Connor said in Claire's ear while he steered her outside. "Don't forget your purse."

CHAPTER ELEVEN

"Thanks for everything. Talk to you tomorrow." Claire got in the car.

Connor opened the passenger side door. "Wait Claire. Gotta few minutes?"

Before she could say yes or no he sat next to her. That happened a lot to her lately.

Claire put the key in the ignition hopeful he'd get the hint.

He didn't.

"I'm sorry about my mom. She can't let any of that stuff go." He ran both palms up and down his thighs smoothing out imaginary wrinkles in his jeans.

Claire guessed she was supposed to ask about all the stuff. She hadn't come for that. She got what she came for. She fished a pill out of the bottom of her bag. Connor reached over, held it open for her.

"It's past time for my medication. I hope you don't mind."

He let out a faint whistle, leaned his back against the seat. "No, not at all. If it's past time, it's past time."

Claire swallowed her pill. "Like I said this isn't the easiest situation for me." Gotta keep the pity coming. She fastened her dilating pupils on Connor. "Whatever happened in the past is over. What I'm suggesting is burying it. Once and for all."

"Wish it was that simple," he said. "My family holds a grudge. They've got a big one against Liam. He left the church, then his wife. My mother took to her bed for weeks." Connor looked toward the house and shook his head. "It nearly killed my father. My mother blames his death on it."

"You're kidding. That's it?" Claire didn't get zealots. What century was this? She thought about her own rebellious youth, her teenage pregnancy. She could imagine Grace and Emmet as her parents driving her out to an empty field and shooting her.

"I know it seems odd to you, but it's the way my parents were raised, what they believed. No one in their family ever bailed on God or marriage."

"Unbelievable." Claire always suspected it was something dumb. Put a gold star by *right again*.

"If that wasn't enough—Liam got rich." Connor picked at the handle of Claire's three-thousand-dollar purse. "Hard to know what pissed everybody off most. If he hadn't made something of himself."

"Making money doesn't mean Liam made something of himself. It just means he was rich. Seems to me you've done okay." Claire had nothing else to offer. "You don't look like a farmer though."

"A farmer?" Connor's brows met his nose. "Oh, the farm. I guess Mom mentioned we live out on the farm. My wife inherited a farmhouse from her parents. We live there, but we don't farm. I'm a programmer."

Claire looked at her watch.

Connor opened the car door and put one leg out, "I better get back. I need to run Mom over to the grocery."

Claire's vitals were somewhat back to normal. Her skin felt like it might stay attached to her bones. The miracle of modern science.

"Wait. Connor?" She almost forgot. "Was your dad a university trustee or a donor? Or was someone in your family a trustee?"

"My dad? Oh no. No one in our family ever sat on any board as far as I know. My folks have no money and even if they did they'd never give it away. No, my dad was just a regular workin' stiff. He worked at the university more than forty years."

Claire turned her full attention to Connor. "He was a professor?"

"No. A janitor."

"A janitor." Claire kept her face still. "I... did he? Well—" Claire wanted to continue but didn't get a chance.

"Why?"

"Umm... I understand they have strict burial guidelines. Your dad didn't meet any of them if he wasn't a donor or a trustee."

Connor shrugged. "Who knows? Things change."

Claire started to explain what Evelyn told her at the cemetery but Connor put a stop to it. With one leg out the door he said, "I've got to be honest. When Mom told me you wanted to bury Liam here it surprised me. I—" He looked like he had a terminal diagnosis to deliver. "Well, Liam hated it here. He hated this town and the university. He said only liberal losers went to it. Bonnie went there. She's back there again. Her father sat on the board for many years. Liam hated our sister. And Mom... no love lost there." Connor's eyes bore into her, relentless. "And he was ashamed that dad was only a janitor. Liam didn't want anyone to know he came from a place like this in my opinion. Or what happened to Bonnie— what she did to herself after the divorce. You can turn your back on the Catholic church but not on the guilt. That hangs on like the Shroud of Turin."

"That was a long time ago." Claire blinked. "Like you said things change. People change."

Connor's eyes stayed latched onto Claire's. "Do you really think Liam would want to spend eternity in a place he despised, with the family he hated, with his janitor dad who shunned and embarrassed him, and the ex-wife who committed suicide because he left her? That's quite a change."

Claire turned the key and the car roared to life.

CHAPTER TWELVE

"Come again? You bought what, where, and for *how* much?"

"Andrew. Stop. You heard me. You just need to do whatever it is you do to get this done. I suppose I'll need to cash out something or other. I have all the contact info for the cemetery director. I'll give it to you before I hang up. Call over there and find out what they need. I already signed some pledge form. They need to fax you a copy."

Claire pulled open the curtains of her hotel room window and looked out over the parking lot. It'd been mobbed with cars when she pulled in. She parked clear in the back.

"Claire, five million dollars is a hell of a lot of money even for you. I have to tell you as someone who's known you for more than ten years this is highly irregular and—" Andrew said.

"It's called a donation, Andrew. I'm a donor."

"Is there a cooling off period?"

Claire felt her eyes do loop-de-loops. "No, there isn't a cooling off period." She mimicked in a singsong voice.

Andrew cleared his throat. "I'm not just your attorney, you know. I hope I'm your friend too. I knew Liam thirty-five years. I can't let you swing in the wind and not try to help you. Especially now when you're dealing with so much."

"I don't need a friend. I need an attorney."

"I can be both, can't I? As your attorney and your friend, I'll just say it—you're going to need to downsize. Liam isn't around to restock the coffers anymore. It's not a bottomless pit of money."

Claire reached for her throat. "Downsize? What are you talking about?"

Would she have to drive an Audi? *Christ.*

"I think you should sell the apartment."

"Our penthouse in New York? Are you crazy?" She clutched the phone, yelled.

"Claire, you're a young woman with a long life ahead of you." She could feel him backing down. "We need to make sure your money lasts."

"Why don't you let me worry about that Andrew?"

"Because I don't think you are. Plus it's more than that Claire. There's no logic to this scheme. It doesn't make sense. I'm worried you'll be sorry later. When more time passes, the wounds heal. You'll regret it and it won't be easy to undo. Maybe impossible."

"I've never been clearer about anything. It makes perfect sense to me."

If anyone understood the wounded Claire did. She saw no healing later down the road. Nor could she imagine regret.

"I'm sure it does... now." He sounded hesitant. "You know, I gave Meg this great trip to Hawaii for—"

"You're telling me I'm broke and you want me to spend money on a trip to Hawaii?"

"Instead of a crypt? Yes. It'd be money well—"

"Mind your own business, Andrew." Claire pressed her forehead against the window.

"I knew Liam's family. I'm not sure he'd want this." Andrew tried a different track. "It seems like a noble gesture, to bury Liam with his father, but now the whole family crypt. I just don't know."

Claire was getting close to the end of her fraying rope. "Well, I do know."

"You also know Bonnie is buried in that cemetery too. Don't you?"

"Yes, of course. So what, she's got first dibs?"

Claire watched as a minivan circled the parking lot in search of a parking spot. What was going on at the hotel? It was loaded all of a sudden. Must be a Bible study convention.

"Well, it just seems inappropriate considering."

"Do you really want to go down the *inappropriate* road?"

Andrew exhaled into Claire's ear. "Claire, *we* need to get that mess settled. We've put it off longer than we should have. She isn't going away. Neither of them will. We've been lucky frankly."

"You're still sending the checks aren't you?" Claire said.

"Yes, of course. But we still need to close the deal. Put an end to it."

Claire hadn't noticed before but the message light on the hotel phone blinked. Someone had called her here. Again. Damn it. She'd forgotten all about her cell phone. With the hotel room phone tucked under her neck she looked around the room. Her cell was on top of the television. The cord nowhere to be seen.

"Claire? Are you there?"

"I've got to hang up. You're three hours behind me. Call the cemetery director. We'll talk about everything else later." Claire gave a protesting Andrew the contact information and watched the minivan circle the crowded parking lot in vain. She waited a few seconds for Andrew to finish writing down the numbers. "Okay? Got it? I really have to go."

She started to hang up when Andrew said, "Claire?"

"What?"

"Liam made a mistake. But he loved you more than anything. You know he did."

The memory of Liam's love sliced through her.

She dropped the phone into its cradle.

S he pushed the blinking light to see what would happen. To her anesthetized surprise a recorded voice said, "You have three messages."

Annabelle's voice said, "Claire, your cell phone is dead. I don't think you've plugged it in."

Could she get on with it without the lecture?

"Anyway, call me when you get this."

Then Jordan. "Mother, nice job with the cell phone. In case you're interested I found out more stuff about your new best friend—Rob Rhino. Or is it Uncle Rob now? Call me."

Annabelle again. "Claire. Hey, I talked to Conchita at the house today. I didn't know you were going to leave Dad's ashes in Pennsylvania. I mean, well, I knew you were talking with his wacko family, trying to make nice, maybe have a memorial. But leave him there? I think Conchita heard that wrong. Lost in translation and all. Call me, please. It's not too late to book that Hawaii thing. I really think you need it."

Claire picked up the phone and dialed. Before it rang she hung up. She didn't need Annabelle's permission. No reason to feel guilty.

Claire yanked the phone out of its cradle, dialed out again. She'd call Jordan. Talk to him about it. Before she punched in all the numbers she slammed down the receiver. Why bother? He'd make smartass trash talk and side with Annabelle. She didn't need the drama.

Liam was her husband. She could do what she pleased with his ashes. Besides it's not like there was a lot of time to talk to Annabelle about it before she left. It was too late anyway. She'd made all the arrangements. Liam was going to be buried in this town, with his viper's nest of a family, in the university cemetery. It's what she wanted. Kids be damned.

****

How many pills had she taken? Vodka nips? The jackhammer in her brain broke through about five feet of concrete. Had she fallen asleep? Her lips caked with she didn't want to know what. The parking lot was jammed with cars. The cheap clock on the nightstand clicked. One minute past midnight, too late to hike two blocks for food.

She lay back down on the slippery bedspread. It made her head hurt to think about Annabelle. Best not to. She remembered Jordan called and left a message too. He'd said something about Rob Rhino. He'd found out more information about Rob Rhino the porn king. She remembered the red car... was it following her? What had he said about his wife's family? His wife had family in this town. His wife was dead.

Curiosity revived her. It was too late to call. No, it wasn't. Not with the time difference. She grabbed the phone and dialed Jordan's home phone. Maybe Steven the ingrate wouldn't answer the house phone.

"Hello?" Maura answered.

"Maura? It's Claire." Claire was always happy to talk to Maura.

"Claire? Is everything okay?" Maura's voice purred.

"Yes." What was that on her lips? Claire licked her fingers and wiped her mouth. "Is Jordan around?" Claire rifled around the bottom of her purse for some Advil. A pharmacy in there but no Advil.

"No, he and Steven left late this afternoon. They closed on that house today. So they went on a long weekend trip to celebrate."

"They did what?" She stopped rifling, elbow deep in her Kelly bag.

"Oh... ah... you know, didn't you... they closed on that house they made an offer on. They'd been looking at it for months. I—"

"Well, that's odd. Why'd they do that? Are they opening some kind of business? It's a commercial property?" She plopped down on the bed, toppled the bag.

"Claire, you better talk to Jordan when he gets back. I'll tell him you called. You take care."

"Maura, is everything okay with you and Jordan?"

"Claire, you really need to talk to Jordan. Good night."

What in the world was going on? She never did trust Steven. Not from the start. A long weekend? They bought a house? Maybe Annabelle knew what the hell was going on. She scowled at the phone in her hand and put it back in its cradle.

Enough was enough. This was too much. Time to call it a day. She took out her pills and took one with a glass of water, pulled off her clothes and jumped in for a quick shower before she crawled under the scratchy thin blanket of the bed. She needed her rest. There was another endless day ahead of her. Maybe in the morning she'd find she'd hallucinated the whole thing.

Wouldn't be the first time.

CHAPTER

FOURTEEN

◆

Traffic was a bitch.

Unexpected in a town that had horse and buggy hitching posts on its sidewalks. Claire couldn't believe the number of cars headed toward the university. The parking lot at her hotel had cleared out but from the looks of things they were all going to the same place. Good thing she'd left early. She'd hoped to dash through the drive thru for coffee but no chance. Not with the congestion.

It took twice as long as she'd planned to get to the chapel. Groups milled in and around the cemetery. They were everywhere. She hadn't considered parking until she saw there wasn't any. It was a few minutes after ten. If she had to search for parking no telling how late she'd be. She was about to start sweating when she saw Joe waving her down like a windmill. He rotated in front of the only empty parking spot. She pulled into it.

He opened her car door. "I saved it for you."

"How nice." Claire got out and they walked to the chapel. "This place is a zoo."

"I should've told you yesterday it's our annual Trustee Week," Joe said. "This weekend kicks off festivities for our trustees, donors, and alumni. It's our chance to thank them, keep in touch. We like to stay connected."

She bet they did—to their wallets. "Must be why my hotel is packed."

"Yes, the university grounds swarm. There're tours, speaking events, banquets, concerts, you name it."

Claire looked around distracted.

"Speaking of, the dean wants to meet you this morning. He'd love to announce your generosity at the Dean's Council banquet tomorrow night. Nothing would please us more than if you'd attend as our guest of honor. However, given the circumstances surrounding your gift, we'd certainly understand if—"

"Can I think about it? We have a lot of details to—"

"Of course. I'm getting ahead of myself. Let's go back to my office."

Joe's office was what she'd imagined. It was, as far as Claire could tell, the only inviting area in the chapel, carpeted with a worn oriental rug in warm colors, the book-lined walls painted a deep terra cotta. Joe offered her one of the four chairs around the small table.

Evelyn came in with a tray of coffee and cinnamon rolls. Thank you Jesus.

"Help yourselves." Evelyn smiled, backed out of the room.

Joe reached across the table to pour coffee. Claire thought she'd gnaw through his arm to get to the rolls. They sat, drank, and chewed. Claire watched the tourists tramp around the cemetery through Joe's office window while she ate.

Joe wiped his mouth with his napkin, "Your attorney phoned. The funds are transferred. We'll close the deal with the property owner in the next few days and start clearing the land."

"How long will that take?" Claire asked.

"Not long. As you've seen there's not much there. We'll clear what little there is and lay sod. We're going to have some lag time nonetheless."

"Lag time?"

"Yes. The mausoleum needs to be shipped and assembled."

"Assembled?"

"Yes. It's prefabricated."

"Prefabricated? Like a... like a mobile home?"

The trailer park for the dead.

"Well yes, simply put. You don't have to go that route. You can go custom but that can take months. Prefab is the quickest."

"Prefab it is then. How much lag time are we talking about?"

How long can it take to make a trailer with some drawers to cram ashes in?

"The last time I—"

Before Joe could finish his sentence a flash of bright green caught Claire's eye. What the— She smacked her coffee cup down on the table with a splash and a rattle and leaned forward to get closer to the window. Several people were weaving in and out of the headstones.

"Claire, is anything—"

She put her hand up. Joe stopped talking. She kept her eyes glued to the ground. They darted back and forth fast, she felt like a lizard stalking a fly. Several seconds passed. There. She saw them again. The bright green clogs. She wasn't imagining things. She zeroed in and went upward. Good God in heaven.

Rob Rhino.

Claire leapt out of the chair and ran out of the office, Joe on her heels.

"Claire, what's wrong? Are you all right?"

"I'll be right back. I'm fine. Stay here. I just saw someone." She ran out the chapel door toward where she'd seen Rob Rhino. The crush of visitors blocked her charge and her vision. Every few steps she dipped up and down to see if she could spot him. Where'd he go?

She blurted "Excuse me. Pardon me" to a few startled tourists as she pushed past them, a bald nut on a mission. About to bolt off the pathway she spotted him.

"What are you doing here? You're following me, aren't you?" Claire said breathless.

He lifted his big head up, his eyes opened wide in surprise. "Hey, Claire Corrigan. What are *you* doing here?"

He moseyed out from behind a grave toward her his hula girl shirt swaying across his hanging belly. The same one from the day before. It looked like her hotel bedspread.

Claire, flustered and frightened, said, "I asked you first."

He stood close to her. "It's cool. No worries. Are you okay?"

Claire's hands were balled into fists. "No. Just tell me why you're following me."

"Hey now, I'm not following you." He laughed.

"What are you doing here?" she said her voice an attack. She jumped up and down, a pissed pogo stick.

"Okay, okay, calm down. You're going to blow a gasket or something." He reached out and patted her arm. "Is the cemetery only open to you?"

"What?" She yanked her arm away. "No, of course not."

"Okay then."

"It's a strange coincidence don't you think?" She shook. "And I don't believe in coincidences. I need to sit down." Before she fell down.

Rob Rhino led her to a stone bench. "Should I see if there's some water somewhere?"

"No, I'm fine. I just... never mind." She sat, put her head down toward her knees and held it with both hands. After a minute or so of deep breathing she collected herself. Sitting next to Rob she saw his badly dyed hair was clean and his rank odor gone.

"My wife Gloria is buried there." He pointed toward a headstone across the path, set several feet away from a cluster of other graves, underneath the peaceful sanctuary of a leafy shade tree. A lone and lonely monument.

His blurted pronouncement made Claire feel kind of bad. She worked her expression, keeping it neutral, didn't want him catching on she already knew Gloria sang with the angels. "Oh I'm sorry. I—"

"It's cool, no worries. It's been years." He looked out across the cemetery, his gray eyes filled. "I come here when I'm in town. It's a beautiful place. Reminds me of her. Everywhere you look, beauty."

Claire felt her own eyes fill, moved by his unexpected simple sentiment. "Yes, this place is spectacular."

"What are you doing here?"

"I'm making funeral arrangements for my husband."

"Oh sad." He shook his head, eyes darkened.

"Umm... yeah."

"Hey, didn't you say your husband died a year ago?"

"You remembered? Yes, he did. It's a long story."

"You are a weird one, Claire Corrigan."

"*I'm* weird? Well, here's a newsflash—"

The red Corvette revved up alongside the path, blackened windows rolled up tight. Before Claire could inquire about its driver Rob jumped up.

"Gotta fly, Claire Corrigan. You take care."

She breathed exhaust as they peeled away. Claire stood. People tromping by eyed her with suspicion. She remembered Joe waited for her and took two steps in the chapel's direction but changed her mind. She was right there after all. So close. Might as well pay her respects. Or something like that. After jostling through a few alumni, she crossed the path, lowered her head in front of Gloria's headstone.

Faithful Husband Father Soldier—Louis David Barnes—1824–1898

J oe paced in the front of the chapel. "Is everything all right?"

"Everything's fine. I just saw someone I never in a million years expected to see."

Claire zipped back to the office, Joe followed.

"Really?" Joe said. "It's a small world isn't it?"

"I guess so."

Bet ole Joe'd be shocked to find out who Claire slummed around with. She felt the heat of a blush climb up her neck at the thought of it.

"You're sure you're all right?"

"Can we talk about the mausoleum?"

"Certainly."

Claire took her seat, leaned down into her Kelly bag, dug for buried treasure.

Joe took out a legal pad, held his Mont Blanc poised over it. "Let's start with the correct spelling of Liam's name. As you'd like it to appear on the crypt."

"Do you have a directory?"

"Excuse me?"

"A directory." Claire leaned forward. "A list of names. Everyone buried here."

Joe sat up straighter in his mission-style chair, peered down his considerable nose. "Well, yes. Is there someone in particular I can—"

"No. It's…" Claire wished she was quicker on her feet— or seat. "I guess with all the history I thought it'd be interesting to scroll through some of the names. See if I recognize any historical ones. You know since I've got time to kill."

Joe rearranged his mouth like he'd eaten something disagreeable. "Really?"

"Yes, really."

What was it to him anyway?

"We're happy to oblige certainly." Joe must've remembered she was worth five million dollars. "We do have a computerized directory. You're more than welcome to peruse."

"How would—"

"Our office is yours." He grinned like a ghoul. "Before you leave Evelyn can direct you to the volunteer desk. It's free more than half the time. She'll show you how to access the database."

****

"Three weeks? Why three weeks?" Grace said.

"Because it's going to take that long to ship and assemble the mausoleum," Claire said.

"I think it's premature to set a date for a service when the whole family isn't sold on the idea." Elizabeth pursed her lips, though it was tough to be sure. Hard to guess her age. She looked more like Grace's sister than her daughter. Identical bad perms.

"What idea?" Joe said.

"The family crypt," Claire said.

"Ahhh... well, are there any questions I can answer for you?" Joe looked back and forth between Grace and Elizabeth. Their early arrival interrupted Joe and Claire's meeting.

"It's for the family to decide." Elizabeth reared back like Joe'd goosed her.

Clearly right at home on the corner of Awkward and None of Your Business Joe pressed on. "Claire has a beautiful spot picked out and a top-of-the-line mausoleum on its way."

Before Elizabeth could put Joe in his place, Grace said, "Elizabeth, your father is already in this cemetery. What difference does it make to you if we move him a few feet? If you feel strongly about it, you don't have to participate. You and William can go someplace else in the hereafter."

Alarmed, Claire hadn't thought of that. "Elizabeth, why don't you think it over? Like Joe said we've got three weeks."

Elizabeth folded her arms over her flat chest like a two-year-old. "Liam hated me. I never did anything to him. He was jealous of me. He didn't even come to my wedding. Why should I do this for him? I know you're bald and all—"

"Claire had an excellent idea. Why don't you think it over?" Joe got off the bench and cast a withering look at Elizabeth. "I'm going to make a call and—"

Elizabeth cut Joe off like an unsightly growth. "All Liam did was lord his money over us. This is more of the same. Why would I want to be in a place after I'm dead that I couldn't afford when I was alive?" Elizabeth said bitter and terse. "Liam was Mr. Moneybags but too cheap to send his own mother Christmas or birthday presents. It broke her heart."

Claire glanced at Grace, looking at her lap. Liam sent her Christmas and birthday presents every year, despite their rift, over Claire's protests. Expensive ones.

Speaking of moneybags.

"Interesting, Elizabeth, your father was able to afford a plot here." Claire sharpened her claws. "Unless I'm missing something, Emmet wasn't a donor or a trustee."

Grace sucked air in Hindenburg gulps. "What are you—"

Elizabeth's head swirled. "What's wrong Mother? What's she talking about?"

"The guidelines say you have to be a donor, or a trustee, or a trustee family member to use the cemetery. Your father was none of the above." Claire almost coughed up a hairball.

Grace turned Incredible Hulk. "Emmet Corrigan was a faithful servant to his family, his God, and this university. When he died he got his just reward."

What did any of that mean? Other than Claire nearly blew it again with her ill temper.

"I'm sure he did Grace. I just wondered about it." Claire tried to look apologetic. "Didn't mean to start an uproar."

"My father's burial was a gift. Isn't that right, Mother? Isn't that what you said?" Elizabeth went whiny. "The school's way of showing its gratitude."

"That's right. Exactly." Incredible Hulk turned into gracious old lady. "Claire just didn't know, that's all."

"Of course." Claire turned to Joe for confirmation, but he was gone.

"Not everyone has diamonds as big as boulders and three-hundred-dollar shoes, but some people have a work ethic and grateful employers." Elizabeth glared at Claire's ring and red kitten heels.

As if you could get Jimmy Choos for less than six hundred dollars. Claire sneered at Elizabeth's serviceable Easy Spirits. She had a bad attitude and bad taste.

"Elizabeth, that's enough," Grace said. "We're all on edge. The sooner this is decided, the better. Claire? Did you bring my son's ashes?"

"Um... oh yes. He's out in the car." Damn it. She'd forgotten him again.

"We're leaving," Elizabeth said. "You can see the ashes in her car. She can follow us out to the parking lot. As far as I'm concerned this isn't a done deal."

"Elizabeth can think about this over the weekend. You have my number at the hotel and Joe's number here if you have any questions," Claire said.

"If you want to go to the store, let's go." Elizabeth prodded Grace along with her hand and a not friendly push.

She just went to the store yesterday. Claire followed them to the door of the chapel.

Grace leaned in toward Elizabeth, sniveling, "I asked Connor to take me to the store yesterday. He said he'd only take me if I paid for the gas."

****

Claire couldn't believe the porn sites that popped up when she typed Rob Rhino's name in the search bar. Not that she looked on purpose. Talk about revolting. Thank the good Lord she'd only gotten a quick glimpse of the foot-long dog. She had to look three or four times to make sure it was even real.

Had Evelyn cranked up the heat? She wiped her head, her sweaty hands together and looked over her shoulder embarrassed, though she sat alone in the tiny volunteer office off the chapel vestibule. She hoped no unwitting volunteers lost their jobs for surfing porn sites. Oh well. They didn't get paid anyway.

Joe'd gone hunting down the dean so Evelyn had given her a quick tutorial. She tried to comb through the cemetery directory but couldn't remember Rob Rhino's real name. Jordan'd told her but she couldn't remember. Her head felt weighted down. Her mouth kept falling open. The tussle with the in-laws had required a quick chaser.

Her eyes moved over the biography of Rob like an Evelyn Woods speed reader. She knew a lot of it already from Jordan. She only wanted to know... there. Raymond Horowitz. She went back to the database.

Didn't find a thing. No Gloria Horowitz. No Horowitz at all. For the hell of it she tried Rhino. Nothing.

Maybe Gloria never changed her name. Back when saying women's lib sounded hip. Claire did another quick scan of Rob's bio.

Married Gloria Metcalf 1970 to 1973. Gloria Metcalf b. 1950 d. 1973. Nothing else.

Claire clicked back over to search the cemetery list.
Ella Jean Metcalf—1880–1948
Randall Metcalf—1875–1927

CHAPTER

SIXTEEN

A nother one not looking at her bald head.

"Claire, I'm delighted to meet you." Dean Lawrence Sumner introduced himself, held both Claire's hands in his dwarfish ones. It felt undignified for a dean to only come up to her nipples.

"I'm sure." Claire crouched, evened things out.

"I can't begin to thank you for your generosity. I'm overwhelmed thinking about it. When Joe told me I nearly fainted." He reminded Claire of someone.

"Don't give me too much credit. I wanted a crypt here." Claire tried not to stare at his mole. Was it penciled on?

"We're so grateful." He pressed her downward. "Let's sit."

Claire untangled her hands, leaned down for her purse. "I'm on my way out. I've been here too long already."

She'd only come out to the chapel from the volunteer office to grab her forgotten bag and then skedaddle. She'd been caught in the dean's snare.

"Your bag and shoes are fabulous." Dean Sumner reached out to feel the bag. "Hermes, the finest leather."

Steven. That's who he reminded her of—Steven.

"Well, I should be getting back to the hotel."

"Can I give you a few things to think about before you take off? I know you're out of state but with a donation that size, well, we'd love to have you on our board of trustees. Please don't answer yet. Your tragedy is fresh. Mull it over." He tapped his little foot. "You don't have to live here to attend meetings. Several of our members join us via conference call. Easy peasy."

"I can't think about that now." He must not think her tragedy was too fresh. A year didn't really count but geez. "I need to settle my husband's burial."

"Certainly you do," he said without pausing to notice her disdainful expression. "But you still have to eat, right?"

"What?"

"The Dean's Council banquet tomorrow night? We don't have to make a big deal over you. Just come have dinner with some of our donors."

Claire took the bait. "Make a big deal over me?"

"At the risk of sounding gauche it's Trustee Week. There are recognition opportunities. Normally a five million dollar gift would be announced." He looked at her like he thought she would finish his sentence.

"To whom?" Claire couldn't fathom. Joe mentioned opportunities.

"Well," he said tapping his chin with a well-buffed fingernail, "to our other donors for one. And, of course, our alumni." His almost violet eyes (had to be colored contacts) circled the chapel.

"And?"

Out with it Lawrence.

"The press. We'd announce it to the press."

"Oh heavens no. I don't want all that fanfare." Claire tried not to look as annoyed as she felt. "How ridiculous—"

"Shall I be frank?"

"Please."

"A sizeable gift, well, a gift such as yours, provides us significant leverage. It could help us get other large gifts." The dean and Joe were the Frank and Jesse James of university relations.

"Oh?" Claire put her bag on the floor, crossed her arms.

"I'm sorry. The timing is terrible. But all our major donors are here this week. If we could announce something—"

"The press release goes to the local paper?" Claire said considering.

"Is that acceptable?"

"Yes. The more the merrier. Radio, news, all of it, if possible."

"We'll call our PR firm immediately. You're an angel." He took both Claire's hands in his slimy ones, looking like he struggled not to appear too baffled at her sudden change of heart.

"I have specific instructions about how I'd like my gift credited."

"Anything you'd like."

"Guess I'll see you at the banquet tomorrow."

"Delightful." He bowed at the waist, his trim silver hair unwavering.

Finally a way to get Elizabeth into the crypt

C laire made the mistake of picking up the hotel phone when it rang.

"I know you're trying to do a good thing. It's so cool. I get it. But—"

"Annabelle, if you think it's so cool, then please support me."

"Claire, you know I love you. You're the only mom I have."

Claire felt the shark jaws of motherly love tighten around her throat. "I need to do this."

"It's too far. We can't even visit his grave." Sniveling sounds carried over the phone.

"There're planes."

"Dad never even talked about his family or that place."

"Can you do me a favor?"

"What?"

"I need more clothes."

Dead air. Then, "That's it? No more discussion?"

Claire didn't respond. The crypt was closed.

"Claire? Are—"

"Clothes. I need them."

"I called that place in Hawaii. Jimmy says you can fly out of Penn—"

Claire picked up the Absolut bottle to throw it, almost cutting off her alcohol supply to spite her face. "Goddammit, Annabelle, I don't want to hear another word about that fucking commune in Hawaii. I'm not going now or ever."

"Claire, you need a rest. That's why you're doing this crazy stuff. Dad's death was hard—"

"I will hang up this phone—"

"Okay, okay. I'll drop it for now." Annabelle sighed, gave in. "What clothes do you want?"

"Ask Conchita to help you. She knows what I like, what's appropriate. She's coming to the house a few days a week even though I'm not there isn't she?"

"I'll have to go over there and find out." Annabelle sounded pouty. "I can't believe you need more clothes. You took too much to begin with."

"I told you I'll be here three weeks." Claire was over the lectures from her kids. "Conchita can FedEx it all to my hotel. She doesn't have a lot to do since I'm here."

She fingered the manila envelope stuffed with correspondence from Holloway, Howard, and Lennox, LLC.

"I'll try to get over there in the next couple days."

"Try? This is important. I called the house and Conchita didn't answer—"

"I have classes, remember? Don't you have Conchita's home phone?"

"Yes, but it's in my cell."

Dead air again.

"Annabelle?"

All quiet on the western front.

"Look, I know. I'll plug in my phone as soon as we hang up. I—"

"Is that it Claire? I really need to—"

"No. What on earth is going on with Jordan?"

"I could pretend I don't know what you're talking about but I won't. You don't really want to know what's going on with Jordy or you wouldn't ask. It's plain as day."

"I thought he and Maura were about to get married."

"*No* you didn't."

"I thought an announcement was imminent."

"*No* you didn't."

Claire started to cry. "What is he doing?"

"He's living his life."

"What about that awful Steven?"

"Steven is far from awful. They bought a house together. They're settling down. It isn't a secret. Jordan's been talking about it for months. You weren't listening."

Claire squeezed her eyes shut to stop the tears. Her chest burned. "I don't understand it. I just don't."

"Claire, don't cry." Annabelle's voice soothed. "Jordy is a good man. What difference does it make if he's gay?"

"Don't say that."

Claire threw the manila envelope across the hotel room. Dozens of envelopes scattered.

CHAPTER

EIGHTEEN

✦

C laire sat on the bed amid a sea of envelopes on the avocado-green carpeting of the hotel room floor. After a shower, she felt fortified. And a hair drunk but only for medicinal purposes. She got on all fours, scooped them up. The room phone rang. Saved by the bell.

Joe Lansing's chipper voice relieved her. "Hope I'm not disturbing you."

Please. Disturb. "No. Not at all. You were on my list to call today, before the banquet tonight."

"Just a small thing. I never did get Liam's full name and correct spelling. We'll need it for several purposes, the stone carving, we do a nice printed program, you might want a small newspaper announcement, etc."

After she obliged, she paused. "Joe... oddest thing. I asked Grace about Liam's father. About his burial at the university. She confirmed he was neither a donor nor a trustee." She flipped an envelope back and forth. "According to her the university gave him his plot as a gift for loyal employment. Does that sound right?"

"That'd be the day. Let me look him up and see what I get. Emmet Corrigan, hmm, it'll take just a few seconds. Oh yes, here he is, Emmet Patrick Corrigan. Someone made an anonymous donation in his honor so he could be buried here. A hefty one to boot—a million dollars. Fairly significant I'd say."

"It wouldn't have been the school?"

"Not a chance. We ask for money, we don't give it away."

"Any way to know who anonymous was?"

"Afraid not. We take that designation seriously." Claire could feel Joe's consideration over the phone. "I'll admit it's a small town. Hard to keep a lid on money like that. But unfortunately, looks like he died right before I moved here. So I don't even know any gossip."

"Hmm, that is too bad." Claire balanced an envelope on Liam's urn. "Would Grace have known?"

"Not necessarily."

"If she did she'd never admit it."

She watched the envelope sail to the ground.

****

Claire picked a random envelope. She pulled a letter out dated three weeks after Liam died. The first one she'd received regarding the matter of Ellen Ryan and Shane Ryan Corrigan. Claire knew it word for word. Every one burned into her memory. The demand letter was the first of many all varying in degrees of hostility. The last promised court intervention if no satisfaction came by the suggested date. Claire reached for the phone.

"Andrew? Sorry to bother you at home on a Saturday."

Not really. Not at the rates she paid him.

"Don't worry about it, Claire. Meg's in Newport with the girls. I'm at the beach house. What's wrong?"

Claire closed her eyes, filled her lungs with as much air as she could breathe in. "I thought we'd talk about Ellen."

Claire could hear Andrew opening drawers. "Let's rip this Band-Aid off and move on. I'm turning on my laptop as we speak."

"How much money are we sending her every month again?"

"Ten grand."

"How much does she want?"

"Haven't you read any of the correspondence?"

"That's what I pay you for."

"She wants twice that. Plus private school tuition. Then college. And a car when he's old enough."

"Liam is dead. I can't believe this is an issue."

"There's more."

"This is a joke."

"I'm not laughing. She wants a piece of the estate."

"Like my dad used to say, want in one hand, shit in the other. Guess which one fills up faster?"

"You want to keep this out of court away from your family? She got the DNA results we demanded. You're on the losing side of this Claire. I'm sorry."

Claire could feel her spine stiffen. "Absolutely not. No piece of the estate."

Claire heard flint scrape metal, the lighter ignite, and Andrew's sharp intake of breath. "Claire, you don't want to fight this out in front of a judge. You'll lose. It'll just be a question of how much. Shane is Liam's son. He might be entitled to a piece of his estate."

Claire lay back on the bed. The tears rolled into her ears. "And he might not."

"I'm sorry. This couldn't be worse. I don't know what to say."

Claire covered her eyes with the hand that wasn't holding the phone.

"Just give me legal advice, Andrew."

"Claire—Ellen could've dragged you into court by now. Or shown up on your doorstep. Contacted the kids. She could've done any number of things to make this uglier. She's erring on the side of reasonable. So far. You want legal advice?" He blew out. "You're going to be paying for a very long time. Shane is only a little over a year old and Liam left a hefty estate. You give this to a judge and I think she'll get everything she wants. You don't want the state to determine the amount. To make matters worse, go to court, the lid's blown off, and it's public. Privacy costs. It's that simple."

"Okay, Andrew. What do you want me to do?"

"Make an offer. A serious one."

"Ten grand a month. Double is ridiculous. Yes to everything else. Plus a million in cash."

"It's a place to start." He hesitated. "Claire?"

"What now?"

"When you get home we need to talk about selling the apartment unless you've reconsidered the crypt. I'm—"

Claire hung up.

A place to start? This mess probably won't end there. Or anywhere. Are there enough pills in the world to get through this?

"Campus for the Cure isn't until Wednesday night is it?"
"You'd think she could afford at least a scarf."

"Hush, Irma. I heard she's a widow. A rich one."

In her three thousand dollar Alexander McQueen dress (worth at least twice that since he hanged himself) she was the belle of this ball. So with her head held high she mopped her forehead and pranced around the auditorium like a million bucks. Five million to be exact. The bitter hens in last year's Escadas could kiss her platinum ass.

"Claire, you look fantastic." Dean Sumner grasped both Claire's hands in his. "That dress is a masterpiece, the best one in the room."

He'd leaned in and whispered so the other donors milling around close by couldn't hear. Claire almost hadn't heard. Her heels made her even taller so his voice echoed somewhere around her ribcage.

"Claire, lovely to see you again." Evelyn Wallace chirped like a bird from across the hall. She tottered over on her pudgy feet stuffed into tight blue satin pumps that matched her dress. She must always coordinate her outfits with her hair color, her shtick.

Claire grasped her plump outstretched hand warmly. "I didn't know you'd be here tonight." Evelyn smelled like Chanel No. 5 mixed with streusel.

"Oh, we Wallaces have been Dean Council donors for generations." Evelyn's eyes scanned the room.

She didn't doubt it.

"Looks like a good turnout," Claire said.

Joe Lansing made a beeline for her to make idle conversation. Claire wondered if Joe'd brought his wife. She'd love to meet the sort of woman who'd marry a funeral director. Did he make her play dead in the sack? If she was like most wives she was good at it. A skill they'd honed right after the wedding cake was cut.

The room neared its capacity. Several round tables were set with white tablecloths and tasteful floral centerpieces, carefully arranged at below eye level to not disturb the flow of conversation.

"Did you sign in at reception?" Dean Sumner looked straight ahead at Claire's chest and appeared to find it wanting. "You don't have a nametag."

As usual she'd sauntered in without a thought or glance to the right or left. "Oh no... I didn't notice a registration area," Claire said. "Sorry."

"Here you are." Evelyn, the eighth wonder of the uber-organized world, peeled the back off Claire's nametag and smoothed it over Claire's left bosom. "There. All set."

They sure knew how to treat a five million dollar donor.

"You're sitting with us at the dean's table, of course." Dean Sumner pointed toward a round table at the front of the room near the dais. "Let's mingle. Several of our council members are dying to meet you."

Sure they were.

Thirty minutes and a hundred handshakes later, Claire's brain felt like mush, her face frozen into a smile only a hack plastic surgeon could appreciate. Half the women in the room had the same one. She inched toward her table, leaned down to Dean Sumner to beg for mercy when a tap on her shoulder brought her round.

"Is that you, Claire Corrigan?"

Her nemesis. King Dong. Mr. Lied-about-his-dead-wife-whom-he-might-have-killed.

"Rob Rhino."

"In the flesh."

"This is unbelievable." She fumbled for the table.

"I know. Can't believe you're here."

He grinned, his best shit-eating kind, not the least bit self-conscious. He'd cleaned up again too. His strings of dyed hair stretched across his bare scalp into a limp ponytail. His expensive suit fit him well and real shoes replaced his green rubber clogs. Rob Rhino in stylish black pinstripes and expensive leather. Claire knew from expensive shoes and well-made clothes.

"Doc, have you met our guest of honor? Claire Corrigan?" Dean Sumner slapped Rob Rhino on the back like a good old boy.

"We know each other. Go way back," Rob said.

Claire's buzz had all but disappeared. What was up with this Doc business? She needed to get to her purse. How many millions did it take to get a cocktail around here?

"Do tell." Dean Sumner clapped his hands like a high school cheerleader.

An elder-statesman-looking fellow stepped up to the dais and asked everyone to take their seats. A collective rumble spread across the room as heels clacked, chairs scraped.

Joe and Dean Sumner sat side by side at the dean's table, no wives in sight. Claire stumbled to her seat. She turned to her side expecting to see Rob Rhino, to demand an explanation for his creepy presence. He'd disappeared. Twisting side to side, trying not to appear obvious, she searched to no avail. The room was packed. He could be anywhere. The loser in the monkey suit still yammered at the microphone. She dug for the only thing she could trust at the bottom of her rhinestone ladybug bag.

What kind of place was this that would let the likes of Rob Rhino in?

And the dean acted friendly toward him? Of all the... she turned to Dean Sumner to ask when she noticed his hand on Joe Lansing's leg.

Jesus, Mary, and Joseph.

She looked away and stared straight ahead.

CHAPTER TWENTY

C laire gulped a glass of cheap chardonnay as soon as one
was poured. Then another. A plate of rubber chicken
and the program passed in a blur. Joe called her name from
the dais. Dean Sumner grasped her elbow, steered her upward
and out of her seat to thunderous applause from the crowd.
She didn't know what he'd said about her. She wasn't listening.
Sitting down again, not so steady, she put her purse in her lap
and searched the bottom. She wasn't bothering with subtleties
when Rob Rhino shook her arm. He'd come from she didn't
know where.

"Wanna dance?"

Claire kept searching her Judith Leiber, ignoring his
absurd offer. "Where've you been lurking? *Doc*?"

He jerked his ponytailed head backward. "Over there.
I'm always at the same table. Come on, let's get a groove on."
He did a little jig.

Claire stopped digging in her purse to look around.
Several couples danced by. She'd been too busy pawing to
notice the music.

"How'd you get in here? How do you know these
people? I can't believe for a second they know what you do."

She turned to her right in time to see Joe and the dean
making goo-goo eyes, their hands clasped firmly together
under the table. Good Christ. No wonder Dean Sumner
reminded her of Steven. Steven and Jord—Claire's stomach
lurched.

She slapped her purse shut. "Let's dance."

He led her by the elbow to the center of the banquet hall where other couples tripped the light fantastic, cheek to cheek. Claire planted her feet, arms at her side. Rob held out his hand, waited. After a beat or two, she took it. To her shocked dismay he pulled her close. He gently placed one arm around her waist, the other near her shoulder where their fingers entwined. She could see over his head. He didn't stink. She could smell his aftershave, crisp, masculine. His grip was firm, protective, seductive. Squirming away crossed her mind but the sweet succor of a man's embrace kept her in it. Her eyes closed for a second, the heat from his palm pressed to her back warmed more than her skin.

A decked-out duo foxtrotted near. "Evening, Doc." The tuxedoed hoofer nodded at Rob as he danced his bejeweled partner by. Rob waved like royalty.

Claire came back to earth. "What's the deal?"

"Told ya. I'm the doctor of—"

"I know—of love." She rolled her eyes.

"It's what I'm famous for." He winked. "A hunka hunka burnin'—"

"Oh God, stop." Claire laughed. "Seriously. Did you crash this party?"

"I've been coming to this thing for years. As a guest. With a date."

Claire froze.

"You have a date?" Her eyes roved the crowd.

"Not that kind of date." Rob laughed. "Margaret Dodd. She's a sweet gal, a widow. Rich as a Rockefeller. Husband was some kind of stockbroker. I introduced them. Known her for years. She doesn't want to come alone but doesn't want another steady."

"Where is she?"

Without hesitation Rob pointed at the bar. "There."

An over-bleached, too-tanned, stick-thin woman with giant breasts had a portly drunk trapped on a stool.

"Perfect."

Rob shrugged. "She likes to party."

"Looks like a stripper."

"She was."

Claire couldn't help but laugh. "This is the craziest town. Guess they don't care who writes the checks, right?"

They kept dancing through another song.

"Speaking of checks. Your gift to the university is unbelievable," Rob Rhino said.

"Yeah, well, I wanted to bury my husband here. Had to be a donor."

"Well, you did it in spades."

Since he brought it up, sort of. "So... your wife is buried here."

Wasn't sure how to let him know she knew he lied about Gloria's grave.

"Yes, she is. She loved this place."

"Why?"

"She went to school here. She's from this town. Her parents still live here."

They moved across the floor to the music. He was better at it than she was. He led her around like a Dancing with a Porn Star pro and she lurched like a clod.

"You said she died a long time ago?"

"Yes. More than thirty-five years."

"Wow. She must've been young."

"Early twenties." He spun her around. "Your husband must've been pretty young too."

"Yes. Fifty-eight."

"Was he sick?"

"No. Car accident."

"Brutal."

"Was Gloria sick?"

"You could say that."

Claire waited. Close to the chest kind of guy. Except about his penis.

The music stopped.

"I saw the headstone you pointed to wasn't Gloria's." She couldn't help herself.

"I figured you would."

"At least the lovebirds went elsewhere," Claire said.

Rob Rhino scanned Claire's now empty table. "You mean Dean Sumner and Joe?"

Claire felt herself blush. "Never mind."

Half the guests in the room had gone. A few still danced, some chatted, a couple holdouts bellied up to the bar. Joe and the dean stood guard at the door bidding goodbye to departing donors and their credit cards.

"Don't tell me you're homophobic," Rob said.

"Of course I'm not."

She wasn't. Of course she wasn't. She—why did he have to get under her skin?

"Don't tell me. Some of your best friends are gay, right?" Rob took a bite of the piece of cake that had been put in front of her placemat while they danced.

"It's just... I—" Claire's eyes filled with tears.

"Hey, it's cool. Don't mind me. I'm an asshole," Rob said patting her back. "Come on now, what's wrong? I'm always pissing you off huh?"

Claire blinked back her tears, laughed. "Yes, you *are* always pissing me off. You need to work on that. And you are an asshole."

Rob looked like a puppy about to lick her face. "Are you all right?"

"Just tired I guess. Long day."

Claire reached into her purse for her emergency hoard. If this evening wasn't an emergency, what was? Seeing no more wine she looked around the table for the water.

"Hey, can you slide that glass of water over here?"

Rob Rhino picked up the glass and handed it to Claire. "You're not gonna take that and drive are you?"

"You're not gonna mistake yourself for my father are you?"

"Seems like you've taken more than enough."

"How do you know how much of anything I take?" Claire felt her temperature rise along with her voice.

Rob pressed his jowls down toward his neck and raised his bushy brows. "Really? You wanna go there?"

"You have a lot of room to talk. Crackhead."

"Crackhead? Me? Been drug-free for decades."

"What? I sat by you on the plane remember? I picked you up on the side of the road. You were barely conscious."

Rob threw his big head back and laughed. "Oh that. You thought I was... oh funny."

"What's so funny about that?"

"I get airsick. Motion sickness. I have to take Dramamine before I fly or take car trips. Makes me loopy. I'm kind of sensitive to it too. Stays with me a long time. I'm not a crackhead. I'm delicate."

Delicate. Right. He takes Dramamine? That's it?

"You're kidding."

A couple she'd met earlier danced by and waved. Claire rustled up a tight smile, waved back.

"Nope. It's one of the reasons I hitchhike. I don't drive. Can't stay in the car too long. I like to go a little ways and then walk."

Rob took a drink of water out of the same glass he gave to Claire and smiled.

She palmed the pill.

****

"I have to talk to Joe and Dean Sumner before I leave. Thanks for the dance Rob Rhino. You sure can cut a rug." She had to give him his due.

"Any time at all Claire Corrigan."

Claire picked up her rhinestone ladybug off the table and walked toward the door when Rob called after her.

"Hey, if you're not doing anything tomorrow drive out to Alex's Warehouse. It's a real gig. You can see my fans. See how the other half lives. Get you a toy or two maybe a movie." He beamed, his missing tooth a banner. "I'll even autograph it for you."

"Not on your sad disgusting life Rob Rhino."

But she knew she'd go. Why not? She had nothing to lose. Not anymore. Besides Rob Rhino owed her. All he did was bug the shit out of her. She wanted to know what happened to his wife. And why he seemed to want her to ask.

****

Joe Lansing and the dean schmoozed another set of major donors on their merry way, probably a few thousand dollars lighter, when Claire approached.

"Dean would you have a minute to talk before I take off?" Claire said.

The dean smiled his warmest *YOU are my new best friend* smile. "Of course we can talk. Joe, Claire and I are going to sit for a few minutes, can you handle the door?" Joe nodded and waved them on while he fawned over the fur coat of a matron with obvious big bucks. Claire and Dean Sumner sat at the nearest table.

"I hope you had a good time," the dean said.

"I won't keep you from your hosting duties long. I have a quick question about the trusteeship."

Dean Sumner perked up.

"Could I appoint someone else to sit on the board in my stead?" Claire said.

"Oh well, I don't know. No one's ever..." Dean Sumner deflated. "No one's asked before. I suppose so. You know you're our first choice. We would bend over backward to accommodate you."

"Oh I know, I know. You've been very thoughtful. But the reason I'm doing this, well this is for my husband and his family. And I know he would want his family to represent me on the board if I couldn't be there." Claire looked at her lap in her best attempt at demure. "So I think his sister Elizabeth is the best choice."

"His sister. Elizabeth. Oh my, well, if that's what you think is best." Dean Sumner couldn't mask his regret. "Of course, I wish you'd change your mind—"

"Well, I'm always just a phone call away," Claire said.

"Yes, I suppose. I know Joe will be surprised. Perhaps a bit disappointed."

"Perhaps. But I think you'll find Elizabeth energetic, enthusiastic. And all of you will warm right up to her."

Like the Hindenburg to a blowtorch.

"Oh I'm sure we will. It'll work out just fine. Delightful."

"*I'm* delighted."

"That's all that matters."

Claire and the dean strolled toward Joe at the door. "Thanks again for your understanding." Claire figured out quick that money bought her anything she wanted here, like everywhere else.

Claire said her goodbyes and waved off kind offers to walk her to her car. She took a last look around the banquet hall. Rob's ex-stripper, rich-as-a-Rockefeller date, climbed up his leg on the dance floor. Not much of a climb given his stumpy legs. She could see him laughing. Claire dropped her eyes to the ground, tucked her bedazzled drugstore under her arm and hurried out the door.

W hat does one wear to a porn warehouse?
She pulled out several outfit combinations only to discard them as not quite right. Too bad Conchita wasn't here to ask. She'd know. She always knew.

The phone rang.

"Hope you don't mind the call—"

"Oh Connor, what's up?"

Claire could hear what sounded like a vacuum running in the background. "I'd love you to come for dinner, here at the farm. All of us could get together."

Could there be a worse idea?

"I don't know. I—"

"It'd be a chance for you to meet my wife Deborah." Connor's voice rose even though the vacuum sound stopped. "And we could get Elizabeth to warm up to the idea of the crypt if we worked on her together."

"When were you thinking?"

Claire kept shuffling through her suitcase looking for appropriate porn star signing wear. Might as well get Elizabeth across the finish line.

"Whenever works for you."

She pulled out jeans and a navy striped boatneck T-shirt. What difference did it make what she wore? For once she probably wouldn't stick out the most.

They settled on a date, he gave her directions, which she wrote on the Do Not Disturb placard that was sitting next to Liam. His urn sat next to the phone and the vodka bottle where Claire left it yesterday. She wondered if the maids looked inside the urn when they cleaned. She was about to hang up when she remembered something.

"Connor?"

"Yes?"

"This is a little awkward." Claire rested her elbow on Liam. She was probably telling tales out of school but so what. "I asked your mother about your dad's burial. You know about the guidelines. She said the university gave him the plot as a gift. A gold watch sort of thing, retirement thanks."

"That makes sense. He worked there a dog's age, you know."

Claire tucked the phone under her ear, pulled on her jeans. "Funny thing about that. I asked Joe Lansing at the cemetery. He told me it's impossible. The university would never give something like that away, so I—"

"Well, maybe they only do it for the old-timers, or they don't do it anymore. Probably before Joe's time." Connor sounded thoughtful. "Maybe he doesn't know."

She unscrewed the top on the vodka bottle. "Turns out they keep detailed records about that sort of thing. An anonymous donor made a donation in your father's honor. A million dollars. That's how he got the plot."

"Say what?"

"Hard to believe. I know."

"Are you kidding?"

"No."

"Did you tell my mother?"

Claire laughed. "No. My asking about your dad's burial wasn't popular in the first place."

"Do you think she knows already?"

"She might."

Connor didn't say anything for several seconds. "Bet she does. She never let on."

"Any idea who'd donate that kind of money?"

"No," Connor said with a laugh. "We don't know anyone with that kind of money."

They were both quiet.

Connor broke the silence. "Except Liam."

"Now you're kidding." Tired of standing, Claire sat on the edge of the bed. "Your family had been long estranged by then."

"Indeed. My mother would've never asked Liam for the money." Claire heard the vacuum start up again. Connor hollered over the noise. "My mother wouldn't have asked Liam for help of any kind."

****

Someone had called while she talked to Connor. Her phone didn't ring this much at home.

Annabelle.

"Okay. I talked to Conchita. She's gonna pack up some stuff and send it tomorrow. You should get it Tuesday. Said she'll go to the house on Mondays, Wednesdays, and Fridays if you need to reach her. She sends her love. She talked to Jimmy. He extended your reservations at the hotel and the rental car place. She's sending your prescriptions. Guillermo's back from Mexico City, whatever that means. Conchita said you'd know. Oh yeah. I'll throw in your mail."

Claire exhaled. It took a village.

****

Claire drove out of town, back to Alex's, where she'd dropped Rob Rhino a few days earlier. How far was it for God's sake? She thought only a few miles out of town. She couldn't keep anything straight.

Claire passed the strip joints, the churches, the massage parlors, and the dive bars without pause. It felt familiar, nothing out of the ordinary. Hard to impress now, We Strip for Jesus, went almost unnoticed. She drove by Alex's preoccupied.

Oh right. Alex's. That's the place. She spun around. The guy honking his horn in the oncoming lane waved his free arm like he was putting out a fire with it.

"Prick."

She careened back and forth across both lanes a few feet before pulling off into the dirt in front of the warehouse. The parking lot teemed with cars, trucks, and SUVs. Only a small spattering of cars dotted the church parking lot across the highway even though it was Sunday. A Corolla pulled out of All Saint's and drove straight across into Alex's. The lascivious were giving the Lord a run for his money. Claire drove around a couple times and got lucky. An old VW van pulled out near the entrance.

At the double doors of Alex's Claire noticed The Last Day for Rob Rhino on the marquee, unblinking. Marquees in daylight seemed sad. The giant porn warehouse with blacked-out windows sitting underneath didn't help. Claire pushed through the heavy mirrored doors with both hands.

"Macho, macho man. I've got to be, a macho man. Macho, macho man."

The disco music, strobe lights, smell of ash trays, and burnt rubber, hit her in the face. She should run. But didn't. The party going on kept her riveted.

Claire walked the center aisle on the Oscar-ceremony red carpet clutching her Prada bag. Metal racks holding God-knows-what, on both sides, stretched as far as Claire's eyes could see, which wasn't far with the dim lighting in the warehouse and her head. The voice on the loudspeaker was saying—no clue—she couldn't understand it over the din. Like lewd lemmings on their way over the ledge everyone scurried in the same direction. Above the pack she saw iron cages suspended from the ceiling. Nude, not-so-skinny women, porn palace hostages, danced inside. One with a live snake wrapped around her neck.

"Macho, macho man."

Yep. Time to run screaming. This was probably a bad idea.

The crowd parted. With might-as-well-be-naked honeys on both arms Rob Rhino held court center stage. A long line to his left curled around the side of the warehouse where men and women of all shapes and ages gripped Rob Rhino merchandise in their sweaty (didn't want to know where they'd been) palms waiting for the Ruler of All He Surveyed to give his blessing.

Claire was about to hightail it out when he homed in on her like a heat-seeking vibrator.

"Claire. You made it," he said loud, shook off the bimbos, and skipped over. A communal groan went down the line. "Come with me."

Claire stood cemented to the spot.

Rob scanned the room. "Don't let this scare you. It's PR. Just for show."

Claire took a tentative step forward. The Village People stopped singing. The naked dancers opened their cages with a clang and started climbing out. Sounded like prison at exercise time. A rope ladder unfolded from a cage and a burly guy in a tight T-shirt with a bright yellow "A" on his chest waited on the ground with a crate and a stick. Must be the snake handler. An identical guy to his right held a robe and a towel. The stripper handler.

"You'd be a hit here you know," Rob said.

Claire peeled her eyes away to look at Rob Rhino and said her first word since entering Sodom. "What?"

"Bald is a fetish."

A vein in Claire's forehead kept time with the strobes. "Leave it to you, Rob Rhino, to use my condition—"

"Even better if you were an amputee. Or a midget."

"Okay, that's it—"

"I'm kidding. There I go again, pissing you off." He started walking again, leading her by the elbow. "Loosen up. Try to have some fun."

"You're nauseating, Rob Rhino."

"You're uptight, Claire Corrigan. Come meet Alex and the girls. They'll love you." He steered her toward the platinum top-heavy titans. "Bald *is* a fetish," under his breath, "so are amputees. And midgets—"

Claire almost said, "Get your mind out of the gutter," but this *was* a gutter so she kept her mouth shut.

Rob introduced her to Cherry and Sundae, the twins, with a straight face. Both girls oohed and aahed over her smooth scalp. More than once Claire opened her mouth to protest but no sound came out—a baby bird waiting for its mother to drop in a worm.

Alex, a jolly, ZZ Top, bearded lug of a man lunged at Claire. "Fantastic to meet you." He pumped her arm up and down like her breasts would inflate. "Are you in the business? You're hot. *Love, love,* what you've got going on up there." He pointed at her head.

Did he say she was hot?

"I'm gonna sign for another fifteen minutes then its breaktime." Rob winked and turned to the pimply faced kid with a DVD clutched to his concave chest waiting next in line. He looked too young. How much weirder could this get?

"Hey son, get over here and get your picture taken with me and the twins, Cherry Sundae," Rob Rhino said their names together, like the dessert, and slapped the kid on his bony back. "It's another twenty bucks but worth it. No, your mama won't like it, but your mama's not here now, is she? She is? Well, let's get her over here. Make it a quintet."

"Over here you've got your basic anal probes, nipple clamps, butt plugs, and penis extenders," Alex said.

He'd volunteered to give Claire a look-see around the warehouse while Rob Rhino finished up with his fans. Claire was anxious to escape the twin's scalp ministrations (Cherry told Claire her head was the same shape as her grandpa's), so she went along.

Penises of all sizes lined one complete wall—large and extra-large sizes. And colors. Fluorescent pink, silver, gold, candy apple red, flesh, and pitch black. Plastic, foam, rubber, fiberglass, and ceramic. Battery operated, strap on, pump-ups, and plain standalone, do-nothin' dicks. One was tattooed, another starred and striped, and one for the crafters—an embroidered patchwork doozy.

"Who buys this stuff?" Claire couldn't believe a whole warehouse could stay in business full of dick stuff.

Alex looked out across the sea of people in the packed warehouse. "You're kiddin' right?"

Claire stayed close to Alex who looked disease free at least. Rob Rhino must think he's trustworthy if he kept coming back. He said they went *way back* or something like that. You know what they say: the perverts you know are better than the perverts you don't. She'd need to get her head examined if she got out of there alive.

"Along here you've got your blowups, your ticklers, your strap-ons, your bangers, pumps, and your basic slings." Alex squeezed a life-sized Angelina Jolie replica with her air-filled legs in a permanent spread eagle and her bee-stung lips in a perfect O. "If we don't have it here, it doesn't exist. And we gift wrap."

"What a relief at birthday and holiday time," Claire said.

Did she live in a bubble? Did these people live among everyone else undetected?

"Here're the films. Rob Rhino territory. They're arranged by category: Anal, Bi, Asian, Black, Evil Empire, Anime, Diabolic..."

He droned on while Claire tried to take in her surroundings. Big flat screens on the wall ran movies on mute. Claire squinted to get a clearer look. A dark-haired man in scrubs (shirt only) was giving his all to a blonde with a nurse's uniform bunched up around her waist. In a hospital setting, of course. *Good God Almighty... how big was his...* Claire clamped her eyes shut. A much younger Rob Rhino. She could've lived her whole live without seeing that in high def.

"*My Granny Is a Tranny... Lard Lovers... Screw My Husband, Please...* and one of my favorites... *Tits Ahoy*," Alex was pulling DVD cases out of the racks, reeling off names to a traumatized Claire.

"All righty then, is there a place to sit down?" Claire did her best to look peaked. Not tough to do.

"And over here's the fetish section... you've got your gimps... your knocked up... your fatties... I could get you in here in a sec with that scalp." Alex stopped. "Oh hey, are you okay? Let's hit the lounge for a minute or two, how's that sound?"

A lounge? God help her. Would CSI know where to look for her body?

He led her toward the back where the restroom arrows pointed to a small quiet area that looked like the breakroom for employees in any company in America. Except for the six-foot erect penis jutting out from the wall. They sat.

"Better?" Alex said.

"Yes thanks," she said to the enormous penis.

Claire turned her chair away from the phallus wall art. Sweat beads lined up like a string of pearls across her throat and forehead. Her mouth felt rough. No moisture. She could feel the panic begin its dreaded ascent from her solar plexus. She thought she'd taken a pill a little more than an hour ago. This place was too much. She reached into her purse for another.

He got her a bottle of water from the fridge and sat down. "So what's your day gig?"

"Mine?" Claire was taken aback. No one thought she did anything. They were right. "Well, I don't have one. Unless you count rich widow."

"A widow? That's a shame." Alex rested his goateed chin in his hand. "Rich is good though. If you can get it."

"So I guess you're not lookin' for a job?"

"No. Afraid not."

She took a tissue out of her purse and dabbed her face, tried not to think of the erection behind her. Guess workplace sexual harassment wasn't an issue here.

"Too bad. We could put you to work in a New York min—"

"No offense, but I don't think I'm the porn type."

"What type is that?" Alex looked amused.

"Well, you know better than me." Claire readjusted her tail bone on the metal chair. "Low self-esteem, poor, uneducated, addicts." Cherry and Sundae came to mind. Rob Rhino, too stupid to get out of the way of oncoming traffic. "Dumb as bricks. I've read the statistics."

Alex yanked the bottom of his beard, resting on his belly, laughing. "Is that so?"

"I've been looking all over the place for you guys," Rob Rhino sauntered in and opened the fridge. "Love my fans. It's a great crowd. But man, sometimes I feel like a piece of meat."

—————◆—————

"I like mine bleeding. Cold and quivering in the middle." Rob Rhino licked his chops, rubbed his hands together.

The waitress looked at the floor. "What can I get you ma'am?"

Claire ignored the slight. "I'll have the chicken and dumplings. Cooked."

Claire wanted to get out of Alex's. So much so that she agreed to walk across the highway with the man of the hour to grab a bite at Ma Pringle's. Plus she felt starved. She lost track of when or where she last ate. She lost track of a lot.

"I love the steak here. It's a tradition." Rob smiled. It didn't seem to take much to make him happy. "Thanks for coming. I didn't think you would."

"That's two of us."

"It wasn't so bad. You gotta admit."

"That place is any decent person's nightmare. Explains a lot about you though."

"You always gotta bust my balls, don't ya?"

"Wouldn't get near 'em." Claire spied the creepy looking guys in the next booth, one pointing at Rob, whispering to his companion. "Alex seemed all right though."

"He's a champ. Between Alex and my manager, they've kept me going."

"Your manager?"

"Yep. He's top of the line. I'm one lucky slob."

"Lucky, I don't know. Slob, yes."

"There you go again, bustin' my balls."

Claire wracked her semi-sedated brain for an appropriate segue to the question she wanted to ask. What's a gracious lead in for *what's the story with your dead wife?* The waitress brought a basket of bread and a bowl of orange-colored margarine. She almost dumped the whole thing in Claire's lap, she stared at Claire's head so close.

"Oh. So sorry. Let me get that. Sorry." The waitress plucked the bread slices off the table and tossed them back in the basket in a hurry.

"Don't worry about it. No problem." Claire pursed her lips, brushed the crumbs off her shoulder.

The waitress turned blotchy pink under her spackled makeup and scurried back to the kitchen.

"You're a champion, you know it? Bravest person I've ever seen." Rob Rhino put his dimpled hand over hers.

Claire let his hand rest. She didn't want to feel moved. She rolled the inside of her cheek between her teeth, fought tears. "I'm not brave. I'm bald. I handle it, that's it."

"No way. You fuck with it. Tell it to go to hell and beat it to the ground." Rob shook his head. "I think you're amazing."

She left his balls alone.

****

The waitress cleared dinner dishes, wiped down the table, and brought their banana cream pie and coffee. She got it all on the table without incident. Claire was running out of time.

He beat her to it. "Why have you waited a year to bury your husband?"

Taken aback, she told the truth. "Because I couldn't decide what I wanted to do with him. What he most deserved."

Rob Rhino turned the sugar dispenser over and poured a steady stream of it into his coffee cup. "Deserved? Hmmm... what did you decide?"

"That he needed to spend eternity with his father, his family."

He stirred, didn't respond. Claire took advantage.

"Why did you lie about where your wife is buried?"

He kept stirring. "I didn't."

"You did. I looked. That wasn't her headstone." Claire pushed her pie plate away. She wouldn't admit she'd searched the cemetery database.

"She doesn't have a headstone," Rob said.

Claire hadn't considered something so benign. "Where is she?"

"Under the shade tree, the most beautiful place in the cemetery." He'd stopped stirring.

"Why doesn't she have a stone?"

"Because I don't want anyone to know she's there."

****

The bell over the door tinkled. A slick, dark-haired, had-to-be-a-used-car salesman in a lavender silk shirt with a Dali thin moustache said, "Hey Rob, let's go. Your fans are restless. You've been over here forever."

Rob stood. "Freddie Eddie, come meet Claire Corrigan." Rob scurried to the register to pay the bill. He yelled as he went. "He's my manager."

Freddie Eddie slithered over, smirked, nodded. "I've heard about you."

Whatever he'd heard, it hadn't impressed him, Claire could tell. *Freddie Whattie?*

She primped her naked sweaty scalp, glanced up at Rob's manager, forlorn. His eyes shone hard, his expression Mount Rushmore. Tough crowd.

"I've never heard about you," she said.

Take that snake.

Why would he have heard about her?

Rob came between them, shoving his wallet in his jeans. He wiped his hands on his hula girls and palm trees. "Hey, Freddie Eddie, you got one of those flyers? For my speech?"

Freddie Eddie had already pushed Ma's door open. "In the car."

The sleek, blood-colored Corvette gleamed at the front door. Freddie Eddie hadn't bothered with a parking space. He leaned into the driver's side rolled-down window, pulled his head out, handed Rob a goldenrod paper.

Claire gaped behind him. So Freddie Eddie was the mysterious driver.

"Here. Come listen to my speech." Rob pushed a flyer into her hand.

Freddie Eddie slammed the car door behind him, started the car.

"Speech?" Claire scanned the paper. "A Twenty-First Century Porn Star? You're speaking at an alumni event at the university? For Trustee Week?"

Rob opened the passenger side door. "Yeah. The Influence of Pornography in the Twenty-First Century."

She stared. That's what it said all right. "Alumni?"

Rob's head wobbled. "Yeah. Got my doctorate. Then I taught there."

"*You* were a teacher?"

Rob laughed. "History professor."

Claire's hand worked like mad at the bottom of her bag while she read the bottom of the flyer, Doctor Raymond Horowitz, or as he's known to his fans, Rob Rhino, adult film and reality TV star. She squawked like an idiot parrot.

"A history professor? You taught history."

Rob got in the car.

"Couldn't get a PhD in pussy."

◆————··◆···————◆

"Mrs. Corrigan? This is Daryl Post. I handle public relations for the university."

"Oh... yeah... uh-huh." Claire tried to sound awake though she wasn't 'til the phone rang. She squinted at the clock. Ten-thirty already?

"Is this a good time? I'm notorious for calling at obscene hours. Thought I'd waited 'til late enough this morning—"

"No, no, fine. Still getting used to the time difference. West Coast—"

Claire'd spent a fitful night. The thing with Rob Rhino, the usual up and down with the pills. They didn't get to close it out the way she'd wanted. His story sure didn't end where he'd left it. She'd found the hotel's ice machine—broken. Her toe throbbed where she'd kicked it.

"The dean said you wanted specific language in the press release?" Daryl jolted her back to the present.

"Oh. Uh-huh." Too much thinking. She rubbed her sore toe. "Well, let's see... I want the Corrigan family, not just me. All the names on the press release. Okay?"

"Names? What names?"

"Umm... me—Claire, Grace. That bitch Eliz—"

"Are you sure this isn't a bad time? I can call back."

Claire rubbed her tongue around her teeth. Tried to find some moisture in her mouth. Nope, none. "I'll call you later with all the names, the spellings."

"Great. That it?"

She opened and shut her eyes a few times, like lid exercises, hoping to find focus. "Umm... what about radio and TV?"

"A gift this substantial will make the local news. Do you want to do an interview? I could get you on the local station."

Interview?

"Hey, my sister-in-law. She could do it right?"

"If that's what you'd like. Sure. You could do it together."

"Ahhh... no. I'll call you back in a couple days ok? Not too late is it?"

"We're not in a big hurry. This is Mayberry. Drying paint is big news."

Claire took down his number with a lip pencil from the bottom of her purse, crawled back into bed. With her slick skull on the cool pillow she stared at the smoke-stained popcorn ceiling, tried to figure out the Rob Rhino enigma. What disturbed her more? His dead wife or his brain? Couldn't put her shaky finger on whatever she felt about it. Like reaching for her hair. She expected to feel something but didn't. There was nothing.

Her thoughts bobbed and weaved through the alleyways of her head. The porn king had a doctorate. He'd gone from history professor to pervert. Claire couldn't fathom why. She thought there were more pills in these bottles. She wished she could organize her scrambled thoughts. Too many broken ones strung together in a strange tapestry with no clear meaning. She and Rob Rhino seemed to be in the same place at the same time a lot. They had in-laws in the same town. They both had dead spouses, soon to rest in the same cemetery. A match made in—Claire didn't bother to finish the thought.

****

Claire sat straight up, looked at the clock. Twelve-thirty. She'd fallen back asleep. She rubbed her eyes with the heels of her hands and threw back the covers. Rob Rhino's porn speech commenced at two. She lurched to the shower. The booze, drug leftover would wear off quick. She perked right up under the bracing water. A few minutes of feeling almost normal. 'Til the sweating, panic, racing heart, mouth dry as a dead man's. Thank God for the pills.

The shrill of the ringing phone tripped Claire up while she grappled with her towel and the cocktail she tried to pour.

"What?"

"Hello to you too," Annabelle said whining already. "You could've just let the voicemail get it. Conchita sent your stuff. It should get there tomorrow. I helped her box it up. You got another one of those letters. From the same place."

Claire's empty stomach churned, looking for something to tangle with.

Annabelle kept on. "I stuck it in the box with the rest of the mail, k?"

"Oh sure, probably advertising. Everyone wants to give me advice now that I'm... now that Liam... you know... hey—" She wanted to talk about something else. "Any word from Jordan?"

"No. They're not back. Extended weekend."

"Oh. I see."

"I think tomorrow."

Claire sat on the bed, heavy. "I see."

"Clairesicle, don't sound so sad." She hadn't called Claire that ridiculous name since she was a kid. Clairesicle like Popsicle, her favorite after-school treat. Annabelle was big on goofy nicknames. She called Liam Daddy Warbucks for obvious reasons. He hated it. Jordan was Jordy. He hated it too, which ensured its use. Claire used to say, "How 'bout aaaaa popsicle?" Annabelle in her babyish voice would squeal, "Yeeeeaaah, but first aaaaa Clairesicle," then she'd throw her arms around Claire's neck. Annabelle, the tender, motherless girl. Claire's eyes clouded.

"I'm all right," Claire said.

"I wonder."

"Jordan never should've moved to San Francisco. Steven lured him there." Claire's soggy hands clenched the towel in her lap.

"Oh Claire, that's not true. Jordy moved to San Fran because he loves it there. Because of you."

"Me? What are you talking about?"

"He told me his favorite memory is the vacation you took with him there. Before you married Liam. You drove to San Francisco when he was just a little kid, just the two of you."

Claire hung her head, almost dropped the phone. The tears came quick, hit the terrycloth with a quiet thud.

"He remembered you were broke. You stayed in some rathole place in Chinatown that smelled like grease and dirty fish tank. The lady at the front desk was like a hundred, didn't speak a word of English," Annabelle laughed. "He worried you'd starve on the trip. You didn't think he'd notice but you only had enough money for one of you to order off the menu. He'd order and you'd eat his leftovers."

Claire knotted a handful of her towel. Damn kid—too smart for Claire's own good even then.

"You took him to the pier, Ripley's Believe It or Not museum, Alcatraz, rode those weird rickshaw bicycles, and took his picture next to a guy painted silver. He remembers every second and can recite whole conversations you had together there. He loves San Francisco because it reminds him of you."

"So what are you saying, Annabelle? This is my fault?"

"No. Claire—"

"It's always the mother's fault, right? Son is gay. Turn on the mother." Claire stood, the towel dropped, leaving her naked. "I'm running late. I've got to go."

TWENTY-SIX

Her brain worked like a sieve.

Procuring a ticket ahead of showtime strained through like so much pasta water. Miss Bossy Pants at will call informed her with regret Rob's speech had been sold out for weeks. Even Claire's naked head couldn't turn up a ticket.

"Here."

Claire spun around. Freddie Eddie in a shiny suit, hair greased up, pointed ears flattened, handed her a ticket. "Let's go."

He waded through the packed reception area, Claire struggling to keep track of him in his lifted shoes. A beaming poster of Rob Rhino greeted her from the center of the hall—A Porn Star for the Twenty-First Century in big lime green letters beckoned across the top. Same Hawaiian shirt and clogs. His closed mouth hid the gaping hole where his tooth used to be. Finally a publicist somewhere convinced him to shut his pie hole into a closed lip smile. Claire elbowed her way through the crowd, ignoring the occasional stare, point, or whisper.

Freddie Eddie led her to a front and center seat, a VIP in the standing room only capacity crowd. She could touch the stage if she wanted to. Rob peeked out from behind the curtain right after her ass hit the cushion. She could tell he was happy to see her, but he didn't approach her.

Freddie Eddie sat next to her. Brother. Did he have that diamond post in his nose before? Didn't he know he was about a hundred and fifty years too old for it? She wondered if he knew about Gloria. He must know. The manager always knows. But Rob said no one knew. Maybe he didn't count Freddie Eddie as a someone. He seemed barely human. Creep.

Jordan hadn't seen anything shocking about Gloria when he looked Rob Rhino up. Wait. He'd left that message the other night, said he found more info. Claire hadn't called him back. Well, she did, but she'd talked to Maura instead. Claire's heart beat faster. Her mouth went chalky. Never mind that now. She was about to lean over to prod Freddie Eddie, who was almost mute for Chrissake, when a familiar face caught her eye. A too-tanned face. Lifeboat-sized tits. The ex-stripper from the Dean's Council dinner. The one she'd last seen climbing up Rob Rhino's leg on the dance floor. Pitiful. Sweat pooled in Claire's armpits. Her legs felt damp under jeans.

The auditorium lights dimmed. Rob Rhino sauntered out to thunderous applause. He moved to the center of the stage, headset on. With two pudgy arms he motioned for the crowd to quiet down. They obeyed.

"How many of you would rather get your rocks off than listen to some old has-been talk about it?"

A wave of raucous laughter moved over the vast crowd.

"Come on now, let's see some hands." Rob peered out over the packed room one hand flattened over his brow like a sailor seeking dry land. "No worries. Put 'em up. Let's get real."

Hands went up. Mostly chuckling, tentative men.

"How many of you got to choose between the two?"

Louder laughter, followed by groans, air slashed by hands going down.

Rob smiled, satisfied. "That's what I'm talking about, my friends. That's why porn in—"

Claire's blood searched the maze of her body, looking for its little helpers. Rob faded from view. His mouth opened, lips moved, she heard nothing. Someone had dialed down the sound. A porn star mime in rubber lime green clogs. She looked at Freddie Eddie—he was laughing—she thought. No sound. Claire's chest tightened. The only thing she heard was her booming heart. Crashing, thundering in her chest.

She looked around, certain somebody would tell her to keep the noise down. Sweat dripped faster than she could wipe. The greasy chicken sandwich she ate in the car came to life, slinked up the back of her throat, pecked and clawed. The ringing in her ears made her want to yell, "Somebody answer the goddamn phone." She jumped up, ran out of the building, stepping on feet and purses on her way. Freddie Eddie stood up, tried to stop her, but she kept going. If she didn't get out, she'd die.

Claire hit the reception area and stopped dead. She felt faint. She reeled to the nearest bench, put her head between her knees.

"Claire? What the fuck?" Freddie Eddie squatted on the ground in front of her. "Get me some water." He motioned to an usherette.

Claire kept breathing deep, long breaths. If she opened her mouth her chicken sandwich would reappear, worse for the wear. The wide-eyed usherette, most likely a student volunteer, rushed over with a paper cup of water.

"Here you go." Freddie Eddie put the cup to Claire's lips.

Claire sat a few more seconds, not moving. Only breathing. The room stopped spinning enough for her to look up. She reached into her pocket, took two pills with Freddie Eddie's cup of water, and put her head right back down. She'd left her purse locked in the car. She didn't want to forget it in the auditorium. The stash in her pocket turned out to be good foresight like usual.

"Christ, another addict." Freddie Eddie stood up. "Of course."

Claire's head jerked up. "I'm on medication. From a doctor." She spit out the words. "Guess I forgot to take it before I got here."

"I'm sure you are. Saw you popping pills in the parking lot at the restaurant. Look at you. How many doctors do you have?"

Claire's already red face burned a deeper shade. "What difference does that make? What's it to you?" She wiped the sweat off her neck with her empty hand.

Freddie Eddie shook his head. "To me? Not a fucking thing. You can OD in the parking lot for all I give a fuck. To Rob? That's something else. He's taken you under his wing. He can't pass up a lost cause. Do us all a favor before this gets out of hand. Go away." Freddie Eddie turned on his Italian leather heels and went back inside the auditorium.

****

Claire fumed and staggered all the way to her car, took another pill. So she took a few pills? Had more than one doctor? So what? Freddie Eddie (what grown man would call himself Freddie Eddie anyway?) didn't live her life. Didn't have a clue what she'd been through. No one did. She stopped a couple times to lean against parked cars to steady herself. Where the hell had she parked the car?

She roamed-stumbled-leaned, roamed-stumbled-leaned for half an hour before finally finding her rental. She pulled the keys out of her pocket and got in the back seat. If she lay down for just a minute or two, she'd be a new woman. Finally the sweating stopped. Her stomach stopped its assault, and the sledgehammer quit bashing at her skull. She stretched out as much as she could in the back, too tall, closed the door, and reached behind her to open the window a crack. Ah. Better. She closed her eyes. Her foggy Xanax-soaked brain ajumble with words, nonsensical, fleeting. Like dandelions in the wind.

What had Freddie Eddie said about lost causes?

****

Flat on her back, Claire stared out the dirty sunroof of the car. She heard voices outside. Someone pushed against the sedan and she rocked in the back seat. She sat up, her bare head stuck to the vinyl made a suck sound when she pulled it away. Cars pulled out of parking spaces, horns honked. She could hear the usual sounds of a busy lot. She leaned back in the seat, rubbed her eyes. She felt better, a little rested.

What happened?

She looked around the inside of the car, out the windows at the parking lot. Scanned her mind for clues. She'd come to hear Rob Rhino's speech. Did she? She wrinkled her brow. No. She didn't think so. She'd gotten sick. Came out to the car to lie down. That's it.

She should see if he was still around. Apologize again to Rob Rhino. Unbelievable. She felt her pocket for her keys. Still there. A relief. She got out of the car idly wondering if the back of her head had seat lines, red marks, from the cheap fake leather, maneuvered through the lot better than before. Put one foot on the curb when Rob Rhino called her name.

"Claire, there you are. I saw you run out. I wanted to stop the show." His face a mask of concern. "Freddie Eddie said you were sick or faint or something."

Claire turned stony. Freddie Eddie. She remembered. "Nothing to worry about."

Rob Rhino looked her over like he was checking for ticks. "Okay, if you're sure."

They stood on the sidewalk while the multitude filed out to their cars. To a man, they waved, called out his name, atta boy'd him on their way by.

Claire smiled. "You must've been a hit."

"I did pretty well considering it's been a while since I've been in front of a group."

"I'm sure it came right back. Like riding a bike." Claire watched the steady stream. "Or a nurse."

Rob laughed. "See how funny you are when you're not all uptight?"

"Hey, Freddie Eddie." Rob called to his manager who had his arm around the wide-eyed usherette. "We're gonna take a breather for a few minutes."

Freddie Eddie saw Claire, smirked and nodded.

"Hold down the fort." Rob turned to Claire. "Feel up to a little walk?"

****

Rob walked with his hands shoved deep in his pockets. Claire wasn't sure where they were, where they were going, or how she got there. There were graves though. Always graves.

The pills relaxed the muscles across her back, shoulders, and neck, kept her heart from falling out on the sidewalk. Did a number on her tongue too. She and Rob Rhino walked around the headstones and the tourists.

"What happened with Gloria?"

Rob kept walking, faced straight ahead. "She had a drug problem. Heroin."

Now *that* was a drug.

"Oh... I—" She didn't know what came next. He clammed up.

"Why don't you want anyone to know where she's buried?"

Still walking, Rob said, "Because I'm not supposed to know where she is."

Claire reached both hands out, blocked him. "Stop. What's the story?"

He stepped off the path, she followed. "When Gloria died, her parents blamed me for her drug problem, her death. I was pretty fucked up. They didn't want me involved with her funeral arrangements, her burial. I felt so terrible, so sorry. I agreed to everything they wanted."

"What'd they want?"

"They wanted her ashes so they could inter them somewhere I would never know and for me to never darken their door again. So I gave them up, just like that." Rob leaned against a crypt. "We'd been in California. The Valley. The porn capital of the world." He spit out the words. "I had her cremated before I brought her back. We were already estranged from her family. They hated me for going into the business, hated her for staying. Her father is a minister, after all."

"But you do know where they buried her. Under the tree, right?"

"No, I buried her there."

"How? I thought you said you gave her parents her ashes."

"I switched 'em."

"You switched 'em?" Claire couldn't comprehend it. "Switched what?"

"The ashes," Rob said his tone even as if it was normal. "Well, not a person's. Fireplace ashes. Not like anyone looks."

"You did not. Tell me you didn't." Claire laughed. She couldn't help it.

"I did." Rob smiled, his missing tooth making him look like a grade-school kid. "It wasn't easy either. I'd already given up the urn. So it was quite a covert operation to break into the chapel and pull the switch."

"Oh my god. You are something else. You broke into the chapel?"

"I had help."

"You had help? Good Christ, it's like *Mission Impossible* around here." Claire didn't think this place could get any more bizarre.

"You can't get through this life without good friends. That's all I can say." Rob Rhino reliving his dastardly endeavors made him laugh.

"So a friend broke in for you?"

"Yeah. A good friend of mine worked here at the school. I have a lot of friends here from my prof days or did. Anyway, he broke in the night before the parent's service and pulled the switch. Gave me back my wife's ashes. No one was the wiser. Gloria's parents went on about their business. They interred some fireplace ashes who-the-fuck-cares where. And

I had my own private funeral service on the downlow." Rob did a little hop.

"You are amazing Rob Rhino. You are." Claire saw him in a different light. A teeny bit better one.

Rob gazed across the horizon. "I'd crossed so many lines in my life by that time, I figured what the fuck."

Claire followed his eyes out over the grounds and off into the heavens. The clouds drifted and rolled in a sky so majestic it might convert the unbeliever. Liam would like it here if he didn't hate it.

"I'm no cemetery expert but this has to be up there with the most beautiful," Claire said.

"Gloria loved it. She'd been coming here since she was a kid to admire it. I could've kept her urn but I had to bury her here in this beautiful, majestic place. The only place I'm at peace." Rob's teary eyes made him look more old-whipped hound than porn star.

"I'm probably pissing off Freddie Eddie. Let's head back. Enough about me. What's your story? I've rambled enough."

"I'm afraid mine is as old as time." Claire put one foot in front of the other. "Right before Liam died, I found out he had a girlfriend. And a baby."

"Whoa, whoa." Rob's rubber heels squeaked to a stop. "Claire, I—"

"No worries," she said in her best Rob Rhino. "It's cool. I'm over it."

"Ah... really?" Rob's eyes moved up and down over her.

Claire stared at Rob's fluorescent clogs, an obscenity of cheer. "Yes. Really. In fact, I'm here to bury Liam with his father in a family crypt. They'd been estranged. I want to bring them together, make peace."

"Oh that's nice of you. Sentimental." Rob's eyes narrowed. "His father is already buried here?"

"Um-hum."

Rob Rhino stopped, tilted his head, took her measure again. "It's nice, right?"

"Yeah. It's nice. I bought a family crypt. For the whole kit and kaboodle."

"Oh well, bygones and all." Rob started toward the auditorium again.

"Liam didn't get along with anyone in his family."

"Oh?"

"His first wife is buried here."

Rob Rhino stopped short. "There was a first?"

"Yes." Claire felt in her pockets for her friends. "She killed herself."

"Oookay..." Rob's eyes narrowed further still. "A happy group."

"Guess she never got over their divorce or some such bullshit." She swallowed.

"I wonder if Liam was in my history class?" Rob chuckled. "Wouldn't that be funny?"

Claire laughed. "No he never went here. He hated this school, thought it was for hippies, pot smokers. Oh sorry. He hated this whole town."

Rob laughed, loud and hard, he slapped his leg and bent over at the waist. "You're over it all right. You're something, Claire Corrigan." He laughed harder.

Claire didn't crack a smile. Her mouth hardened in a kiss-like pucker while she waited for Rob Rhino to come to his senses.

"Are you done?" she said.

"I'm sorry, it's just—" Rob wiped his eyes. "Whoo. You've got James Earl Jones sized balls. That's some revenge scheme. Five million bucks—wow."

"I'm not going to deny it," Claire said. She touched her scalp. "Why should I? You're right. I'm getting even. And I spent a boatload of Liam's precious money, which he'd hate, for the privilege. So what?"

Rob pulled himself together. "So what is right. Claire, come on. Are you serious?"

Claire stood ramrod straight. "I've never been more serious in my life."

"You do know Liam is dead. Odds are he won't know."

"Maybe. Maybe not." Claire wasn't a spiritual woman. In this case she hoped she was wrong. She clung to the convenient, ridiculous idea of eternal life. "Depends what you believe."

Rob sighed. "You're right. I'm not religious. I believe in love. I'd like to think the good in us can triumph over the bad." Rob jammed his hands in his pockets. "I want to think Gloria and I will be together again. But that's not the point— that's romance. What you're doing is revenge."

"And?" Claire leaned against a headstone.

"And? Revenge is wasted on the dead. Liam's been gone, what? Over a year? Why did you wait? How long did it take to decide you were pissed off?"

Claire jerked and sprang off the headstone like a bird had just crapped on her head. "This is why. I'm bald, you asshole. I'm bald and it's his fault." The passing visitors made a wide berth around the campus odd couple, frowning at Claire's yelling on sacred ground. "It looks like I'm going to stay this way forever. I'm stuck here alone to deal with his girlfriend and her kid, and I have to do it with no goddamn hair. If I'm miserable for eternity Liam can join me."

Rob Rhino filled the short distance between them and held her hands. "Claire, it won't matter. Whatever you do to or for the dead doesn't matter. I know. It won't make you feel better. It won't make you any less bald."

Claire's hands went limp, her bottom lip trembled like a child's. "It's all I've got left."

****

They walked back to the parking lot. She rattled the keys in her coat pocket, felt her hand brush up against her pills. They met Freddie Eddie loping toward them.

"Where've you been?" Freddie Eddie said "You disappointed your fans. They thought you'd mingle longer. I'll bet Alex's is packed next weekend. I handed out flyers."

"I'm sure you took up the slack," Rob Rhino said. "You break enough hearts in my absence."

Freddie Eddie winked and chuckled. "Just a couple."

"A real pleasure to see you again, Claire." Freddie Eddie bowed at the waist. When he straightened up his eyes looked like whatever he felt about seeing Claire again was the opposite of pleasure.

Claire gazed over his head, stayed silent.

"I'm gonna walk Claire to her car then we can take off," Rob said.

Freddie Eddie waved goodbye and headed in the opposite direction.

"I rode over with him," he said.

"Where are you staying by the way?" Claire left the subject of Freddie Eddie alone for the moment.

"I own a house here. Nothing fancy."

A never-ending wonder, Rob Rhino. "Why does that surprise me? Right about now nothing should."

"No, right about now nothing should." He shook his heavy head, smiled a rueful smirk.

"Well, here's my car. I can take it from here." She unlocked the door.

"How long are you staying?"

"Three weeks if you can believe it. Long story. Mausoleum shipping time and everything."

"Oh well, I'll probably see you around. I'm here for the next few months. I usually stay for the spring and early summer, before it gets too humid. I'm around campus for the rest of Trustee Week, plus out at Alex's most weekends."

"Alex's." Claire clucked like a hen.

"It's a gig, isn't it?" He looked pleased. "Freddie Eddie's helped me ride the wave pretty hard the second time around."

Speaking of. "What about Freddie Eddie? Does he know about Gloria?"

"No. No one does."

Claire didn't know if she should feel flattered or not. "Why did you tell me? Me, of all people?"

Rob kicked at a piece of gum stuck to the asphalt. "I believe in love."

TWENTY-NINE

The parking lot was at a standstill. Twelve hundred visitors headed out at the same time, nobody moving. A toss-up to see who'd get out first, the suckers in their cars or the stiffs six feet under on hold 'til the Second Coming. Claire'd bet even money.

Her car edged forward while she dug around in her purse for something to do. She grabbed a big lump of something and yanked it out. Her cell phone cord. Guess that meant it wasn't plugged into her phone. Which meant her phone wasn't plugged into the outlet. Again. Still. *Where was it anyway?* On top of the TV in the hotel room probably. Oh well, the kids knew the hotel number.

The car moved forward a tad. Some lady in a BMW honked. Like it'd help. Claire rolled down her window all the way, reached into the bottom of her purse for her pills. Stop. She put both hands on the wheel.

It started with the dentist.

He'd had that genius idea to do her root canal with no anesthetic. Hello? Doctor Mengele calling.

He'd said, "Mrs. Corrigan the nerve is dead. But the tooth is abscessed up into your nose. The area I'd have to numb is very tender. I'm sure I don't need to tell you. The pain from the needle would—"

"What do you suggest?" Claire'd asked.

"I can do the root canal without novocaine. You won't feel a thing." The look on her face was the international symbol for *not on your fucking life* so he'd added, "I'll give you some

Valium to take before your appointment. You'll be relaxed as a newborn kitten."

Doctor Mengele sent her home with more Valium than he'd probably intended. At seventy-three he'd threatened to retire for years. Claire watched him shake a few pills from a big bottle into a small one, all the while blabbing about his new fly rod. On her way out the door, he'd handed her the big bottle. She'd kept her mouth shut and kept walking, big pill bottle in hand.

That night, as a dry run, she'd tried one. Doctor Mengele was righty-o. The runaway thoughts and choking panic that'd haunted her most of her life slept for the first time.

She'd mentioned her wonder drug to her Pilates instructor who gave her some lifechanging advice. "They're still giving out Valium? That's for old ladies. Harmless. Like Advil. Anytime you go in for any kind of medical procedure, no matter how harmless, you can get that stuff. Just tell 'em the procedure makes you nervous, and, bam—you get it."

Then she'd looked it up online to see what else she could get it for.

Over the course of the next year Claire had two mammograms, a CT scan for unexplained side pain and an MRI when the CT scan was inconclusive. Then three unnecessary root canals, two wisdom teeth removed, complained of insomnia, suffered from restless leg syndrome, and fibromyalgia.

Her days floated off in a serene haze, her nights in a dreamless catatonic-like sleep. For a time. When she'd suspected Liam had a steady on the side, the runaway thoughts and panic woke with a vengeance, she accelerated her fake illnesses and the Valium dosage then chased them with a small glass of wine or two in the late afternoons.

Claire pulled out of the parking lot and onto the outer campus road where traffic moved quicker. When Liam died and her hair fell out, she got a whole round of new doctors.

Dermatologists, specialists, a shrink or two. She'd found the perfect setup and a different yet similar drug. And an ace in the hole with her hairless widowhood. A well-placed tear brought out the prescription pad every time.

Then she discovered she could buy the drugs online. And from Guillermo.

She turned onto the main road out of the university. She reached back into her purse. Her pulse quickened, her mouth felt full of yarn. She decided to take a pill (just the one) when the car died. *What the—?*

It slowed almost to a stop. The car behind her swerved, the driver hung out his window, hollered something about her mother. It felt impossible to steer. The wheel would barely move. She pulled hard. The sedan rolled slow, came to a complete stop about six inches from the sidewalk.

Shit. Shit. Shit.

She banged the steering wheel with both hands. *What's the deal with this goddamn car?* She just put gas in it the other... at that station on... *shit crap shit.* She'd never put gas in it. The last person to put gas in this heap was probably rental car lip-ring boy back at the airport.

Now what?

She'd call for help. She looked down at her purse. Hit the steering wheel once more for good measure. Goddammit. Call on what? A cord? She leaned her wet forehead on the wheel. Guess she'd have to hoof it. Her hotel was a few miles away. No idea where a gas station was obviously. She'd find someone to ask. Have to deal with the staring, the awkward politeness, or rudeness. Claire opened the door without looking. An oncoming car nearly slammed into it, skidded out of the way, horn blaring. She jumped back. Didn't any of these hicks watch where they're going in this Podunk town?

After looking in all directions she got out and started walking toward her hotel. Not five feet from the car she heard a familiar voice.

"Claire Corrigan?"

Rob Rhino.

If she wasn't in such dire straits...

Claire stopped to turn around. Rob and Freddie Eddie drove next to her at a crawl in Freddie Eddie's 'Vette.

"We'll pull over right up there." Rob Rhino pointed to Freddie Eddie who did what Rob said.

"What's up? Something wrong with your car?" Rob Rhino walked as quick as his stub legs would let him, his clogs squeaking and slapping on the sidewalk toward Claire. Freddie Eddie stayed in the car.

"It's out of gas."

Rob dropped his head and wagged it back and forth, "You're kidding. Claire Corrigan. What am I gonna do with you?"

"Take me to get some gas."

"Two-seater car. Hang on." Rob did a quick waddle back to Freddie's lech-mobile and leaned into the driver's window. In a few seconds he doubled back to where Claire stood helpless on the sidewalk. Freddie Eddie peeled away from the curb.

"Where's he going?" Claire said.

"Gas station, I hope."

"By himself? How does he know what kind to get?"

"No telling what kind of trouble you'd get into alone. Unleaded. It's a rental. Won't need premium grade."

"Aren't you smart?" Claire had a less generous observation on the tip of her tongue for Freddie Eddie and his ridiculous car but since he'd gone to get her ass out of a sling, she swallowed it. "Let's go sit in the car. Only thing it's good for right about now."

They walked the few feet back to the sedan and got in.

"Now we're even." Rob Rhino said.

"Even? Huh?"

"Yeah, I kinda owed you one."

"For what?" An odd duck, this porn star.

"You picked me up on the highway and gave me a ride that first day." He rapped the dashboard like a snare drum. "This is karma I guess."

"If that were true you'd have run me over first."

Rob cracked up. "Well, I wasn't gonna mention that part."

Claire's mouth felt parched. Beads of moisture lined her upper lip like tiny soldiers. She wiped them away with the back of her hand and reached into her purse. Claire felt one of the many pill bottles at the bottom but didn't pull one out. She didn't want to take a pill in front of Rob Rhino. Why she cared she didn't know. She caressed the pill bottle in the dark recesses of her Kelly bag.

I believe in love.

She glanced up to find him looking at her arm sticking out of her purse. His eyes moved to hers. Caught with her hand in the pharmacist's jar.

"You can wean off those things." He looked stern, professor-ish.

"Why would I?" Her doctor (doctors) never said she should. "Not like it's heroin."

"You're gonna end up dead nonetheless." Rob glanced out the window.

Claire yanked her arm out of her bag. "Not everyone dies of an overdose like Gloria."

"What makes you think Gloria died of an overdose?"

"Didn't you say—"

"I said Gloria had a drug problem."

Freddie Eddie pulled up alongside her.

Claire felt exasperated. She rolled her eyes. "How'd she die then?"

"I killed her."

CHAPTER

THIRTY

They put gas in her car and Rob insisted on following her to the hotel. Better safe than sorry. Freddie Eddie made stern faces at her and only grunted when necessary. Claire drove to the hotel, pulled into the closest open space in the parking lot still full of Trustee Week revelers. Freddie Eddie idled behind her. Rob jumped out.

"This is me. Days Inn." Claire got out, locked the rental, tossed her keys into her bag. She'd taken a few stress relievers as soon as Rob jumped out of her car when Freddie Eddie delivered the gas. Her anxiety on a rampage after Rob's bombshell.

"Oh so this is where the princess sleeps on the pea."

The murderous porn star seemed casual as ever.

Claire licked her peeling lips, wondered if he could hear her blood running, smell her sweat, her alarm. "I appreciate all the help." Damn Jordan for being right.

A dual cab truck roared up behind Freddie Eddie, revved its engine.

"Better get going before Freddie Eddie starts kickin' ass."

"Wait." Claire crept close to Rob's ear. "Why'd you kill her?"

"She needed to go."

****

Housekeeping dollied up the biggest FedEx box anyone there'd ever seen. They had to send someone back for something sharp and heavy duty to get it open. Claire had a few hours to sort out its contents before heading to the farm for the last supper with Liam's family. Conchita'd worked her usual magic. All were well chosen, wrapped in plastic, shoes in cloth bags, a few coordinating purses, ready to wear.

Her pills were neatly boxed as promised. She opened them. Three full bottles. Enough to kill a horse or make this trip palatable. Guillermo knew where to go on vacation.

A manila envelope of mail. She dumped it out on the bed. This month's *Vogue* (surprised Annabelle didn't snag it) a handwritten note from Conchita letting her know that she'd kept all the bills. A brochure from Inner Peace Palace in Hawaii, junk from AAA, a subscription reminder from *Bon Appétit,* and a letter from Ellen's attorney.

A letter from Ellen's attorney. One.

Claire held the manila envelope upside down and shook it. Where was the other one? There should be two. When she spoke to Annabelle yesterday, she'd said there was *another* one. Where was it?

Claire looked at the postmark. It was dated just a few days ago so it was the most recent. The first letter was missing. Annabelle. She picked up the phone and dialed. Her own voice on her answering machine greeted her. She dialed Annabelle's cell. It rang once and went to her voicemail. Even Claire knew that meant it was turned off.

Goddammit.

Claire's panic began its insidious takeover. Calm down and think. Maybe it's lost. Got thrown away by accident. Any number of things could've happened, none of them bad. Maybe it fell out the envelope and into the box. She hopped off the bed and searched. Didn't take long since the box was empty. Nothing. Not on the floor either. Maybe Conchita'd kept it. After all, she knew about the whole mess. Conchita knew everything. Perhaps she didn't want Claire to get upset while she dealt with Liam's family. Annabelle'd intercepted the second letter before Conchita could see it and keep it too. That explained it.

Whew. She'd feel better if she could talk to Conchita to confirm. She looked around for her cell phone where she kept Conchita's home number stored. Where is it? It used to be on the TV. Not anymore. It wasn't next to Liam either. Just the bottle of vodka. The phone was dead anyway. She'd have to wait until tomorrow, call the house.

She opened the latest from Ellen's attorney. Andrew said it was too early to hear anything about their offer. She scanned it. Same illegitimate son, different day. Must've sent it before Andrew made their offer. She tossed it in her open suitcase that'd sat on the floor since she got there and lay back down on the bed.

She'd been too preoccupied to give tonight's dinner much thought. Best probably. All things Rob Rhino took up the space in her brain. Claire's lids felt weighed down. She gave in, closed her eyes.

****

The incessant ringing in her ears woke her up. Damn it. She stretched out across the bed and snatched the receiver.

"Are you all right?" Jordan said. "We just got in. Annabelle left a couple messages. Hard to know if she's just her usual slightly hysterical self or what."

"What are you talking about, Jordan?" Claire closed her eyes again.

"She thinks you're off the deep end. More than usual."
Don't start.

"Is that so? Speaking of, where've you been?"

"Do you really want to talk about that?"
Yeah, on the twelfth. Of never.

"Not now."

"You sound terrible. How much crap are you taking?"

"I just woke up. What did you need Jordan?"

"Need? Nothing. Just wanted to make sure you were okay."

Claire could hear commotion in the background.

"I'm fine. What's all that noise?"

"Steven. He's cleaning around me."

Steven. Great. Change the subject.

"Hey, didn't you say you had more Rob Rhino info?"

"Oh yeah. Still hot and heavy? Don't tell me. Let's see... let me find it, I printed it."

She could hear drawers opening, Jordan shuffling things around.

"Oh here we go. You'll never believe this. He was a history professor."

"Crazy, right?"

"You knew that already?"

"He told me."

"You saw him again?"

"Yeah, never mind go on."

"Every time I talk to you the tale gets more lurid. Where was I? Oh right, his wife died of a drug overdose in nineteen... wow... how long ago was that?" He paused to calculate. "Thirty-five years. So you're probably right, the guy's a wasted druggie."

Claire's eyes snapped back open. "It says drug overdose?"

"It says... let's see... actually it says drug related. That's code for *she was a junkie*."

"Yeah, probably right."

"Anyway, thought this was interesting, he's made most of his money producing and distributing."

"Producing and distributing what?"

"Films. Porn. Amateur mostly."

"Really? He never mentioned that."

"Lover boy's holding out on you."

"Go on. Is there more?"

"He's a partner in the company."

"Did you say amateur porn?"

"That's what it says."

"What's the difference?"

"Seriously?"

Rob Rhino and a nurse zipped through her mind. "Seems to me they all look pretty amateurish."

"And you'd know this how? No that's okay. I'd guess amateur porn doesn't use contract actors or scripts, no real production value. Just weirdos off the street filming in the garage."

"Oh you'd *guess* huh?"

"You asked."

"Why would Rob Rhino produce a film with no production? How is that possible?"

"Well, maybe he'd wrangle the weirdos. Run the handheld. I dunno. He was a teacher, maybe he taught—"

"Stop. Ick. What a bizarre world."

"Now all of a sudden you're a prude? Well, you'll love the name of his production company."

"Can't wait."

"Fresh Flesh Films."

THIRTY-ONE

"Your face is still pretty. Around the edges." Deborah smiled, patted Claire on the leg.

Claire looked around for help. None came. Connor gazed at his wife with indulgent adoration. Grace sat huddled in the corner with Elizabeth. Elizabeth's husband William sat next to Claire observing her head like a mutant germ in a Petri dish. They'd finished Deborah's mother's recipe for Yankee pot roast with all the fixins and moved from the mauve painted dining room to the dusky blue painted living room (it worked in the eighties) for... for what? Who cared? No liquor at dinner. Claire didn't hold out hope for any after.

"Raquel Welch has a line of wigs that look just like real hair. She's on QVC all the time." Deborah blathered on, so helpful. "I almost bought one myself just to change it up, didn't I sweetie?"

She nodded her round head with its own Curl Up and Dye bad perm at Connor who agreed with enthusiasm. "She did. Honest."

"Doesn't it get chilly in winter?" William found his tongue. Too bad.

"California is mild," Claire assured him. She had to hand it to these people, they could get down to it.

"Oh right," he said.

William then went off on a tangent about temperature and weather patterns while Claire tried to absorb her surroundings. The farm was QVC and Franklin Mint purgatory. No doubt Deborah planned to keep the whole living room in its original wrapping along with the certificate of authenticity to cash in for their early retirement.

Claire'd arrived fashionably late. Deborah clucked and fussed over her like the terminally ill prodigal daughter. She and Connor seemed a good match—Eager and Beaver.

Right after Claire made her entrance she zipped into the restroom. Eager and Beaver's happiness at her presence made her want to induce her own coma. Elizabeth and Grace's disdain for her offered a welcome balance. Claire hung by William—the family's Switzerland.

Dinner passed with small talk. It occurred to her not one person asked about Annabelle since she'd arrived in town. Nor had they mentioned any other children. She hadn't seen any photos of any either. She guessed they assumed or didn't care whether or not she and Liam had any children together.

She looked at the grim faces around the table. If anyone wanted to talk about Annabelle, or Liam for that matter, they weren't going to do it here. She thought Grace might ask again about Liam's ashes. Not a peep. She showed no interest in Liam dead any more than alive. None of them did. They didn't ask a single question about his life. Deborah shuffled them all out to the living room.

Claire needed to get her business settled and out of this snake pit.

"Isn't that right, Claire?"

"Hmm? Sorry... I—" She fantasized about all of them in drawers in the mausoleum.

"I said you haven't spent much time on the East Coast? Isn't that right?" William said.

"No, that isn't right. We own an apartment in Manhattan."

"That's only two hours from here." Elizabeth looked like she'd taken a swig of sour milk with lumps in it.

"Yes it is." Claire nodded.

Was this a geography lesson?

"Well, it's nice you're here. No matter what anyone says." William looked in his wife's direction, sheepish, like a kid who'd just peed his pants. If she heard him she pretended not to.

"Well, now that you mention it." Claire wanted to get out of there. "We should discuss Liam's memorial service, the family crypt and everything."

With bat radar Grace and Elizabeth moved in closer. So far Grace'd shed no tears, no Kleenex turned up wadded and torn in her hands. She appeared made of sterner stuff this evening perhaps fortified by the group. Strength in numbers.

"You know what I'd like to do." Claire rubbed her head in case they forgot she was bald. "I'd like to lay the past to rest, bury Liam with his father and eventually the family."

"And we don't even know her." Elizabeth's voice climbed on Claire's last nerve.

Claire went on. "I'm sure you know by now I made a significant donation to purchase the newest addition to the university cemetery. As you also know it's a requirement." Claire stared at Grace looking for a sign that she knew Claire just got a dig in. Nope. Talk about a death mask. "There'll be a lot of local press about the gift. Of course, I'd like it to be from all of us. The whole family."

"What do you mean from all of us?" William said.

"The press release will say the gift is from the Corrigan family and will spell out everyone's—all of your—names. As well as mine equally."

"How much is the gift?" Only Elizabeth would ask that question. Claire counted on it.

"Five million dollars."

"Merciful father in heaven." Grace fanned herself with an invisible fan.

"What sort of press?" The second question only Elizabeth would ask.

"Newspaper, radio, TV."

"We'll be famous." William smacked Elizabeth on the back and she flew forward. "William really. Have some class." Elizabeth righted herself on her chair.

"My goodness, five million dollars. I've never known anybody with that kind of money," Deborah said.

"There's a couple things I'd like to ask you to do for me, Elizabeth." Claire met her sister-in-law's swooning eyes. "I've been asked to sit on the board of the university. I can't. Or I should say I won't, because I don't live here. I'd like you to do it for me. As the family representative."

Elizabeth's head swelled to twice its size. "Me? A board member? There?"

"Who better? If anyone'll fit right in it's you. When I told Joe Lansing, you remember Joe, that I wouldn't consider it he thought of you immediately. Said you were the perfect choice. I agreed, of course." Claire felt her nose to see if it'd grown a few feet.

"Well, I do know how to conduct myself in any situation. I did attend the DeVry secretarial course that one year." Elizabeth's nearly nonexistent lips pursed and her sparse lashes batted like a coquette's. She fluffed her bad perm with one man-hand. "You said there're two things?"

"Yes. The interview."

Grace sat up along with her daughter. "Interview?"

"TV interview. I'd like Elizabeth to do it since she'll sit on the board, family rep and all. Probably this week."

Elizabeth's head nearly blew off her neck. "What? Television? William did you hear that?" She popped his leg so hard he yelped.

"My goodness this is really something." Deborah rubbed her chapped hands together.

"This is assuming we go forward as I suggest, of course," Claire said.

Elizabeth looked stunned. "I wouldn't hear of doing it any other way."

Game, set, match.

A hard tap on her shoulder jerked her head around.

"Are you feeling all right?" Connor said offering up her purse.

****

Claire left Elizabeth and Deborah in the living room yapping about what Elizabeth should wear for her fifteen minutes. All bodies accounted for, if not quite dead yet. Too bad the sweating and the palpitations put a cramp in her victory. She needed to duck into the bathroom then hit the road back to relative civilization. She trooped down the hallway, this season's It bag in a hopeful grip. The devil really did wear Prada. Whispered voices as she passed the kitchen alerted her, drew her in.

"Are you sure she's not sick?" Claire couldn't see from her spot in the dark hall but it had to be William.

"She's not. Unless you count dope addict as sick."

Was that Grace? Dope addict—what did she know? Who said *dope* anymore?

"That'd explain the way she looks."

Claire clung to the wall, stiff, straight, a cigarette and blindfold away from an execution.

"Connor said she'll probably croak soon." Grace didn't bother to lower her voice.

Claire felt her mouth and eyes drop open like trap doors.

"I don't doubt it. I've seen concentration camp victims better lookin' than her."

What was the jerk formerly-known-as-William talking about? This outfit cost more than he made in six months. Big talk from a doofus wearing short sleeves and a bow tie.

"Those black circles under her eyes. Jesus, she weighs like, what, eighty pounds soakin' wet? And she's tall," jerk William continued.

Claire's fingertips went to the puffy bags under her eyes.

"You can see her collarbone from a mile away," Grace said. "And talk about soaking wet. She sweats like a teamster."

"Yeah, I noticed that. Blech. And it's cold in here with the refrigeration on." William coughed as if to make a point.

Claire dropped her head, humiliation too heavy to keep it up.

"Liam always did like the fragile ones. Like Bonnie. He sure could pick 'em," Grace said. "She liked her pills too remember?"

"She used to call Elizabeth when we lived in that apartment over on Center Street when they first moved to California, crying, high as a kite," William reminisced.

"Here too." Grace sighed. "She always wanted to talk to Emmet. Not that she did." Grace made a sharp snort sound. "Like I ever knew where Emmet was. Bonnie didn't like me. Neither did her parents. Especially after. They blamed all of us for her slittin' her wrists."

"This one doesn't like you much either looks to me." William chuckled. "What's the deal with the hair again?"

"Says it fell out. But you never know with those California weirdos. She could be one of those Scientolo—"

Claire hurried down the hall, hand over her mouth. She got to the bathroom door but it was closed. Goddammit. Tears pooled in her eyes.

Who did these yokels think they were talking about?

She raised both fists to bang on the door when flickering lights and the unmistakable smell of hot wax caught her attention. On a low table at the end of the hall candles burned. She walked toward them mesmerized. Who lit the candles? They weren't lit before were they? She hadn't noticed any of this when she'd used the bathroom earlier.

In smoky silhouette, like some voodoo sacrifice, three framed photographs stared down at Claire from the wall. Shadows jumped across them, candle wicks dripped and hissed. Up close the acrid smell stung Claire's nose. One black and white photo looked like young Liam, a graduation picture, maybe college. Another of an older man who bore a strong resemblance to Liam in a suit with a flower in his lapel. Emmet—she bet. Maybe at someone's wedding. The last one in color. A white-faced Deborah, young, cradling a newborn wrapped in a lamb-covered blanket, tight, cocoon-like, its eyes closed. Was it sleeping or dead? Claire could see her grimace reflected back in the glass.

So Connor and Deborah had a child. No one mentioned it during all the talk about the family crypt. The colors in the baby's photo had faded with time. How much time was hard to tell. Ten, fifteen years? She looked down at the blazing candles. At least twenty votives in glass jars alongside a two-foot statue of the Virgin Mary.

Hail Mary, full of grace.

Holy Mary, Mother of God,

pray for us sinners, now and at the hour of our death.

A shrine at the end of the hall of tears.

Claire's false peacemaking mission gave her a feeling of crushing sadness. And guilt. Her stomach hurt. Her eyes traveled from Liam's picture back to Emmet's. What was it like for the two of them before it went bad? Were they ever close? If they could speak now what would they say? Grace said Emmet would want to be with Liam in death. Would he? Claire knew what Liam would say. This particular road to retribution was paved with Liam's protests.

Maybe Rob Rhino got it right. Revenge was wasted on the dead.

Claire's tears finally ran over. She brushed them away. The last thing she needed this late in the game was second thoughts. Or a conscience. She looked again at the baby. Just an infant, never lived at all. She reached up and touched the small glass-covered face. Claire covered her eyes like she'd seen an eclipse unprotected. She didn't want to know about anyone else's loss but her own.

About to try the bathroom again, a darkened room by the shrine, door ajar, beckoned her. She pushed the door open. In the blaze of the candlelight she could see the nursery furniture. The crib, changing table, dresser. A rocking chair with a thick pad, most likely handmade by Deborah. Even in the glimmer the furniture looked new. Like a sleepwalker, Claire wandered to the middle of the room with its thick carpet, ruffled curtains, and stuffed animals. Smelled like fresh paint.

She went back to the bathroom to knock when the sounds coming from inside stopped her. She put her ear to the cool wood. No mistaking it. Whoever sat behind the closed door was crying. Claire leaned back and looked down the hall toward the front of the house. Grace and William still stood in the kitchen gossiping about her. Elizabeth and Deborah plotted Elizabeth's rise to national fame in the living room. Claire laid her palms against the door.

Connor.

Claire rested her forehead on the smooth surface, closed her eyes, and listened. She wrapped her arms around herself as a stand-in for the man alone in the bathroom who needed comfort she couldn't give, whose heart was broken.

C laire unplugged.

She stood in her hotel bathroom under the glaring light, naked in front of the mirror. Sans Chanel, Burberry, Prada, McQueen, or Carolina Herrera. No expensive designer label to cushion the blow. Not even a mid-priced one like DVF or DKNY.

Just Claire.

She touched the sharp edge of her collarbone where it jutted out at the bottom of her neck, flesh pale as the belly of a tuna and just as wet. She could see veins and count ribs through papery skin. The sight of her breasts sharpened her breath, the sad empty flaps of stretch-marked skin, slashed tires of her womanhood. Lips cracked and chapped a purplish inhuman color. Her already big eyes bulged out of an alien-like head. Even when she shut them the ghoulish image stayed branded on her brain.

She could only see herself from the waist up.

A small mercy.

I've seen concentration camp victims better lookin' than her.

She toppled over to the bed and fell down on it. Pissed, she noticed the maids left the empty vodka bottles next to the new half-full one. If they were going to sneak sips of her sauce they could at least throw out the empties.

Claire needed to get these next couple weeks over with, been here nearly a week already. She'd see if Joe could hurry along that damn crypt. She needed to get this memorial service out of the way. As a shrink would say—closure. She needed to stop thinking about Liam and how much he'd hurt her, shamed her, and go on with life.

But what about Ellen? Always Ellen.

Claire's eyes filled. What was the use? She still hadn't heard anything from Andrew. Ellen would probably drag this thing out for years. Claire's tears ran unchecked. She struggled up onto her elbows.

Drunk-dialing cheered her up at home.

The nice lady at information (though she kept saying, "You're slurring ma'am. I can't understand you") told her there was no listing for a Rob Rhino. Or a Roberto Hoskowitz. Or Reynaldo Harmon.

What the hell was his real name?

What was that he'd said about love?

Did he think she was beautiful?

After a couple more ridiculous designation combinations and some miraculous operator intervention she finally got it right.

"Claire? Jesus Christ. Where are you?" Rob said.

"In this black hole of a town. Where do you think?"

"At your hotel?"

"Duh."

"Are you all right? I can't believe you're calling me. What's wrong?"

"Guess a lot of shit is wrong." Claire felt the room changing shapes. "Do you think I'm ugly?"

"Ugly? What the... well, you could use a few pounds."

"Blah, blah..."

"It wouldn't kill you to wear a rug now and again."

"Fuck a rug."

What imbecile would call this asshole for anyway?

"And fuck you too," she said.

"I'm just sayin'," his voice brightened. "Hey, I could hook you up with a bodacious set of knockers. On the cheap too. Just the thing. I know a—"

"You're a hideous—" Claire's sobs cut off her insults.

"Hey now. There I go again. I'm an asshole." Rob's voice purred. "I was just messing with you. Trying to cheer you up, make you laugh. I'm an idiot."

"You are an asshole." Claire kept crying. "And an idiot."

"You're not ugly Claire. Mean as a snake, but not ugly." He made *mean as a snake* sound endearing. "More like a fixer upper."

Claire wanted to ask him about love but in her crazed state she didn't know how, couldn't put the letters in the right order. "Love. What about love?" she said in a low slurred mutter.

"You're stoned. How much shit did you take? I'm coming over."

"They think I'm dying. No reason." Claire threw it out there like a fishing line.

"Who?"

"Liam's weirdo family. Fuckers."

"We can talk about them when I get—"

"You don't know where I am."

"Yes, I do."

"Did you say you killed your wife?"

****

"I never should've told you that. I'm sorry."

Rob's odd presence in her room threw her off. More off than she already felt.

"I just wanted to scare you. So you'd stop taking all those pills."

Claire couldn't focus. She couldn't remember how he got in her room. Had she called him, let him in? Why was he there?

"I wasn't scared." She wasn't, was she?

"I know. But I wanted you to be. So you'd stop." He kept talking but she stopped hearing. Like the day he gave his speech. She watched him, acted like she comprehended, yet didn't really.

Was he saying something about Gloria?

Why was he always wearing the same clothes?

She looked down at herself on the hotel bed. She had on a T-shirt barely covering her butt, the top of her stick legs. She grabbed the bottom of it, tried to pull it down, make it longer. Rob sat across from her on a nubby chair, his hair unnaturally black, wild. He reached for her.

"It's okay Claire. I've seen it all. I'm a history professor, remember?"

He made a lopsided smile, scanned the mess of a room, picked up two empty vodka bottles off the floor. "Did you drink all this tonight too?

Claire's eyes closed, her lips felt made of lead. She fell over on her side. Rob yanked her up, shook her. She couldn't see him, but even in her pitiful state she knew he wasn't smiling anymore.

"Is this how it's going to end? Like this? Here in this shithole?"

She didn't answer.

He shook her harder still. "You're gonna go out like some street junkie?"

Her head flung backward with a vicious sting. He slapped her. She opened her eyes wide. Her hand touched her face where she could feel the imprint of his hand, his fingers. The skin stung like a burn, throbbed.

"What's it gonna be Claire?" He smacked her again, dragged her off the bed. "Tell me. Wake up and tell me if you want to die."

"I'm gonna be sick."

****

She laid her head on his chest, pressed against a coconut-covered tree.

"Don't you have a family in California?" he said.

She couldn't move her mouth, her jaw sore from vomiting, the force of his hands. She could only nod.

"Kids?"

Claire nodded again.

"They've already lost their father. Don't be this selfish Claire." He hugged her tight against his gut.

"Why do you care?" Claire's vocal chords, ragged, uncooperative, eked out frail sounds.

"I just do." He held her out away from him. "Why don't *you?*"

She wondered what it felt like to kiss him with that gap in his teeth. Would her tongue fit in it? She felt herself getting warmer, hot. She wrapped her leg around his.

Claire's trashed brain cells flung a memory to its surface, urgent. "Was it an accident?"

"What?"

"When you killed your wife?"

Rob squeezed his eyes shut. "I told you. I didn't. I was just trying to scare—"

Claire pried them back open with her fingers. "Was it? An accident?"

"Would it matter?"

Claire felt bile rushing up her esophagus. "I hope so."

—————◆—————

"You've reached Annabelle. Leave a message."
Shit.

Still turned off. Claire called like a stalker, to no avail.

Her head pounded, hands shook. Snippets of the night before tortured her, made her cringe. Liam's family, the dead baby.

Rob Rhino.

He'd been there, at her hotel 'til the wee hours she guessed. She woke up alone. She bent at the waist, a dry heave, and jerked back up. God forbid.

Somewhere a vague whisper of memories... she sat on the bed, smoothed her hand over the sheets, tried to recall. Claire could still smell his musky scent in her room, lush, ripe. She licked her lips, inhaled. She could still hear his whispers, feel the flat of his hand against her face, taste blood from the inside her cheek. He'd held her, she couldn't breathe... the choking... his hands had been on her, rough. A fleeting vision of skin, tousled covers, hovering shadows. Sweet entanglements, little deaths, silent halleluiahs. Hot, fresh, flesh.

He'd brought her back to life.

Like hanging on to fog, her thoughts flittered away.

She didn't know anything for certain. Other than she didn't want to think about it or know for sure. She covered her face with both bony, bruised hands. If she never saw him again, it'd be too soon.

****

She'd stayed away from the diner down the street since that first day. But she didn't know of anywhere close to eat. The place clamored busier than ever. Trustee Week must mean big business in a little town like this. She stood in the crowded doorway with the other schmucks waiting for tables and tried to decide whether or not she wanted to stay. She needed to settle her stomach, eat bread or something. The usual points and stares made the drive-thru a more attractive option when she heard her name over the racket.

"Over here, Claire," a long-fingered hand waved atop an outstretched arm encased in a lavender long sleeve. Nice cufflinks from what she could see squinting but a little gaudy.

Claire elbowed her way through the waiting diners to stumble to Joe Lansing's booth.

"Come join me." Joe motioned toward the empty side across from him.

The thought of another meal spent like a leper made Claire grateful to see Joe. He felt like an old friend compared to the gawkers. She slid into the booth. "Are you sure? I don't want to intrude."

"Are you kidding? Delighted."

She knew he'd say that. He glowed. Queen for a day.

"What are you doing in this neck of the woods?" Claire didn't have any idea about his usual neck of the woods.

"We don't live too far from here. I pass this diner every morning on my way to work so I often stop in for breakfast. Lawrence and I aren't compatible breakfast eaters." Joe chuckled.

Claire put down her bag and smoothed her powdered cheeks. She'd put makeup on this morning for the first time in months in an effort to hide last night's episode (she knew Deborah's mother's Yankee pot roast had smelled funny). She'd tossed a cashmere pashmina around her neck to hide the finger-shaped bruises near the bottom of her cheek, neck, and collarbone. Good thing Conchita thought ahead and threw that scarf in the box. She would, having slapped Claire to her senses a time or two herself. By the look on Joe's face she could tell the combined affect was more Baby Jane/Norma Desmond than she'd anticipated.

"Are you feeling all right?" Joe said.

"Having trouble adjusting to the time change. Not twenty anymore, you know." Claire rubbed her cheeks in case her blush wasn't blended.

"When I hit fifty it all went downhill. Everything's around my knees now." Joe eyed her scarf.

He'd just ordered so the waitress brought Claire a menu so she could catch up. They got coffee and ate their breakfasts over talk about the crypt, the upcoming memorial service, the odd unfinished piece of business here and there. Joe dug a piece of paper out of his man purse to take notes.

Claire munched her toast, sat back in the booth, and looked Joe over. A solicitous, gentle man underneath his gold-digging (grave-digging) exterior. Funny, Joe didn't seem too swishy. Not like the dean.

"Lawrence tells me your sister-in-law, the charming Elizabeth, will take your seat on the board of trustees," Joe said.

"She seems the logical choice."

You poor bastards.

"She won't be worse than a lot of them." Joe took the last bite of his blueberry pancake.

Claire buttered her English muffin. "By the way, I saw Rob Rhino's speech a few days ago." She balanced her knife at the edge of her plate. "At the auditorium."

"Ahhh... Doctor Horowitz, the infamous history professor." Joe laughed. "Quite a character."

"Quite. Surprising though. The speech, the topic." Claire sipped her coffee. "It's not like he's a professor anymore. He's a porn star for Chrissake. Isn't anyone offended?"

"Perhaps a few." Joe stacked their plates, put them to one side. "But this *is* a liberal arts college. The dean is quite progressive."

"Takes all kinds," Claire said her nostrils pinched.

"Well, Rob's a good man." Joe wiped the crumbs off the table onto the floor. "When he's in town he volunteers at the hospital's rehab program, at our literacy outreach center, hands out food to the homeless. Not what comes to mind when you think of a porn star."

"A real saint."

"His father-in-law doesn't think so." He pushed the stationery he'd been taking notes on toward Claire, pointed at the list of names running down one side.

She stopped mid-chew, pulled the paper toward her. "What?"

"Jesse Metcalf. Gloria Metcalf's father. You know Rob was married, don't you?" Joe tapped his buffed fingernail on the university letterhead. "He's a trustee emeritus."

"Yes I do know. I *didn't* know Rob Rhino's father-in-law was on your board. This *is* a small town."

"Honorary now, he's old. He shows up at the annual events to ramble on about how much he hates Rob. After all this time." Joe smiled the satisfied smirk of a blue-haired old lady at a coffee klatch. "You know poor Rob lost his wife many years ago. Drug addict I've heard."

Claire's ears almost flapped. "Why would her father hate Rob for that?

"Who knows? Better to blame someone else for her drug habit I guess." Joe motioned for more coffee. "He's so old no one can make sense of anything he says anymore. Nonetheless he's a father. Can't blame him for not appreciating the finer points of porn. Rob was a history professor when he married her after all."

"What would possess him to change careers?"

"Probably genetics." Joe laughed.

Claire laughed too. "What about her mother?"

"She's a recluse. No one ever sees her, but she's alive as far as I know," he said. "She's rich, which explains the trustee seat. Rob's wife isn't buried here though... something weird about that whole thing. Can't remember what, way before my time." Joe shrugged. "*As the World Turns.*"

Claire squinted down the sides of the letterhead, printed in a tiny elegant cerulean font. "How many trustees are there?"

"Thirty governing, ten emeritus. Or is it emeriti?" Joe laughed. "I can't keep that straight."

Distracted, Claire said, "He never married again?"

"Not that I know of." Joe poured more cream in his coffee. "Once is enough for a lot of us.

Claire's coffee went down the wrong pipe.

"You were married? To a woman?" She didn't mean to sound so astonished. Or offensive. Not out loud.

"Surprised?" Joe laughed.

Too late to pretend she didn't come from three generations of white trash. "I'll say. I thought... well... you and the dean. I thought you were—"

"Gay?"

"That's it."

Joe laughed more. "Yes afraid so. Card carrying. But I pretended I wasn't. So I married a wonderful unsuspecting woman and ruined her life." Joe stopped laughing. "And had a kid just for kicks so I could drag her through the whole mess too."

Claire's coffee cup froze midair halfway to her mouth.

"I'm sure that's more than you wanted to know." Joe took off his glasses and wiped them with his napkin.

"No, well, I... I'm sorry. I had no idea." Claire put her cup down. "How long were you married?"

"Ten years. A decade of keeping the closet door and Pandora's Box shut."

"That's heartbreaking." Sorrow tiptoed, fragments crept to the surface.

"Yes, terrible lonely years for her. Then several more to heal, to forgive."

"No, for you." Claire didn't realize until she said it that she meant him. "All that pressure, the faking, then the guilt."

"Well, we all got lucky in the end. Our daughter is healthy, happy, married now. How she came through relatively unscathed is a testament to her mother. My ex-wife went on to marry a man worthy of her but unfortunately she died of cancer last year. And five years ago I met Lawrence." Joe opened and closed his eyes, blinked back tears. "Not before kissing a lot of toads."

Pictures, flashes like butterflies caught in a net, worked free behind her eyes.

A dark-haired child tap, tap, tapping across the asphalt playground in his Payless five-dollar cowboy boots, cherished for their heels. His boy pumps. Every Halloween embraced with fervor the littlest drag queen. Lips pressed against a young forehead hot from trying. A mother mourning a son who wasn't.

"It's not luck Joe." Claire'd torn her English muffin into a pile of crumbs. "It's courageous, you and Lawrence. You deserve your happiness."

Joe reached over and put his spindly hand over Claire's. "You're a good person, Claire, and a lovely breakfast companion."

She fingered the bruises near her jaw.

"Hola?"

"Conchita?"

"Si?"

"Conchita? It's me, Claire."

"Si."

"Conchita. I said it's Claire."

"Si hola como estas?"

Claire took a deep breath, counted to ten. Conchita spoke better English than Claire. Yet she loved this Abbott and Consuela phone routine and did it any time Claire called. Jordan liked to say that Conchita loved to *yanko* Claire's *chaino*.

"Conchita, I've been in an accident. I have about an hour to live."

"Oh good one, Claire, good one." Conchita laughed. "Maybe you should talk to Guillermo instead."

Claire got no respect. If she wasn't so lazy she'd fire her and look for a new... a new... what was Conchita anyway? What did you call a person who knew where all your illegal drugs and bastard children were? Oh that's right—*employed*.

"Hey, thanks for packing up all my stuff and sending it. Perfect choices like always."

"No problem." Conchita could pack a suitcase like most people could make a peanut butter sandwich. Without thinking in no time flat. "How are you really?"

"How long do you have?"

"I knew you should've stayed home. Away from those people."

"Well, I'm on the home stretch. Umm... is Annabelle around?"

"No, not today. She only comes by to raid your closet." Conchita made clucking sounds. She worked her ass off to put her two kids through college. Twenty year-olds in two thousand dollar outfits didn't sit well with her. "I keep telling her she has her own place now. Time to fly the nest. Our little chica is too spoiled."

"Good luck with that. Hey, I've gotten a couple letters from Ellen's attorney since I've been gone. Only one made it into the FedEx. Did one get left there?"

"Ay chihuahua. That woman. Not that I've seen."

"So you didn't keep it there on purpose?"

"No. But I would've if I'd seen it. She's waited this long. She can wait a few more weeks."

"Shit. If you come across it call me at the hotel. My cell is... not working right. Try to keep Annabelle out of the mail. No. Better yet I'm going to be here a while. Forward it. Keep the bills. And if you see or hear from her tell her to call me pronto."

"Si señora."

"Adios amiga." It made Conchita happy when Claire threw her a bone.

Not good. Where'd that goddamn letter go? If Annabelle opened it...no that couldn't happen. It couldn't.

Claire put the receiver in its cradle and rested her forehead on Liam who was right where she kept leaving him by her cell phone. Both still dead.

****

The message light blinked. Claire pressed it hoping to hear Annabelle's voice. Two messages. Daryl Post, the university's PR man called to let her know Elizabeth's television debut was scheduled for tomorrow afternoon. Dean Sumner would appear as well to talk about the university donor program and

Elizabeth would speak *briefly* about the Corrigan family gift. The dean or someone from his office would call later to get info about Liam so they could say a few words about him on air. A press release went out to all local media. Yadda, yadda, yadda. Well, there's some good news. She hit two for delete and continued on.

"Claire, it's Connor." Claire's already sour stomach clenched. "Hey I ah, I'd like to talk to you about the crypt. The service and everything. Give me a call tonight at the house. I'd like to have coffee or something away from the family. I can come wherever's close to your hotel. Thanks."

Great.

No Annabelle either.

****

"You've reached Annabelle. Leave a message."

Goddammit.

She'd called her cell like a compulsive maniac all day. Claire beat the phone receiver against the dresser. A good-sized dent appeared in the cheap plywood and only the phone's ringing stopped her from whittling it down to firewood. Could she get her hands on an axe?

"Andrew, tell me something I want to hear for a change."

"She'll take a one-time cash settlement. Ten million. Everything else goes away."

No beating around the bush. He had that going for him. "Ten million? Are you high?"

He coughed, choking strangled sounds so forceful she thought a lung might hurl through the receiver. "Ahh... no," he finally said.

"You must be. Or you have a head injury." Claire's heart jumped, kicked, did somersaults.

"Claire, it's a good deal."

"For who?" Claire felt like she'd been dropped into a vat of acid.

"You're gonna pay close to five million over time anyway with the child support, tuition, etc." Claire could hear birds in the background. "That doesn't include any part of Liam's estate or any adjustments she might ask for over time."

"Adjustments?" Claire said loud.

"Child support is never a closed issue until they're of age."

"Forget it. I won't consider it."

"I don't understand Claire."

"Really? You're an Ivy League graduate. Get your head out of your ass." Claire trembled with fury. "Let me say it again. My answer is *no fucking way.*"

"So you want to go to court? 'Cause that's where this is going."

"I guess we'll see, won't we?"

"Then you're not willing to negotiate? Look we're going to have to sell the apartment anyway. Maybe let Conchita go. And do you really need a ten-acre estate now that Liam's gone, with all that maintenance?" He took a breath. "Keep in mind this would get rid of her. One payment and she's gone forever. Her and the kid. That's got to be worth something to you."

Andrew might as well have been humming elevator music. "Jordan and Annabelle didn't get anywhere near ten million. They got a quarter of that and won't see another penny 'til I'm dead. If there's none left, that's what they'll get. They aren't guaranteed another cent. Why would I hand over ten million dollars free and clear to his bastard?" The phone slipped in Claire's sweat drenched hand.

"We could negotiate down. But I don't think they'll go for it."

"Well, isn't it your job to persuade them to *go for it?*"

"Claire, I'm just playing devil's advocate—"

"Why don't you try playing my attorney for a change? My answer is no."

"I'll see what they say."

"You do that."

THIRTY-FIVE

Connor wiped his upper lip, his eyebrows, fidgeted in the diner booth. They'd agreed to meet at the diner during his lunch hour. The waitresses were getting used to her baldness now. Not so much staring.

"Your mother gave me the impression she wanted to weigh in on some of these arrangements."

Connor slapped his water glass down. "Oh don't worry about that. She let me know what she wants." With pale hands he wiped the spilled water with a twisted napkin.

"Okay, let's hear it."

Claire craned her neck and head forward, wished more than ever her damn eyebrows weren't gone. She hoped the wrinkles in her forehead worked as a kind of Morse code for the hairless. Connor called this meeting, now he wasn't talking. He must think she had all day. She did, but still. He didn't know that.

"She wants some special hymns," Connor said.

"I'll never remember." Claire searched her bag for something to write on. Joe'd left the university letterhead with his scribbled notes behind by mistake. She'd collected it off the table. Might as well make good use of it. A passing waitress surrendered her pen. "Write them down." She gave both pen and paper to Connor.

He roused. "Ah, the illustrious board of trustees." The pen clicked against the Formica as he wrote. "Guess Bonnie's dad is still around. What a nut job. He always blamed Liam for his unstable daughter."

Bonnie's dad? First Gloria's father, now Bonnie's? Both trustees? Claire's ass left the booth pronto so she could lean across the table.

Connor pointed with the ballpoint. "He's listed as a trustee emeritus—Elgin Grady."

Jesus H. Christ. Was everyone a trustee emeritus?

"Bonnie's parents are still living?" Claire said still ass-up.

"They're breathing far as I know. More religious fanatics."

"This place I full of 'em."

"Elizabeth ought to have a high time tonight."

"Tonight?" Claire plopped back down.

"Didn't you know? She's beside herself. It's Trustee Night or some such crap. All the trustees past and present have their shindig. The dean invited her personally. I assume that means all these codgers," he pointed to the emeritus list, "will attend too."

****

The bottom-of-the-sea tin can aroma of Connor's tuna-on-rye sandwich tested Claire's grit, still not 100 percent since her weird night with Rob Rhino. She straightened the high collar on her Thomas Pink button down, hoped it hid her bruises, fiddled with her multiple-strand Mikimoto pearl necklace. Connor shoveled mouthfuls of his lunch, one arm guarding the outside of his plate, eyes fixed on Claire, the standard prison dining room stance.

She studied him, his inmate-style eating, tried to conjure up the dead baby photo. Had she imagined it? What had she overheard Grace and William blathering from her spot pressed up against the ugly wallpaper?

"Are there no other grandchildren besides Annabelle?" Claire never knew when her Tourette's would rear its barking head.

Connor's last bite of sandwich hit the plate. His mouth full of fish sagged open like she'd just stretched a nylon over her head and pulled a loaded gun out of her purse.

He took a drink, wiped his mouth with the back of his hand. "Umm no... no more."

Claire stared him down.

"Elizabeth and William couldn't. They tried for several years." Connor twirled the ice around in his glass.

Claire gave him her don't-make-me-go-there-'cause-you-know-I-will look, peering down, neck bent.

"Deborah and I, we, we had a baby." Connor's face burned bright red, he'd started to sweat. He looked like Claire, except for all the hair. "It's been years ago. Twelve to be exact."

Claire leaned forward, cutting him no slack.

"He died shortly after birth, heart defect—congenital. Nothing anyone could do." Connor took a drink of Coke with the fork still in the glass. "We didn't want to try again. Didn't want to risk it."

"Oh I'm so sorry to—"

"Don't be, it's been a long time."

"He's not... not at the university cemetery?" Claire already knew he wasn't. She needed something to say.

"No. He's at Creekside, the other cemetery across town."

Claire's thoughts turned over like bingo balls. "Won't you want him laid to rest with all of us in the crypt?"

Connor jumped up, threw a twentydollar bill on the table. "I'm late. I need to get back to work."

THIRTY-SIX

"We hope our gift helps the university—" Elizabeth, with lips so lacquered she could barely open her mouth, squealed at the dean. She stared, glassy eyed, hillbilly in the headlights.

"The Corrigan family's generous gift endows the cemetery and will help pay its upkeep long past my tenure, I can assure you." Dean Sumner smiled into the camera.

Claire sat on the edge of the hotel bed, glued to her TV watching Elizabeth and Dean Sumner on *Hip Happenin's with Hobbs*. Elizabeth looked downright frightening. The camera added ten pounds all right, plus a striking resemblance to Milton Berle. Claire couldn't remember the last time she'd enjoyed herself so much.

Her medication certainly helped.

The alcohol helped kill the E. coli, peritonitis, or whatever horrible virus she'd picked up out at that godforsaken farm. She sipped from one of the glasses she'd taken out of the bathroom, squinted at the set.

Definitely a fresh perm and not just on the dean.

Where in the name of Ethel Merman had Elizabeth found that outfit? Just seeing her in it was worth five million. The wrist corsage was a nice touch. Giggling, Claire kicked her bare feet.

The local yokel Charlie Hobbs lobbed goofball questions at both the dean and Elizabeth as if they were three-year-olds. Given Elizabeth's answers and the star-struck look on her face, probably a good policy.

"You told us earlier that this colossal gift—and five million dollars is nothing short of colossal—is in honor of your brother Liam and your father. We talked a little bit about your brother but can you tell us something about your father?" Charlie crossed one maroon leisure- suited leg over the other, his white loafers keeping time with the cheesy background music.

Elizabeth sat at the edge of the red white and blue couch, back ramrod straight. Her false eyelashes periodically stuck together, which made her look like she'd pulled the straw out of the gin bottle right before air time. She cleared her throat loud every time she spoke.

"Well, Charlie," she looked around the studio like a beauty pageant contestant, "my dad, Emmet Patrick Corrigan," she enunciated the name like Charlie'd gone Helen Keller, "supervised the sanitation department at the university for over forty years. He made sure the campus stayed beautiful, the buildings remained in good repair and clean, the *cleanest*, and the bathrooms—"

"That sounds just swell." Charlie leaned forward and patted the dean on the back. "And this lovely lady is the newest trustee. Is that right, Dean?"

"Yes, she is. She represents the Corrigan family. We're lucky to have her, yes, we are." He smiled. Claire thought she could see *help me* behind his eyes.

Charlie asked a couple lame questions until the crappy music squawked louder, cut him off and he was forced to sign off. Claire shook her head laughing and got up to turn the TV off. She was about to congratulate herself on a job well done when her phone rang.

"Annabelle?" Claire said.

"Claire Corrigan?"

She held the phone away from her ear.

Goddammit. Him again.

He'd left messages, worried about her. She'd ignored them.

"I need to talk to you. Can we meet somewhere?"

"Rob Rhino. Look, I'm fine." She could feel her face getting hot, remembering. Her hand crept to her still tender throat, bruises fading but still visible. "I think I ate rancid meat out at—"

"Right. Good. I mean, whatever. I just saw your sister-in-law on TV."

"Elizabeth?"

"Yeah, her."

"So?"

"So I need to talk to you."

"About what?" Claire could feel her blood moving fast, her scalp prickling.

"I knew your father-in-law and your husband."

Claire schlepped into the diner. She felt sick of the place, the same old gum-smacking waitresses, shitty food. Now she had to listen to whatever ridiculous fable Rob Rhino'd cooked up. He probably wanted to get back at her for whatever happened the other night, for performing the Heimlich maneuver or whatever the hell he'd done on her. The two blocks seemed too far to walk, so she drove, beating Rob there.

"What now?" Claire heard her shrewish voice. She slurped her water. "How could you possibly know my husband or anyone in his family?" She hoped her indignation hid her deep shame.

"Claire. Hey now, it's cool." Rob Rhino slid into his side of the booth, his rubber green clogs flapping against his heels. He motioned to the waitress.

"I doubt it. Sounds the opposite of cool."

She searched him over the rim of her glass for any sign. He looked dorky as always. No knowing smirks, no intimate glances. She wondered if he expected thanks for having come to her aid. "Start talking."

"I spoke to him on the phone—your husband. A coupla times." Rob patted his girl covered shirt, his face blank. "I never met him in person."

"Speed this up." Claire's tongue flicked the ice cubes in her glass. The dreamy sedation she'd so enjoyed while watching *Hip Happenin's with Hobbs* died a tragic death.

The waitress asked if they wanted anything, as if all was well in the world. Rob ordered them both cheeseburgers. Claire stared straight ahead.

"I didn't recognize the name. I knew Emmet Corrigan as Pat the janitor when I was a prof." He fidgeted in the booth, got comfortable. "He'd been retired quite a while when he died. I didn't see him too much the last few years. He and Freddie Eddie never hit it off."

"There's a surprise."

Claire crossed her arms over her chest. The sweat beads started under her bra, armpits, and upper lip. She grabbed a handful of napkins, thought a minute... oh right. Emmet Patrick. She wiped her neck.

"Don't know if I ever knew his last name. When I heard your sister-in-law talk about the head of the sanitation department today, I knew it was him. He used to joke about that," Rob said.

Elizabeth didn't have an original thought in her head.

"Pat was my friend." Rob's eyes watered. He clasped his hands in front of him. "He's the one who switched Gloria's ashes, broke into the church."

"Liam's father was the ash thief?" Her heart beat a little faster, she dabbed her upper lip and forehead.

"Yes. God love him."

Claire moved the napkin holder closer, yanked out a handful. "Well, I never—"

Rob went on. "I went into the porn business. Gloria and I left town. She died. The years passed. Freddie Eddie and I hooked up with a distribution company, got into producing and distributing. I wanted out from in front of the camera."

Doctor Rhino, naked but for his stethoscope, whooshed through her memory.

"Good idea, go on."

"We distributed amateur porn, regular schmoes off the street, no script. Keep in mind when we started it was pre-internet. Before everybody and their horny brothers could use their cell phone cameras to film their honeymoon and put it on YouTube. There was money in amateur stuff in those days."

Claire had no patience for Rob's prance down memory lane.

"Is this disgusting story going anywhere?" She swiped her sweaty collarbone under her pashmina.

"Alex'd just moved into that warehouse. We'd film there. That's where Pat came in."

Rob Rhino stopped talking while the waitress set their cheeseburgers down. Claire took a big bite of her burger. "Came in for what? Clean up after your sordid sexcapades?"

If her mouth hadn't been full she might've yawned.

"Not exactly." Rob spread mustard on his bun.

Claire stopped midbite. "What do you mean, *not exactly*?"

Rob laughed, chewed up cheeseburger flying out the hole where his tooth used to be. Rob patted his lips with his napkin.

"By then Pat was Father Pat, the very naughty priest."

"Emmet Corrigan was a porn star?" Claire said it so loud everything in the diner came to a halt. Heads turned in their direction. After a few seconds of no motion, their waitress hustled over.

"Ma'am is everything all right?"

Claire shut her out.

"Mild disability." Rob smiled a weak apology, pointed to his head. "Mental."

The confused waitress shuffled back to the counter.

"You're gonna get us kicked out of here. Keep it down." Rob put his greasy finger to his lips.

Claire sat forward, her sopping wet chest flush with the table. "Are *you* mental?" Her voice came out in a hiss. "Emmet Corrigan disowned his own son because he got divorced, left the church. He was a devout Catholic, fanatical." She picked up the pile of napkins, patted herself down.

"Well, that explains the frock coat and collar—"

Claire slapped the table with her open hand like a school mistress. "This isn't a joke." She thought she'd die from the heat. She knew she flushed red as fire.

"For fuck's sake Claire, take a pill."

Claire slumped back against the vinyl booth. "What?"

"Take a pill. You need the drugs. You're a fucking mess. Take a pill so you can get through the next hour without having a seizure or something and take off that wrap or whatever the fuck it is."

Claire wanted to tell him to go to hell, mind his own goddamn business, but if she didn't take a pill she knew there'd be trouble ahead. She took off the pashmina, fussed with the collar of her shirt around her blue jaw and neck to see if recognition would flicker.

He frowned. "Jesus, Claire. Call the rehab center. I left the card for you on the dresser, remember? I volunteer there. They're great, get you started while you're here."

"I missed my regular dose that's all."

Rob Rhino pursed his lips, said nothing else about rehab or her bruises.

"I can't believe it. Emmet Corrigan in porn," Claire said moving it along.

Rob Rhino reached to the side and put a box on the table. "Look familiar?"

Like passing a ten-car pileup on the interstate, Claire couldn't look away.

On the front of the DVD box stood a man dressed as a priest who resembled Liam—only older. A lot older, with a girl, hopefully legal, in a plaid miniskirt with plump double Ds pushed out over the top of her unbuttoned white blouse. The Catholic school girl uniform X-rated style. That's the best they could come up with? Originality wasn't a requirement she guessed.

Claire picked it up, held it so close her nose brushed the cardboard. Pat looked a lot like he did in the picture at William's shrine. "What was he thinking? His family acts like he ascended into heaven with Christ."

She traded the box for the menu, fanning herself, eyes blinking fast.

"Porn's not so bad." One of Rob's over-dyed eyebrows headed up toward his over-dyed combover. "Consenting adults..."

Claire waved her hand, exasperated. "Believe me, it's not on their agenda. Saint Emmet. I heard it with my own ears."

"He had his contradictions. Lonely, bored, getting old. Dangerous combination."

"It's quite a leap from lonely old man to...to Friar Fuck for God's sake."

"Well, he *was* a man, Claire. He'd been patronizing Alex's for years. When we started filming in the back, he hung around. Got a kick out of it, so to speak."

Claire screwed up her face, still fanning. "Pathetic."

"After a couple years, he joined in. Energetic for an older guy. Those crazy Irish." Rob chuckled, remembering.

Claire put the DVD back on the table. "Speaking of old. Wasn't he?" She pointed to the box. "Christ, he died five years ago. He was like two hundred. Had to be too old for this."

"In this country, yeah, for sure." Rob bit into a pickle. "In Japan, no siree Hiroshima. All Father Pat's films went straight to Asia. They love their old folks."

Claire looked up over the menu. "Insanity."

He smiled, a satisfied grin stretched out his floppy face. "Not insanity. Niche as a matter of fact," Rob said.

"What is?"

"Elder porn."

Two words that don't ever belong in the same sentence.

"Of all the crazy, disgusting—" Claire flapped the menu harder.

Rob shook his scraggly head back and forth. "Elder porn is big over there. They live to be like five hundred. And now with Viagra? Yoko bar the pagoda. Of course it's just the men who are old. Chicks still have to be young."

"Only you, Rob Rhino, could corrupt an elderly church-going man."

"Hardly. He had ideas I'd never heard of. There was that thing with the plunger and the collection plate—"

"And Grace, of course, had no idea." Claire tried to imagine her mother-in-law in leather, spiked dog collar, whip in hand.

"Pat used to say if you wanted to know where the Dead Sea Scrolls were all you had to do was look between their sheets."

Let the church say amen.

Her heart calmed down a bit, she felt cooler.

"Anyway, she didn't know, didn't want to know. Until he died."

"He spilled his guts on his deathbed?"

"Might as well have. He died on set. In a confessional with Parishioner Patty."

F orgive me Father for I have sinned.

Claire studied Rob Rhino, now a balding, dumpling-shaped lothario with missing teeth, then looked back at the video. Grace Corrigan's saint of a prehistoric husband had died dressed like a priest, humping a blonde bimbo in a fake confessional. She burst out laughing 'til she cried.

"This was worth the trip." She wiped her tears with her hands. "Emmet Corrigan a porn star. Of all the improbable—"

"I knew you'd like it." Rob laughed too.

Claire, still laughing, handed her empty plate to the hovering waitress. "I'm afraid to ask what Liam had to do with this mess."

"When Pat died we had to call his wife."

Claire sucked in her breath for a second then laughed more. "You talked to her?"

"Freddie Eddie did."

Just the thought of Mr. Personality and Grace was too much for Claire. She laughed so hard her sides ached. "I actually feel sorry for Freddie Eddie."

"Grace wasn't pleased."

"I don't doubt that for a second." Claire laughed still but put some effort into pulling herself together.

"When poor Pat keeled over they took him straight to the hospital. Freddie Eddie called her, like five times. She wouldn't come. Finally she told him to call her son Liam."

So she had known Liam's number.

Rob scratched his chin. "We tag-teamed. So I called him."

"I can't believe it."

"Freddie Eddie shoved a phone number in my hand, said call the son."

"What'd he say?"

"Not much. I told him what happened. His mother wouldn't come make the arrangements, next of kin, all of that. He said something like I appreciate the call and hung up."

Claire shook her head. "That's so Liam. Direct, to the point, polite. Given how they'd treated him, I'm not surprised. He must've been shocked though."

"If I remember right, it took us at least two more calls to Grace and one more to Liam to get poor Pat identified. But Liam never budged."

"He could take a hard line."

"We felt sorry for poor Pat. We were gonna make a hefty donation in his honor—"

Claire knew where this was going, "You're the anonymous donor?"

Rob stopped. "You know about that?"

"Joe Lansing told me. He said an anonymous donor paid for Emmet Corrigan's cemetery space." Claire looked Rob up and down, his bald spot, his pock marks. "It's you."

"Not just me. All of us at Fresh Flesh Films chipped in." Rob Rhino's droopy eyes filled up. "I could never repay what Pat did for me."

"Thought you said he and Freddie Eddie didn't get along."

"Freddie Eddie gets along with money and Pat's films made it." Rob poked the table with his index finger to make his point. "I guess he did it for me more than anything."

"How did it all get resolved?"

"Only by force." Rob shook his big head. "The hospital told us if she didn't get down there they'd send the police out to find a next of kin. We knew Pat wouldn't want the police parading his secret life all over town. They gave us an hour to get somebody down there."

Claire felt like she was part of her own reality show.

Rob kept talking. "So we went over there."

"Get out."

"She let us in only to keep the neighbors from seeing us at the door. Freddie Eddie told her the deal. She never made a peep. We told her we'd take care of the university burial and vowed discretion. She held the door open, pretty much kicked our asses out it."

The thought of Grace suffering was Claire's favorite part of the story.

"I don't know what to say." Clarity hit her. "All this happened while Liam and I were married. He never said a word."

"You never know about people."

"A lot I never knew about Liam."

"It's a crazy life, right?" Rob Rhino ran his hands through his ratty hair and sat back in the booth.

"I can't figure out why she'd give you Liam's number. What'd she think he'd do?"

"There's a sister too?"

"And a brother. They both live here, always have."

"Probably didn't want them to know, why poison the other fruit? She might've hoped to rustle up a little sympathy, look victimized by the husband with the secret porn life. Get Liam to rush to her aid, forgive past grievances. Take care of the whole mess so she didn't have to."

"Sounds like Grace."

He threw up both hands. "So that's how I know the Corrigans."

Claire shook her bald head. "Grace Corrigan's got her nerve. Holier than thou is her middle name. She went on ad nauseam about Emmet's piety and Liam's sins. Yet all this time she's known her husband was a big fake." She grabbed her purse, got ready to leave. "Can you imagine anyone in more denial than that whacko family?"

Rob Rhino smoothed his moustache, scratched his nose. "Hard to imagine."

****

"Looks like Freddie Eddie's here." Rob Rhino said eyes fixed on the parking lot through the diner window.

"What's he doing here? Did he drive you?" Claire's foe.

"No. I took a cab. I called Freddie Eddie right before I left though to have him come pick me up in an hour or so. We're gonna zip out to Alex's. Freddie Eddie gets nervous if I don't let him chauffer me. Especially this week."

"Why?" Freddie Eddie seemed like a clinger.

"Gloria's dad. Freddie Eddie thinks we still have unfinished business. The guy's a religious nut. He's out and about a lot during Trustee Week."

"Jesus freaks aren't in short supply around here."

"A fire and brimstone preacher if there ever was one." Rob laughed. "Freddie Eddie worries he wants to speed me on my way to hell."

"Are you worried?"

"Nah. He's got one foot in the grave. What's he gonna do, gum me to death? I can take him." Rob grinned, black hole showing. "Besides, I've been coming back here for thirty years. If he meant me harm I've been an easy target. He's a nut but a lazy one."

"I'll be so glad to get back to California. You all make our weirdos seem catatonic." Claire put some napkins in her purse for the road. "Does Freddie Eddie know about all this... the Corrigan coincidence?"

"Not yet. He'll sure be surprised. Small world."

Claire stood. She felt better. Wouldn't last long.

"I guess so," she said. "If that's what you can even say about it. It's quite a story. Not sure what to do with it."

"Nothing, I hope." Rob stood too. He'd already paid their check. Such a gentleman for a porn star. "What's to be gained after all these years?"

The look on Grace's sour face for one thing.

"Nothing, I suppose. Sleeping dogs and all that." Claire headed for the diner door.

From behind her Rob Rhino laughed, "Claire Corrigan you are the end all."

"What now for Chrissake?" Claire stopped.

Rob pointed down at Claire's feet.

They were bare.

Claire walked across the asphalt in her bare feet with whispered ouches and ows. Like those half-naked natives who walked on hot coals. Hopefully no one saw the crazy bald lady doing the high-step across the hot, dirty asphalt parking lot in bare feet, talking to herself. Maybe she looked like a rain dancer. Maybe she just looked like an idiot.

She climbed the steps to her room, two at a time. As she got closer she could hear the TV still on. She got to the door, dug her key card out of her bag. Damn things never worked right. After the fourth time the green light lit up, staving off full meltdown. She pushed the door open with one dirty foot, dropped her bag with a thud.

Annabelle jumped up, muted the sound, "Claire, don't kill me—"

Claire, not easy to surprise, stayed rooted to the spot, stunned. "What in Christ's name? How did you get in here?"

"I know, I know. I had to see you to talk to you. In person." Annabelle stood in front of the flickering kaleidoscope of the TV, her long dark hair spilled around her. "I told them I was your daughter. Family emergency."

Claire didn't blink.

"I gave the blue hair at the front desk a hundred dollars to let me in."

"You flew in? Today?"

"Yes."

"How did you get from the airport to here?"

Was Claire in a hotel or the *Titanic*? Her nausea made the room sink, go sideways.

"Car service."

For a zillion dollars. Fucking rich kids.

Claire slammed the door shut, reswallowed the half-digested cheeseburger rebooting on the back of her tongue. She sat on one of the chairs at the small table by the window. Bribed the front desk. Great. A serial killer for all they knew. Inbred rednecks. Since when did Annabelle get so good at greasing palms?

"I've been calling you for days. Why didn't you answer, tell me you were coming?" Claire's stomach cramped, she leaned over a little.

Annabelle opened her lips, started to answer.

Claire held up her hand, "No, better yet, why didn't you *ask* me if you could come?" These goddamned entitled kids. Damn Liam. Leave them a couple million dollars right out of the gate. Annabelle Marie Antoinette'd her way across the country and Jordan shacked up with Steven in his massage parlor/love den.

"Because I knew you'd say no, that's why." Annabelle started to cry. Her gray eyes (just like her father's) welled up.

"You're right. I would've." Claire felt the walls go up around her. Like Alcatraz. Her chapped lips almost welcomed the sweat forming over them. "Annabelle, you coming here doesn't change anything. I'm going forward as planned, and your ass is going out on the next plane."

Claire eyed Liam in his urn. She didn't think Annabelle noticed he sat next to the TV. Claire wanted to keep it that way. Didn't want her to get any ideas.

"It doesn't matter. That's not why I'm here. Not really." Annabelle wiped her dripping cheeks and reached into her backpack, held out an opened envelope. "This is."

The letter. In all the excitement with Rob Rhino, Claire'd forgotten about it.

Claire got up, took it from her, flopped back down, squeezed her eyes shut. Panic, like a suicidal scorpion, worked its way up from her ankles. Her lungs felt like pinpricked balloons.

"Claire? Oh my god. Are you all right?" Annabelle's voice squeaked. "Where are your shoes? Jesus, where've you been? What's going on here?" Her head made a full turn around the room, even cleaned up it looked *Girls Gone Wild*. She studied Claire's jaw and neck. "You get in a bar fight or something? Never mind. I'm sure I don't want to know."

"Give me my purse," Claire said more of a cough than a request.

Annabelle threw Claire's bag on the table in front of her. Like a madwoman Claire dug out her pills. With shaking hands she swallowed two. Annabelle ran to the bathroom for water.

"You look like hell," Annabelle said trying to get an even better look around Claire's lame attempt at disguise—her shirt collar.

Claire laid her head back on the nubby chair. "What would possess you to read this? It's none of your business." She took a napkin out of her purse and wiped her neck.

"Because I knew it had something to do with why you're here, your craziness." Annabelle sat on the floor at Claire's feet. "I was right."

Claire kept her eyes shut, to keep the room from spinning out of control. Her whole body felt contracted, muscles cramped. This couldn't be happening. The one thing she didn't want. The thing she'd tried so hard and spent so much money to avoid.

"I didn't want you to know."

"I take it the other letter, the one I sent with your clothes, is more of the same?"

Without picking her pounding head up, Claire nodded.

"This thing's been going back and forth since Dad died?"

Claire nodded again.

"He was born around the time Dad died, a couple months before?" Annabelle sounded like the orphaned child she was when Claire first met her.

Claire's chest rose and fell her breathing deep, ragged. "Yes," she said in a whisper.

She laid her head in Claire's lap and wrapped her arms around her wet calves. Without lifting her head or opening her eyes, Claire smoothed Annabelle's hair. The skin on her trembling hand thin, translucent. Claire could hear her own tears fall on the wooly cushion underneath her ears. The heat from Annabelle's body radiated through the damp legs of Claire's jeans. She inhaled the comfort of her familiar scent, sweet, like cherries.

Annabelle. The motherless, now fatherless, girl.

CHAPTER FORTY-ONE

"What are we gonna do?"

"*We* aren't gonna do anything."

Claire stepped into her leopard print ballet flats. She and Annabelle had spent a restless night in the same bed. Between the chills, nausea, and the stomach cramps, Claire hadn't slept more than a few minutes at a time. "I don't want you to worry about it. You're going to get on the next plane back to California."

"I meant today, here."

Annabelle put her hair in a ponytail and looked out the window. Seemed she didn't fully grasp the situation with Ellen and her son Shane. Liam's son. She'd stayed silent about it the rest of the night. Claire wasn't sure what that meant but she wanted her to go home.

"Annabelle." Claire didn't intend to take her on a tour of Bizzareville. "We need to see about getting you out of here. There's nothing you can do."

"I want to see my mother's grave."

Not what Claire expected. She couldn't conjure a response.

"You've been to the cemetery haven't you?" Annabelle said.

"Yes, of course."

"Do you think we can find her?"

Annabelle looked like she'd just come up for air from the bottom of the pool.

"I know someone who can."

****

Bonnie Colleen Corrigan. Her headstone stood near a shade tree and wasn't far from the chapel. Joe Lansing looked it up, no problem, and drew them a nice map. Claire and Rob Rhino must've walked past it and not known it.

Annabelle and Claire stood in front of the stone for a few minutes in silence.

"I don't remember if I came to her funeral," Annabelle said.

"You were only a baby," Claire said.

"No flowers."

"No, guess not."

"People probably lose interest after a while."

"Maybe we came in an off week." Claire said. "Could've been some a few days ago for all we know."

Poor kid.

Annabelle looked around. "This place is really pretty. I like it here. You know, if you have to be dead."

"Yes, it's quite something, peaceful, beautiful.

They walked.

"What could've been so bad she didn't want to live?" Annabelle said.

"I think some people are too delicate for this world."

They stopped at a bench and sat.

"Maybe some people are just fine 'til they marry my dad."

****

Just what she'd wanted to dodge. Claire turned to face her stepdaughter.

"It's true," Annabelle said. "My mother killed herself... and...and...look at you." She covered her face with both hands and sobbed. "You're the walking dead."

Claire reached into her pocket, felt her stockpile.

Soon this would be over.

While Annabelle wasn't looking, she gulped a buffer.

"Your mother's death was not, absolutely not your dad's fault." Claire rubbed Annabelle's back. "You know that. Everything is screwed up in your head right now. I'm fine. I am."

Annabelle put her hands down. "Have you seen yourself? You're not fine. Everything is screwed up in *your* head." She started sobbing again.

Was it? Claire frowned. She didn't know what she was anymore. For now she needed to make it right for this young woman who'd lost too much. That's all she knew.

"Annabelle, your father loved you, loved us. But he wasn't perfect. He made a mistake. One you never should've known about. Don't let that wipe out what he meant to you for a lifetime."

After he gets what's coming to him maybe I'll feel that way too.

Annabelle sniffled, "Aren't you mad at him?"

Tread lightly.

"Well, I can be mad at him and still recognize what's true can't I?"

"I dunno."

"Well, you will. Takes time."

Annabelle brushed the hair that'd escaped from her ponytail away from her face. "Speaking of time, how long are you going to be here?"

"Didn't I tell you? The crypt takes three weeks." She tried to figure how long she'd already been there. The inside of her head felt like mashed potatoes. "A couple more weeks I guess."

Annabelle didn't seem to care much about the answer.

"What did you hope to accomplish by coming here?" Claire took Annabelle gently by the chin and turned her face toward her own.

"I don't know. I saw that letter. I wanted to see you."
Annabelle's eyes overflowed. "I'm scared. I thought you
wouldn't come back."

Christ, how bad do I look?

"Why would you think that?" Claire said.

"Just a feeling. You... you're barely hanging on, Claire."

Claire sighed. "I need to get this behind me. As soon as
I do, I'll get better."

She would. She'd look into going vegan. Maybe she'd
get a colonic.

Annabelle looked skeptical.

"We better get back," Claire unfolded out of the bench.
"You need to get home, forget about all this and get to school."

Annabelle stood, words shot out of her mouth like coins
from a nickel slot. "Give her what she wants."

"What?"

"Give Ellen the ten million."

"How in God's name do you know about the ten
million?"

Annabelle faced Claire full on. "I talked to Andrew. We
decided it would—"

"*We* decided?"

Had an anvil fallen on Claire's head?

"Claire, these decisions need to be made by... someone
else. You're not competent to—"

Claire grabbed Annabelle by both shoulders, with
strength neither of them realized she possessed. "If you know
what's good for you, that sentence will stay in your ignorant
mouth."

CHAPTER FORTY-TWO

Claire took Annabelle to the diner for lunch on the way back from the cemetery. It was the most comfortable choice. Claire tried to calm her rattled nerves, find some perspective at the bottom of her Prada. Annabelle sniffled, wiped tears, whimpered apologies.

"I thought I could help. I'm sorry, Clairesicle, I—"

"Don't you ever talk to Andrew again, is that understood?"

On the heels of food poisoning was she getting the flu? Would it ever end?

Annabelle nodded, ribbons of tears running down her perfect unlined face. "He said you'd never survive a trial. Or dragging the whole thing out. I—"

"Andrew doesn't have a clue about what I'd survive."

Annabelle's cell rang. Conchita with her flight arrangements. They'd have a couple hours to throw Annabelle's stuff together before the car service came.

Picking up where she left off, Annabelle said "He's looking out for you, Claire. For us."

Claire would've jumped out of the booth if she hadn't been so weak. "Don't be ridiculous. You're a naïve babe in the—"

The waterworks started down Annabelle's cheeks again. "You're sick, Claire. Not in your right mind. You need to come home with me, see someone, a professional, for an evaluation. I tried to get you to go that place in Hawaii. Andrew says there's a place here. As your family we need to step in, do the right—"

"Do what right thing?"

Annabelle looked at her hands. "Well, we could force this, Claire. You don't have to agree to—"

Claire leapt across the table, silverware clattering, grabbed Annabelle's too expensive T-shirt front. "You and Andrew think you'll have me committed?" Claire's breath blew into Annabelle's face. "Who do you think you're dealing with?"

The waitress headed to their table turned on her Dr. Scholl's and headed in the other direction.

"See? You're out of control." Annabelle sobbed, tried to worm away.

Claire pushed her toward the booth, flung herself backward, sat with her head in both hands. With a sigh heavy as bricks she met Annabelle's wide eyes.

"What would possess you?"

Annabelle wiped her running nose with the back of her hand. "I'm just trying to help. It all came out wrong, but I'm worried about you. We all are."

Something stank. "What's in this for you?"

Annabelle glanced down at her lap. "I am worried about you. I am."

Claire lunged across the table again, mashed her stepdaughter's cheeks together with an iron grip. "Do not fuck with me."

She crumpled like a piece of tinfoil. "Andrew said if I helped bring you around on this, he'd pay me, make it worth my while."

The waitress snuck in with their lunches, hurried away without eye contact.

"Pay?" Claire said. "You just inherited two and half million dollars."

Was she kidding?

Annabelle turned pink. "I spent most of it."

Claire dropped her fork on the floor. "You spent most of it?"

"Okay all of it."

"That's almost unbelievable." Claire's body felt like jelly.

"It's not like a couple million goes very far these days." Annabelle's whine made Claire's skin feel like it shrank three sizes. "I bought that condo, my Beemer, I went in on that yacht with Kimmie and Dale. I have to have clothes. Now I might have to get a job. I—"

"How did you pay for your trip here?"

"Andrew."

Judas and his silver.

"What's in it for him?"

"Nothing, Claire. He was Dad's best friend. He promised to take care of—"

Annabelle's phone rang again. Saved her from getting Claire's French dip thrown in her stupid face.

"Jordy, hey... what?" Annabelle's eyes, big as the plate her Chinese chicken salad sat on, glanced at Claire then away. "No she's right here." Annabelle got up, ran out the diner door. Claire followed, telling the waitress, "Be right back."

"At home? Did Steven bail you out?" Annabelle paced, wiped at her eyes, her still wet face.

Claire ripped the phone out of Annabelle's hand so hard her stepdaughter tripped backward on the sidewalk.

"What the hell is going on?"

"Mother, it's not a big deal." Jordan said. "I didn't know you were sitting right there. Annabelle's got a big mouth."

"Answer me."

"Don't freak. I got arrested. I—"

Claire felt the sidewalk come up. "You got arrested?"

A passerby, already staring, stopped. She flipped him off.

"I said don't freak." Jordan's voice started to rise. "I'm already home. Bailed out. Taken care of for now."

"Arrested for what?"

Bad taste in men?

"Drug possession."

Claire reeled. "Drugs? What the fuck are you talking about?"

"I had some pot in the car, Mother, a little coke. Nothing earth-shattering. First offense—"

Claire looked up at Annabelle who rocked on her Chloé wedges with her arms crossed, shaking her ponytailed head. "Now you're some pot smoking coke head?"

Jordan laughed, a sharp short sound. "Really, Mother?"

"Yes, really." Claire almost hopped up and down with anger, disappointment. If she hadn't been so sedated. "You were not raised to do drugs. That Steven, this is his—" She spit her words.

"Don't go there."

"You've never taken drugs. Not even prescription, not since your ADHD medication when you were a kid."

Claire couldn't believe her ears. This all had to be a nightmare.

"I didn't have ADHD, Mother."

"You did too. You used to get that medication, remember? Every month like clockwork."

"Yeah, I remember. You took it all"

Claire grasped for her head. It hurt. Before her arm reached its target she winced and dropped it. The IV stuck in her vein pulled when she tried to move it. Her brain was a mass of disconnected scenes, moving pictures, recollections in triple time. She thought hard, bits of chaos, bright lights, madness, ran through like worker ants. A dangerous jumble, mixed up like everything else she didn't like thinking about.

"Claire?"

She turned. Her head throbbed, felt huge. Were her eyes burnt? A nurse. Smiling in that way they do. Like you're about to croak or they wished you would. Maybe she was about to. The nurse's teeth gleamed like perfect eighty-eights. Claire shouldn't knock it. At least the last person she'd see looked happy.

"How are you feeling? Better I hope."

Better than what?

"I feel like shit. Am I in a hospital?" Claire looked around her room. She was the only one in it. "I'm in a hospital, right?"

"You are. I'm afraid you overdosed last night."

"How long have I been here?"

The nurse picked up her chart, looked at her watch. "Looks like about twelve hours." She listened to her heart, did all the nurse stuff, while Claire tried harder to remember the night before. Other than the hospital acoustics, the cold steel, the white coats that came first to her addled mind, there was nothing. Annabelle, Jordan. Goddamn ungrateful brats. She'd taken a nap or tried to after a bawling Annabelle got whisked off in the limo... couldn't sleep.

"The doctor will be in to see you soon. Oh and your fiancé's here. He slept in the hall all night. Since they brought you in. He's worried sick about you."

"Fiancé?"

"Rob, Rob Rhino. Quite a character. He's well known around here." Nurse smiled, made notations. "He sure seems devoted to you." She put the chart back and left.

Claire felt her wrist for a pulse.

She must not've survived the overdose and gone straight to hell.

****

Rob Rhino bustled in, his rubber clogs squeaking across the tile floor.

Did the man own another shirt?

She followed his candy green feet across the floor. Her head felt a little better. She might not have to crack her own skull open like a walnut. *All right* was a stretch though.

"Rob Rhino, if I wasn't so exhausted, I'd strangle you. My fiancé?" Claire felt too frail to sit up or lift her head off the pillow.

If she expected him to look sheepish she was mistaken. "Listen, you'll thank me when you get the skinny. It's against the law you know."

Claire managed to lift her head a little. "What's against the law? Having you for a fiancé? It should be."

"I see you're not too sick to bust my balls." Rob laughed too loud for a hospital. "No, Miss Priss. It's against the law to try to kill yourself."

Claire rolled her eyes. "Kill myself?" Her voice a snake-like hiss. "That's ridiculous. I never... is that what you think?" She breathed the heaviest sigh she could. "I suppose that's what everyone here thinks?"

"Yes, that's what everyone thinks. Claire, you popped a whole bottle of pills, *again*. Plus the booze."

So she had some hooch. Not like she drained the bottle, bottles, or drank every day. Okay not a ton every day. Who was Mister-Cock-of-the-Walk to judge?

Claire rewound the last couple weeks in her spinning head on speed dial. The porn palace, the religious fanatics, Liam's *Sopranos*-like family and their patriarch—Father Pat the parishioner-plugging priest—and realized she didn't care what everyone thought. They think she tried to kill herself? Whatever. Bingo was her name-o.

"So okay. Let's say I did. It's against the law. Am I going to jail? How does having you for a fiancé help? Sympathy vote?"

Rob rested his scaly elbows on the metal hospital bed railing. "They can commit you to the psychiatric ward for however long they think is necessary."

Claire's head left the pillow for that one.

"As it is, you'd better behave. It's up to the doc how long you stay."

Claire gave Rob the stink eye. "So far, having you for my betrothed hasn't done diddly for me."

"Not so fast. They like it better if you have somewhere to go and someone to go there with. If you don't blow it they're probably going to let me take you home sooner rather than later no matter what kind of fruitcake you turn out to be."

"Are they? You must be awfully charming. Even more than I thought."

"I introduced Doctor Levinson to his wife."

****

The nurse came in with a little blue pill.

"You're giving me these?"

Claire couldn't hide her surprise or relief. Her head felt better but she'd started to sweat. Her pulse began its usual hokey-pokey. Rob moved out of the way.

The nurse nodded. "You can't stop cold turkey. The doctor will talk to you about it when he comes in later." She handed Claire the pill with a paper cup of water.

Claire swallowed the pill with a pale trembling hand. "They tell me you brought me here."

"No. We found you, called the ambulance." Rob Rhino sat in a plastic chair that he'd pulled up close to Claire's bedside. "I left a bunch of messages, you never called back. I got a bad feeling. Freddie Eddie and I headed over and found you. You were unconscious. We couldn't revive you."

Freddie Eddie. Why did it have to be him? She didn't remember it.

"I wanted to sleep, that's all." The look on Rob Rhino's face made Claire nervous. "I didn't die. I'm fine, right?"

"Barely."

Rob looked like a man who'd seen a ghost. Claire knew he had.

"You're lucky they didn't need to put you on a respirator. I thought they might. Gloria—"

"I'm not Gloria."

"No, you're not."

"Did Gloria have to go on a respirator before she died?"

"No."

They stared at each other.

"Did the front desk let you into my room?" she finally said.

"Of course. We called from the car. Said we thought you'd overdosed. The paramedics met us there."

"You did what?" Claire's mortification drilled her to the mattress.

"Claire Corrigan, stop with the pretense. You almost died." Rob Rhino gave her his professor face. "I'd have said you were in a gangbang with a horse and a peg leg if I'd had to."

"Of course you would've. In all my years—"

"You're welcome."

Claire stopped. She folded her hands in front of her and looked down at her blanket covered lap. "Thank you, Rob Rhino." She glanced up at his baggy face. "I mean it. I'm such an asshole. Thanks for giving a shit."

Rob tilted his head to one side. "I'd say with that scalp more like a dickhead than an asshole."

"Laughter's the best medicine." A young man with short curly hair in a white coat said. He walked over to a still laughing Claire and stuck out his hand. "I'm Doctor Levinson. You look much better than the last time I saw you."

FORTY-FOUR

"How long have you been taking Xanax?" Doctor Levinson sat in the chair Rob Rhino vacated when he left the doctor and Claire to *get acquainted*. Traitor.

"Only as needed." Claire balled the blanket up into her fists.

Doctor Levinson sat quietly for a few seconds, crossed his legs, and folded his hands over his knee. "Months? Years?"

"I don't keep track."

He cleared his throat, waited a few seconds. "When did you lose your hair?"

"How do you know it's lost? Maybe I shaved it."

Presumptuous ass.

"Just a wild guess." He smiled, too superior for Claire's taste.

She hoped her displeasure showed on her hairless face. "Year or so."

He seemed young for a doctor. That was a sign of advancing age. Everyone else looked young. She supposed he was a shrink. Come to evaluate her mental health. Better cooperate. She had a dead husband to get even with.

"Alopecia," the doctor said.

"So they say."

"How long have you been taking Xanax with alcohol?"

"I don't usually." Claire crossed her ankles under the blanket and her arms across her chest. "I wasn't thinking."

"Do you know how much Xanax you took last night?"

Seemed like not enough right about now.

"No."

"Let's just say you ought to play the lottery."

Claire cut to the chase. "I wasn't trying to kill myself. I was trying to sleep."

"Do you normally take a whole bottle of Xanax and a bottle of booze to sleep?"

"No, of course not." Claire's patience was as thin as the sheet.

"You have some bruising around your jaw and—"

"Rough sex."

Mind your knitting, Doogie Howser.

He flushed crimson, rearranged his chair, coughed.

Claire bailed him out. "The pills have stopped working. They were making me feel worse, more nervous. Like I was having a heart attack sometimes. I sweat all the time. I've had to take more. A lot more than I realized, obviously."

The doctor nodded, reached for her chart at the end of her bed, clicked his ballpoint pen so he could write. "You've built up a tolerance. You have to take more to get the same benefit. When the drug wears off, and it does quickly after you've taken it so long, you start to feel withdrawal symptoms, because you're an addict. So you're battling the withdrawal and trying to sedate yourself. A double whammy. You're constantly on the edge of overdose." He clicked his pen closed.

"Now what?" Claire said.

Sounded like a junkie hamster on a wheel and she'd never get off.

He leaned forward and put her chart back. "We need to wean you off the drugs. It's imperative that you do *not* stop all at once. You can have a seizure."

Wean. Did she want to wean? What about a different drug? A better one? This was the twenty-first century for Chrissake. If the Xanax worked she wouldn't have had to take so much of it.

"I started taking Xanax because I needed it. If I stop taking it, what good will that do? I'll still need something won't I?"

Probably not smart to ask that. She should wait and talk to Guillermo. She'd probably never get out with questions like that.

"Needed it? For what?"

Doctor Levinson grabbed her chart and clicked his pen again. She'd probably have to marry Rob Rhino now to break free of this cuckoo's nest.

Don't get me started, Doogie.

Claire pointed to her head with its lost hair and made her *no duh* face.

"Xanax isn't prescribed for alopecia," Doogie said.

If she killed the kiddie doctor, how long would she have to stay?

"No, it isn't. But it is for panic attacks and anxiety," Claire said, "which the alopecia didn't help."

Doogie considered her for a few seconds. "These types of drugs aren't for the long-term treatment of anxiety."

Claire could feel her mouth go dry, her hands and feet start to tingle. Breathe, breathe. She shut her eyes for a few seconds. When she opened them Doogie still sat at her bedside, yapping.

"I'm not going to lie and say this process is easy. It's not." He looked down and wrote in her chart. "But the good news is there are other drugs you can take, longer term that can be helpful while you're detoxing. But I don't recommend you do this on your own. I strongly advise a rehabilitation program. We have an excellent one at this hospital, as you know."

How would she know? Oh right. Her fiancé, the rabid volunteer. And Annabelle and Andrew.

Doogie paused, looked at her with thoughtful deliberation. "In a rehabilitation setting they'll help you deal with why you feel so anxious all the time. Until you get to the root of your anxiety your recovery is limited."

He got up out of the chair and stood next to the bed.

"What's bothering you, Claire?"

****

The nurse came in again with another blue pill and a new yellow pill that the doctor wanted her to try for shits and giggles. Satisfied by Claire's vitals that she still lived, nurse fiddled with her IV, made more notes on the infamous chart, then left. After giving her a reassuring pat on the arm, Doogie murmured something about food for thought and promised he'd be back in the morning. Ready or not.

To tell the truth, Claire felt better in the hospital setting. Taken care of. Like when Liam was alive. Someone looked after her. She relaxed, let whatever flowed through the IV run its course through her veins.

What's bothering you, Claire?

****

She dreamt, remembered.

"*What's this?*"

"*Looks like a piece of paper.*"

Claire held it out to him, rattled it, frightened and furious.

"*Don't be an asshole. What is it?*"

Liam took the statement from her, his expression cut from concrete. "It's a Vanguard statement." He held the paper out again, as if he meant for her to take it back.

"*Okay, don't be a fucking asshole. I know it's a Vanguard statement. Why is a Vanguard statement coming to our house for Shane Corrigan? Who is Shane Corrigan? Better yet who is Ellen Ryan?*"

"*I have no idea.*"

Liam turned toward their dresser and took off his Patek Philippe watch like he did every day when he got home from work. Just another day at the office.

Claire grabbed him by his custom-made shirt and jerked him around to face her. "I'm not an idiot even if you treat me like one. You and Ellen Ryan are the custodians on this account. Who are these people?"

Claire felt like she would choke. Her grip on Liam's shirt was death-like. She knew who they were. He knew she knew it too. The only question was—how long would the dance go on?

He wouldn't meet her eyes. A dead giveaway.

"I called Andrew already," Claire said. She let it hang.

Liam turned to look at her. His face handsome, painfully so. Claire brushed her hair out of her eyes. Wouldn't want to miss anything on the day her life went down the shitter.

"You already know. Why are you asking?" Liam put both hands on the dresser and stared at the wood.

"What was I supposed to do—wait for you to volunteer it?"

"I don't know, Claire. Who knows what you do?"

The sound of Claire's open hand meeting his cheek with all the force she could put behind it rang loud in their master suite. He took it like a man.

"How dare you? This isn't about me. It's about you and your tramps. And your bastard." Claire heard herself yelling. She didn't try to wipe the tears that ran down her face.

Liam slammed the double doors to their bedroom shut. Claire didn't know why he bothered, no one else was home. She'd made sure.

"I'm afraid not. It is about you, Claire. About us."

"Don't think for a second you're going to blame me. You think you're master of the universe. You can have it all. You'll trade me in for a younger model to impress your cronies. You're such a pathetic cliché."

Claire paced their cavernous room, her voice boomed, bounced off the walls, the vaulted ceilings.

Liam covered the distance between them and grasped her shoulders. "I'm a cliché?"

He pulled her close, hissed his words. "That's rich coming from a trophy wife. You want to know who has it all? You. You have everything and didn't work for any of it. You go to lunch, Pilates, shop, drive your

Mercedes, have your own parking spot at Neiman's, yet all you do is bitch and whine while I pay your fucking bills."

He shook her, her hair tossed around like a rag doll. "That's if you're not stoned. You want to talk about pathetic?" He held her inches away from his face, she could smell his mouthwash.

Claire was caught off guard. For a second. Then she rallied.

She yanked free. "Is that right?" She held up her left hand with its diamond and platinum rings. "We're married, remember? Ever hear of the wedding vows? Faithfulness? You don't get to pick and choose the ones that suit you. That's what commitment is." Claire's righteous indignation fit like an Hermes glove.

Liam ran both hands through his salt and pepper hair. "Vows? You want to recite vows? Okay, let's get after it. Just so happens there's more than one, Claire. What about love and cherish? How about honor? Or was I the only one who uttered those?"

Claire almost stomped her feet. "What are you talking about? I loved you. I honored you, our home, our family. I've raised your daughter for Chrissake. Raised her like my own and you know it."

"Get the violins." Liam yelled too. "You honored our marriage? What marriage? You love me? How would I know?"

Claire stared at him. "What do you mean by that?"

"Just what I said. What makes this a marriage? How could I tell you loved me?" Liam sat down on the chaise so hard it almost tipped over. "When's the last time we had sex?"

"What?"

"Sex. I'm sure you're vaguely familiar with the term."

Claire wiped her eyes. "I don't know when. Since you asked, I'm sure you can tell me."

"You bet I can. A year ago."

"A year? Please. Let's not get ridiculous. It hasn't been that long."
He lied. Of course he would.

"Yes, it has. You graced me with your presence on our anniversary. So it's been more than a year. And even then I had to wheedle. Not my finest moment or yours. Nice impression of a quadriplegic though."

Claire shut her eyes. He was right.

"There's more to marriage than sex you know. More to love."

"Like what?"

"Are you kidding?"

"Do I look like I'm kidding? I could've gotten a roommate or a nanny. It would've been cheaper. I wouldn't have to trade in an expensive German import every other year. Intimacy is what makes a marriage what it is and not just a friendship, an acquaintance."

Claire wasn't going to let him off the hook. Not like this. Not this easy. A secret kid for God's sake. A sob slipped through her lips.

"You're a pig. What about illness? Or if one of us had been in an accident and couldn't? Then it's carte blanche? You can do whatever you want with whoever you want?"

Liam jumped out of the chaise.

"We're not sick. You're not sick. There's been no accident. You avoid me like the fucking plague because you don't want to have sex. There's nothing between us. We don't sit together, we don't hold hands, no physical contact of any kind. You won't be alone with me unless it can't be avoided. That's not love, Claire. Not any that I recognize. And it's certainly not a marriage."

He went to her. She stood, not moving. She wanted him to hold her and never touch her. She wanted him on his knees.

"What are you? A horny sixteen-year-old boy who can't control himself?"

"No. I'm a grown man who wants a grown-up wife and a real relationship."

"Well, grown-ups in real relationships don't chase the first piece of ass they can find the first time they don't get laid."

Liam's eyes opened wide, like someone shoved a knife in his back. "This has been going on for years. The only time you're interested in me is on payday."

"That's not true and you know it." Claire felt shocked at his audacity.

"Yes, it is. You can't look me in the eye and say it isn't."

Claire couldn't.

"I'm not as worthless as you think. There were kids to raise, multiple households to run. I had responsibilities as your wife. You're successful because I helped you. Endless dinners, parties, and entertaining rounds of bores here, abroad... those demands are tiring and you never appreciated any of it."

"How demanding do you think my life is, Claire? I work a sixty-hour week when I'm taking it easy. I don't recall any thank you cards coming my way. And you didn't raise our kids alone. I raised them too. I'm not too tired. I don't consider our sex life a burden. To me it's a bonus."

Claire could think of no rational response. "You're trying to take the heat off yourself and your sins. The fact is I loved you. I was faithful, and you betrayed me."

"I don't know what you feel for me Claire, but it isn't love. Gratitude? Loyalty for taking you and Jordan in? But whatever it is, it's not enough."

Liam looked away. She thought he'd started to cry.

She wasn't about to feel sorry for him. "Why didn't you tell me how you felt? You never once talked to me about it. You deal with two hundred employees every day, I'm sure you could handle one wife."

Liam laughed a brittle sound. "By the time I get home from work, I'm lucky if you're still coherent enough to string a sentence together."

It was Claire's turn to laugh. "What a joke. I'll tell you why you never talked to me about it, Liam. Because then the problem might've been fixed. Maybe I would've wanted to change. But then you couldn't justify your women. Assuage your Catholic guilt. No this way you could tell yourself your sad story. I'm so misunderstood and neglected. I deserve this."

Claire'd struggled out from under his assault and hit a nerve.

Red-faced he said, "You think you know everything. You don't."

Not about to surrender the upper hand, her rage reached its boiling point. "Don't I? I know I'm not going to sit idly by while you run around with whores and father their bastards." She balled up her fists and started to strike him.

Liam grabbed them midswing. "Claire, I'm sorry. I am. If I could take it back—" His voice lowered. She could barely hear him.

"Couldn't you have had the spine to divorce me? Did you have to lie and humiliate me this way?" She spoke loud enough for the both of them.

The master's universe imploded.

"It happened. I didn't plan it. I tried not to humiliate you by not telling you, which only made it worse. I tried to handle it."

"Handle it?" Claire felt an eruption coming on, volcanic, historic. "I guess you've been laughing at me, right? What a dumbass Claire is... you and your baby mama behind my back... it's a real drag I'm stoned all the time. Until it isn't. Makes it a lot easier to sneak around when I'm semiconscious."

"No, Claire, it hasn't been like that—"

She put both hands on his chest and shoved him. "Get out and don't come back. You're right Liam. I don't love you. I never have. Do you know what I feel for you? Hate. I hate you." She shoved him again, harder.

Liam grabbed the keys to his Range Rover and headed toward the closed doors with Claire on his heels, her hysteria climbing like the Donner Party through the Sierra Nevadas.

She screamed at his broadcloth covered back. "I wish you'd die."

Claire woke gasping and pawing at the air. She fought off an attacker, someone holding a pillow over her face, suffocating her. Only there was no one, only regret and her addiction.

FORTY-FIVE

"Morning, Claire, how's the deathbed?"

Rob Rhino strolled in carrying a Dunkin' Donuts bag and a small bouquet of baby pink roses.

"Rob Rhino, you're something else."

Claire hoped the donuts were for her. She was starved. She hadn't eaten since lunch with Annabelle. She'd been in the hospital more than twenty-four hours but hadn't felt like eating even though her stomach's contents had been thoroughly vacated. She didn't think the crap they'd brought her on a tray looked worth eating anyway. Deep fried fat rolled in sugar. *That* was a food group.

"A girl can't be in a hospital room with no flowers." He gave her the flowers, flushed like a schoolboy.

Nurse had removed her IV. She took the spray with feeble hands and held the beautiful blush-colored buds under her nose, inhaled their sweet scent. "They're the loveliest flowers I've ever seen." They were. He was one gracious porn star. "You're so thoughtful, really." She handed them back. He set them on the table next to her bed.

"Trained by the best."

Rob Rhino rewarded her with his finest toothless smile.

"Gloria?" Claire looked at the donuts.

"Uh... no, ma'am. That would be Grandma, thank you very much." Rob handed her the bag. "You get to pick first. I'll eat whichever ones you don't want."

"Grandma?"

"Yeah, she brought me up. My mom died when I was four. Dad split way before that." Rob put a chubby hand into the donut bag and came out with a maple bar. "My grandma took me in and raised me. One hell of a good woman. She died when I was seventeen, left me a little money, which is how I got my undergrad degree here. Private school was beyond my means without her help."

"So no family?"

Claire couldn't remember eating anything as good as the cinnamon sugar goodness exploding in her mouth. The soft dough slid down her throat slick as wet noodles.

"No. Just Freddie Eddie. He's close enough." Rob talked with his mouth full.

Claire savored her cinnamon twist. Freddie Eddie. Close like fungus. Or chiggers.

"Speaking of family, I don't want mine to know where I am. They—"

They're felons and Linda Tripps, but they're all I've got.

"You've done so much for me already. I hate to ask you to do anything else—"

"Anything." Rob was already wiping his hands on a napkin, ready to jump into action.

"Could you check the messages on my hotel room phone? All you have to do is push the blinking light if there are any." Claire talked with her mouth full too.

"Can do."

"Oh but I can't call them from here. The number will show up on their cell phones. They can't find out about this... this... unfortunate accident. They'd..." Use it against me.

"Don't you have a cell phone?"

"I think it's around there somewhere. Maybe near the TV. Can you grab my purse? The tan Prada bag—"

Rob Rhino looked confused.

Claire explained. "It's the only Prada bag there. It has P-R-A-D-A on the outside by the clasp. The phone cord's in it. I hope." Claire swallowed her bite of donut. "Can you check on Liam? He's the one in the urn. By the TV." Just taking a couple bites of donut tired her out, despite the sugar rush.

"For sure gotta check on Liam. He probably ran amok while you were gone. Had a kegger."

****

"Jordan says—Mother, if you're not too pissed, give me a call so I know you're reasonably well. My whatchamacallit isn't as bad as you think. Really." Rob looked over the paper he'd dictated her messages on. "Jordan's your son?"

Claire tried not to move any facial muscles. "So they told me at the maternity ward."

"Okaaay." Rob glanced over the top of his bifocals. "Continue, please."

"Next up... Annabelle? Says you probably don't care, but she made it home." Rob's voice went falsetto. "Please, please, please, don't be mad at me. I know I look bad 'cause of the money, but I thought I was helping Clairesicle." Rob laughed. "Clairesicle? Like icicle? Perfect. Who's Annabelle?"

"My stepdaughter who would benefit from an ass whipping." Claire narrowed her red bleary eyes at Rob Rhino. "Are there more?"

"Two from Annabelle. The second one because you haven't called since she left the first. She's worried. You look like something the dog drug—"

"I get it. Anything else?"

Rob's PhD sized brain whirred. "She was here?"

"Unfortunately. Next?"

"Grace." Rob stopped, smiled. "Almost called her back myself. Rehash old times. Have a few laughs."

Claire smirked. "What'd she want?"

"Has her dearly beloved been exhumed?" Rob twitched his bushy upper lip. "She hates to be a pest and all. Poor Pat."

Claire wrinkled her naked brow. "Now she's in a hurry. Bloodsucker."

"And good ole Joe Lansing says the mausoleum is ahead of schedule."

"Seriously? For once, some good news." Was she the first person in history to have her mood considerably brightened by a crypt delivery?

"Not by much, just a few days."

"I'll take what I can get. I'll need to call him right away."

"No, you'll need to get some rest. Another day or two won't matter. Dead is dead sister friend. And Liam still will be in a day or two."

Normally an argument would've ensued. A new normal moved in. Claire kept her mouth shut.

Rob paced as he read. "Here's a promising one—Conchita called." He stopped, his eyes misting over as he stared off into the distance with a goofy smile. "I knew a girl named Conchita once. She had this weird nipple and could pick up quarters with her—"

"For God's sake can you just give me my messages without the disgusting commentary?" Conchita did seem limber, now that he mentioned... maybe... no. God, now he has me doing it.

"Okay. Last but not least, someone named Andrew. Needs to hear from you pronto while you still have a prayer."

"He said that?"

Rob consulted his paper. "Yep."

"Fucker."

"Oh my, not a friend of yours?"

"He's my attorney. Supposed to be handling the mess with Liam's kid and his girlfriend. Instead he's conspiring behind my—" In no shape to revisit ground zero she stopped. "Is that it?"

Rob handed her the hotel notepaper with the scribbled messages on it. "Here you go. If you need written reminders. Good luck deciphering my handwriting."

"Thanks again, Rob Rhino. I'll be glad to get out of this booby hatch. Never thought I'd say it, but I'll be thrilled to see that ratty hotel again."

"Yeah, well, about that." Rob pulled up the chair to his usual bedside spot.

Claire didn't like his tone.

"What do you mean *about that?*"

"The hotel... you see... umm." Rob licked his lips.

"Spit it out would you?"

"They kicked you out." Rob ducked down in the seat.

"They what?"

"You can't stay there anymore. Vamoose. The overdose. They can't have that kind of thing at their establishment. At least that's what the manager told me."

The same manager of the fine establishment that let Annabelle into her room for a hundred bucks?

"You've got to be kidding."

She could see he wasn't.

"What now? My clothes, the car, Liam—"

Could her life get worse?

"Got it all under control. We took all your stuff to my place, Liam too. Freddie Eddie got your keys out of your purse, drove your car there." Rob's usual shit-eating missing tooth grin took up most of his fleshy face. "You're gonna bunk with me."

Welcome to worse, a lot worse.

FORTY-SIX

Her cell phone had thirty-three old messages on it. She ignored them. Was there anything else she wanted to know? Claire called Conchita to update her on the situation. Sort of.

"The hotel was a dump. Turns out the dean is offering up a nice cottage near the university for the rest of my stay. When you drop a load of cash here they accommodate you." The lie ran like melted butter off her tongue.

"Christ must be descending from the heavens if you've actually plugged in your cell phone. I'll get Jimmy to get your money refunded from the dump." Claire could tell she wasn't sold on the university's generosity story. Conchita was a tough sell.

"Can you let the kids know the deal? I've got a ton of crap to do yet. No time to yack on the phone. You know how they like to go on and on."

No way would Claire talk to Annabelle until she figured out what to do about that whole debacle. Jordan needed to cool his cocaine-fueled jets before she'd reward him with a phone call.

Claire wished she had the strength to think of plan B. But so far plan A wasn't working out so well so maybe she ought to suck it up. Rob Rhino, her roomie? Why did she have to pick now to give up her drugs?

Doctor Levinson worked out a weaning schedule and started her on it. He reminded her that the new yellow pills weren't like the old ones. They'd take three to four weeks to kick in and weren't sedatives. He was hopeful she'd have good results but reiterated he'd prefer she check into a rehab center.

"You're more than welcome to see me on an outpatient basis when you and Rob are here in town if I can't talk you into an inpatient program."

She had to admit she already felt a little better than she did before although she had no reason to. Maybe she felt hopeful. The mausoleum would be here sooner. Her job here was almost done. She could see an end date. The burden she carried felt lighter and soon it'd be tucked behind a concrete slab.

The doctor and Rob Rhino conferred in the hallway while Claire gathered up her meager belongings and got dressed in the clothes she wore when they brought her in. Rob had taken all her other clothes from the hotel to his place. He'd had on the same outfit since he'd been in town. Bringing her a fresh set of clothes wouldn't make the top of his list. She'd need to remember to peek in his closet when he turned his back. See if he owned anything else.

"Well, Claire, I think you're ready to go." Doctor Levinson handed her a prescription. "Your fiancé here will fill this and take good care of you. He assures me." He winked at Rob, looked like Doogie Howser again. "He sure takes care of a lot of people in our rehab facility."

Claire tried not to visibly shudder. "Oh he's a regular Gandhi."

Rob put his arm around Claire's shoulders. "That's right, honey bunch. We'll get you home, tucked in, and I'll take real good care of you."

He'd pay for that. Smartass.

She fidgeted out from under his smelly armpit. "Thank you, Doctor Levinson." she said and left it at that. What could she say? Good call sending her home with the perv and his giant prick?

Claire and Rob Rhino headed toward the hospital doors and the outside. Claire moved slow. The overdose had taken a lot out of her. Not that she'd been in great shape before. Annabelle was right. She looked like something the dog drug in well before her hospital stay.

"Freddie Eddie's waiting. He brought your car since it has more than two seats."

Claire stopped dead. "Freddie Eddie? Is he still chauffeuring you around?" All she needed was Freddie Eddie looking down his pierced nose at her. "Isn't Trustee Week over yet?" Claire stuck her bottom lip out.

"Yeah, a few days ago." Rob pulled her arm gently to keep her moving. "He's worried about you too. He insisted on coming to the hotel with me when you overdosed. You should thank him."

"I'm gooey over it." Claire gave him major stink eye.

Rob pushed through the double glass doors, maneuvering a complaining Claire. Freddie Eddie waited at the curb, engine running. When he saw them he jumped out of Claire's rental and popped the trunk.

"She doesn't have anything remember?" Rob Rhino said his voice a boom, so the back rows of the lot could hear. "It's just me and her."

Freddie Eddie slammed the trunk, slithered around to the passenger side, and opened both the front and back doors.

"Claire." Freddie Eddie nodded his head at her and gestured for her to get in the front seat. "Glad to see you're feeling better. You gave us quite a scare." His eyes flickered over her jaw and neck. If he had an opinion about their condition he kept it to himself.

Claire met him with defiance. If she'd planned to shop for a fight he disappointed her. Freddie Eddie looked, for lack of a better description, sad. But for who? At least there was no smarmy attitude, no thinly veiled *I told you so*. She felt disarmed, not quite sure how to respond. So she didn't. She got in the car—in the back.

Claire wanted to lie down in the back seat but didn't dare. Not with Thelma and Louise in the front seat. She looked at the back of their heads as they drove through the quiet Pennsylvania streets. One balding badly dyed combover porn star and the other badly dyed greased back *West Side Story* reject.

Freddie Eddie turned on the radio. Rob Rhino squealed. "Tammy Wynette. Who doesn't love her?" He sang along, off-key, loud.

Freddie leaned in toward the center of the car, closer to his duet partner, in full torch and twang they *stood by their man*.

"Her catalog suffered after she and George called it quits." Freddie Eddie told Claire in the rearview mirror. His mouth spoke soft, his eyes glinted hard.

Claire rolled down her window and put her head out, like a trapped bald dog.

How bad could the psychiatric ward have been?

FORTY-SEVEN

The house that porn built was grander than Claire'd imagined. She didn't know for sure but she'd bet it was in the nicest part of town. It looked nicer than any part she'd seen. A far cry from where Liam's mother lived. And not exactly the *nothing fancy* Rob had described earlier.

Like most things in town it looked at least a hundred years old, red brick, possibly historically significant. The large yard, no doubt kept perfect by a professional, buzzed with bees and hummingbirds. The wraparound porch had a *Better Homes and Gardens* magazine welcoming feel to it, right down to the wicker furniture and rag rug. Not a place a porn star would fit in, much less call home.

"I thought you said your place here was small, no big deal?" Claire slammed the car door behind her and headed up the stone walkway. She shook off Rob's hand on her arm.

"Compared to your estate, I'm sure it is," Rob said.

"What makes you think I live on an estate?" Claire stopped.

Both Freddie Eddie and Rob Rhino came to a standstill, stared at her, eyebrows lifted.

"Never mind." Claire continued toward the house. "It's beautiful. Seems big."

"Five bedrooms." Rob opened the front door. "These old houses always have lots of bedrooms. Back in the day families were bigger."

Freddie Eddie went straight into the house down the long hall next to the impressive staircase and disappeared in the back.

Rob Rhino's grandma must've come back from the grave to decorate. Where would a man like Rob Rhino get doilies? Claire could see her reflection in the wood floors where they weren't covered by carpets. She supposed the old lady décor was called Victorian or Early American—Claire got those mixed up—and fit the house.

"Wanna tour?" Rob said.

"Love one." They strolled through some of the rooms. "Don't tell me you did all this yourself."

Claire couldn't believe they hadn't come across a bean-bag chair or a lava lamp. No Daisy Duke posters and not one of the curios had an erection. She'd only seen part of the first floor though.

"Nah. Afraid not. Had a decorator—Mavis Applebee. She's famous." Rob leaned against the wall of the dining room tastefully covered in velvet flocked paper. "I haven't lived here long. It's quite an upgrade from the house I owned before. This one is a historical landmark. I wanted to respect the period."

"You're a marvel, Rob Rhino."

They got to the end of the hall that Freddie Eddie'd last been seen ducking down. Claire was shocked to see a large office in complete working mode. With a young girl behind a computer screen. Tastefully dressed.

"Oh Melissa. I forgot you were here today." Rob slapped his hand on his forehead. "I'm sorry. Did you find everything okay?"

Melissa smiled. "Yes fine. No worries. I've been coming a while now. I know where everything is." She looked at Claire's head, then the ground, then her computer screen.

Freddie Eddie intervened. His specialty.

"Melissa, this is Claire. She's a good friend of Rob's. She'll be staying here a few days. She's in town for a family memorial service." He was a smooth operator.

Claire's lips made a slight smile—tight, fake. She probably looked like an embalmed corpse. "Hi, Melissa. Nice to meet you. I won't be in the way."

"Melissa helps us out with all the paperwork, orders, scheduling, you name it," Rob said. "She's the brains of the outfit."

"Really?" Claire felt surprised. Surprised he knew a woman with a brain. "I guess I thought your gig at Alex's and the reality show was it. Oh and I guess the film distributing but—"

"Rob's got lots of irons in the fire." Freddie Eddie leaned back in his ergonomically correct desk chair. "We've got another reality show starting up in the fall. He's got tons of merchandise, T-shirts, lingerie, baseball caps, vibrators, lube, coffee mugs, mouse pads, with more in the works. There's Fresh Flesh Films, of course. A few legit film offers, some other TV roles coming up. Some talk shows. Speaking engagements, personal appearances, his charities, and he's working on his autobiography."

Claire was impressed. "Wow. You're a conglomerate, a brand."

Freddie Eddie laughed.

"He's the biggest dick on campus."

****

Rob held her elbow like a country squire as they climbed the wide staircase. She didn't shake him off this time. Claire felt pooped. They poked around some of the bright spacious bedrooms upstairs. The closets were not. They stopped at the room Rob chose for her, the girliest so far. Pink floral wallpaper, window seat with a mauve tufted cushion, and porcelain figurines scattered about. The room's centerpiece was the king-size crochet-canopied bed sitting directly in front of an ornate fireplace. Claire's clothes covered half the room. Rob tried to fold, stack, and arrange in neat piles.

"I put some stuff in the closet, whatever fit. Your shoes are all in there. Holy mother of God you've got a lot of shoes." Rob whistled through his missing tooth gap.

"All women do. You forget."

"I put the unmentionables in the dresser over there." He lowered his voice to a whisper and pointed to the tall oak chest of drawers.

Rob Rhino manhandling her underwear. Nice.

"This is a magnificent room. The whole house—" Claire glanced around the room. She loved it. It was the house she wished she'd grown up in. If only.

"And Liam's there." He pointed at the nightstand by the bed. Liam's urn sat on a tea-stained crocheted doily.

"He's been passed around like a joint at a frat party." Claire said. "Soon he'll be where he belongs."

Rob clucked his tongue against the roof of his mouth. Looked like he had something to say but thought better of it.

She'd seen three of the five bedrooms. He hadn't said if one was his. She hadn't asked. She preferred denial. The cock king's domain was better left a mystery.

Who was she kidding?

She'd die to know what it looked like but preferred the self-guided tour. Not the VIP one with the dick docent.

She started to sweat. "What time is it?"

"Shit. Your pills." Rob reached into his pocket and gave her a pill.

"Now you're carrying pills in your pocket? That's a shift." Claire swallowed.

"I'm taking care of everything. No worries. It's all cool."

"Hey, what about your gig at Alex's? I hope you're not going to bail because I'm here."

"Nah. I've already been a few times. Just found out I've got to make a trip to LA. After your husband's memorial. The reality show deal, so I've got to cut my engagement short out there for now."

Claire sat on the bed. Heaven. She toppled over, her smooth head landed on a pillow. Rob put her legs up on the antique white duvet, took off her loafers.

"Excellent idea. You get some rest. You can see the rest of the house later."

"Rob Rhino?"

"What?"

"Are you really writing your autobiography?"

"I don't know. Freddie Eddie wants me to. We have a publisher chomping at the bit."

"What would you say about Gloria?"

He climbed on the bed, kicked off his ugly clogs, wriggled his sock-covered toes, lay down next to her. Claire didn't yell at him to get off.

"I'd say for a few years I had everything."

Claire felt so tired. The heat from Rob's body made her even sleepier.

"What did you love about her?"

"Truthfully? The way she made me feel about myself." Rob put his arms behind his head. "She was so beautiful, perfection. Everybody knew she was too good for me. But she didn't see it that way at all. I have a thousand faults but when she looked at me she saw the good stuff first. That's a life right there."

Claire couldn't break the spell to ask about her death. He seemed so happy.

"You must've loved her very much."

"Still do."

Claire's lids drooped. She rolled onto her side, toward Rob Rhino, rested her bare head on his hula girl-covered shirt, a constant comfort. He didn't yell at her to get off.

"What about you, Claire? What would you say if you wrote a book about yourself?"

She snorted. "Good God. I'd never write about myself. I'm too horrid."

Rob laughed. "That's true. And you're a bad dancer."

Claire laughed even though she wanted to sleep more than anything. "You're an asshole."

"You're not so bad." Rob reached for her face, gave it a soft rub. "You'd do the right thing if it came down to it." He felt her forehead like a fevered child. "You're good. Under all that anger there's heart."

Claire yawned against his beefy chest. "Is that right?"

"You have a thousand faults Claire Corrigan. But do you know what I see when I look at you?"

Claire felt her weary eyes getting teary, her heart softening. "What?"

"You're really bald."

The bed beneath her creaked. Claire rolled over, restless, agitated. She took deep breaths like Doctor Levinson told her to, tried to calm herself.

"Close your eyes and watch the light show behind your lids," he'd said.

Self-soothing without an overload of pharmaceuticals wasn't her strong suit. She wrapped her arms around herself.

You'd do the right thing. She wanted to believe Rob Rhino, her new friend.

Would she? Had she ever? Claire started to cry, rocked herself back and forth. All she wanted was the absence of pain. Even when she did the right thing it felt wrong.

Claire's stomach knotted. She looked to make sure the bedroom door was shut, reached for her purse on the floor and her phone. It took several minutes of digging through her wallet for the number but she found it. She could barely make out the numbers anymore, scribbled in faded pencil on paper torn from a prescription pad. She punched them out.

"Volunteers of America. This is Abby. Can I help you?"

Claire didn't know what to say, right out of the gate. It'd been so long.

"Hello? Volunteers of America this is Abby, can—"

"Yes, yes, hello."

Claire cleared her throat. "Can I speak to—"

"Ma'am, I can hardly hear you. I think we have a bad connection or something." Abby yelled like she hoped to set the example.

Claire'd been whispering. She swallowed, spoke up. "Can I speak to Mercedes Miller?" She cleared her throat again. "This is... it's her... her daughter. Claire. Claire Corrigan."

"Do you know what unit she's in?"

"Yes."

I pay for it. Of course I know.

"She's in Jonah's House."

"I'll transfer you."

Jonah's House. Claire hated the biblical names. As if it softened the blow of total lockdown. Like Ronald McDonald House made cancer fun.

"Hmmm?" The voice on the other end sounded dreamy, childlike.

"Mom?"

"Who is this?" Coquettish, flirtatious.

"It's Claire. Your daughter."

"Oh... Claire." Disappointed, skeptical. "Where are you?"

"Same place. California."

No point going into it all. Far from her still.

"How are you feeling, Mom?"

"Is Dad with you?"

"No, Mom... he's—"

"Is he coming to get me?" Mercedes's girlish tone changed to grown-up quick.

"Dad passed away a long time ago, remember?"

Claire could feel Mercedes's damaged brain churning over the phone. "Did you ever have that kid?"

"Yes, Mom. His name is Jordan. He's all grown up, remember?"

"Oh I remember now. I remember." Mercedes said in a whisper.

"How's the weather there, Mom?"

Was there a dumber question?

"Hmmm? I'm having soup. You hate soup."

Claire had to laugh. She did hate almost all soup. "Yes, I do. You remembered."

"I remember you. That's what. Are you still so pretty? Remember how pretty you always were?"

Claire laughed, felt her head. "Well, not so much these days, Mom."

"You got your looks from your mother," Mercedes said her voice strong.

Somewhere in a mind destroyed, a truth wormed to the surface. Mercedes had once been as beautiful and exotic as her name. She struggled on. "Your dad said he thought I was the most beautiful girl he'd ever seen."

"I'm sure he did." Claire wanted to end the call.

"Remember what your dad used to say about you?"

"Yes."

You're worthless. All girls are.

"He used to say you were a real beauty. A long tall drink of water and all the men would want you." Mercedes giggled. "Wasn't that funny?"

"Something like that."

Creepy, yes. Funny, no.

"Is he there with you?" A note of suspicion crept into Mercedes's voice.

"No, Mom. He's dead."

"That's what you said." Mercedes sounded like she didn't believe it. Like if it was true Claire probably had a hand in it. "You always were trying to steal him from me."

"Are you eating, Mom? Getting exercise?"

Was that what you said to people in the loony bin?

"Yes. I think so. I like the pudding. It's chocolate." Mercedes sounded like a child again.

"I'll send you some." Thank God for the internet. You could have anything delivered. Appease your guilt with a single finger stroke.

"Have your dad bring it when he comes." Mercedes said in a let's-play-school-and-I'm-the-principal voice. Before Claire could tell her, again, that her husband died a long time ago, Mercedes said, "Never mind. I can make it myself when I get home."

"Okay, Mom." No use. She should hang up.

"Are you still rich?"

"I just wanted to say hello, see how you were doing, Mom. I should let you go."

"Let me go?" Mercedes said her words a whisper again. "I'll say."

Claire'd stayed on the phone too long. "I've gotta go, Mom. I—"

"Your father's dead, isn't he?" she hissed, accused.

"Yes, you know that."

"He's dead because he worried himself to death about you. Always sneaking out. Running off with boys in the middle of the night." She started whimpering.

Worried? Wasted out at Lucky's or Dixie's was more like it. When he wasn't pinching me on the ass or beating the shit out of you.

"Mom, I was just a kid."

"He's dead. And you left me there. You left me alone. Then you left me here—"

Claire realized she was pouring sweat. Her hand ached from clutching the phone. The veins on both sides of her neck bulged against her skin, pulsing.

"I couldn't take care of you Mom. I was just a kid." Claire said in the softest voice.

"Where's your father? Put him on the phone right now—"

"Mrs. Corrigan?"

Claire jumped. "Huh? What?"

"Mrs. Corrigan? This is Nancy Wright. I'm the day nurse. Please don't let what your mother says upset you. She isn't having a good day today."

Claire's mouth felt full of sand.

****

"Looking for something?"

Shit.

Claire rifled through her clothes looking for her stash of pills. No luck. She'd hardly napped at all and was armpit deep in a mess of designer duds when Freddie Eddie snuck in and startled her.

"My cell phone." Good recovery.

"Is that right?" Freddie Eddie looked snarky. "That one?" He pointed at the bedside table and her phone. Right where she left it after she'd talked to her mother.

"Oh well." Claire got up off her knees. "There it is. Hiding in plain sight." She faced Freddie Eddie. They were the same height. "I guess we can go downstairs then. Or do you want to lurk around here some more?"

She moved toward the door, snatched her phone off the table. He sidestepped in front of her, blocking her way out.

"What is your deal? Get out of my way," she said pissed.

Freddie Eddie didn't move an iota, his face a sculpture. "You need to go back to wherever it is you came from."

Claire tried to push past him. Even though they were evenly sized, he was compact, solid as a boulder, unmoving. "Why don't you mind your own business?"

"Rob is my business."

"He's a big boy. Or haven't you noticed?"

Freddie Eddie grasped her wasted shoulders with both his hands, not as harsh as she expected. "Go home. I'll take you wherever you want to go." His smooth ferret-like face moved next to hers, she could count his pores. "Or this won't end well."

"Up already?" Rob met her at the bottom of the stairs. Freddie Eddie bounded down behind her, mumbled something about seeing them tomorrow and went out the front door.

"He goes in and out," Rob said. "Kinda the bad part about having the business here. No real private life. People come and go like any other office."

Claire watched Freddie Eddie's Corvette peel away from the curb.

Rob circled his baby chick. "Are you all right? You look like you've seen a ghost or something."

"Fine. I'm fine." She didn't want to meet Rob's eyes. "I should make some calls."

"Wait right here." After a few seconds he came back with her purse and her cord. "Come with me, the most comfortable place in the whole house." He beamed.

Like the rest, the room was in the same rich hip granny style. Except for the ugliest tackiest biggest loveseat Claire'd ever seen. A hideous pea-soup green color, the monstrosity sat directly in front of a flat screen TV with some kind of console in its center. A crocheted afghan hung on the back of one side in shades of lime, like his clogs. Claire made a face. Not a nice one.

"You don't like it?" Rob said.

"Well, it's... it's... I'm sure it's comfortable, it just an unusual choice considering the rest of the décor."

Rob cackled. "Yeah, well, a man's gotta have his chair. Sit."

Rob went to her side of the loveseat and pulled a lever. Claire flew backward.

"It's a recliner." Rob clapped his hands with childlike glee. "You can recline both sides or not. Independent of each other. An engineering miracle."

Claire laughed. Furniture that did tricks. Comfy. Maybe she loved it.

Rob reached for the center console. "If that isn't cool enough, this is an ice chest." He pulled out a cold beer.

She definitely loved it.

****

Rob Rhino nominated himself beer Nazi and wouldn't let Claire imbibe. Instead he made her a cup of the best hot chocolate she'd had in her life. Not that she'd had a lot of it.

"Mexican chocolate. That's the secret. And real cream mixed with the milk." Rob gave her a steaming mug with her pill and covered her legs with the afghan.

He was good to her. He probably would've been a good father. Except for the porn. Everyone had their quirks. Freddie Eddie hated her the jealous old... what was he exactly? Probably a closeted queen.

"Okay, make your calls. But be quick about it." He sat on the other side of the reclining loveseat. "I'm going to be right here to make sure you're not overdoing it." He pulled a book out of a side pocket pulled his lever and leaned back.

Did the damn thing fold out into a plane too?

Claire dug out her wallet with all her phone numbers. Better call Grace first. Get that over with. Grace sounded perturbed. More than usual.

"Had the flu," Claire said to cut off Grace's moaning about not hearing from her. "Really took me out of commission the past few days."

"I finally called the chapel director myself. Whatever his name is, John I think."

Oh I'm fine now. Thanks so much for asking bitch.

"Joe Lansing. His name is Joe." Claire looked over at Rob and rolled her eyes. "What did you need, Grace?"

"We *need* to decide on the arrangements. I let Mr. Lansing know what I wanted. He told me he'd pass it on to you."

"We did decide on the arrangements. I met with Connor a few days ago. He said you told him what you wanted to pass on to me. He passed it on."

"What? I... he... oh well, he must've misunderstood."

"Whatever."

Bunch of weirdos.

"Grace, if you talked to Joe, it's settled then. Just in case I'm going to give you my cell number. I'm not staying in that hotel anymore."

"Oh?" Grace said.

Nosy hag. She'd perked up for that morsel.

"I'm staying with a friend," Claire said.

What was it to Grace anyway? Like she cared.

"I didn't know you had friends here."

"You don't know anything about me, do you?" Claire couldn't pass that up.

She knew Grace was still on the line only because she could still hear her vampiric breathing. Then, "I know Liam didn't cotton to the church—"

The artful dodger.

"No, he didn't."

"But I'd really like to have a mass. A Catholic mass," she said the last part loud and slow. Like Claire's mother used to when she was speaking to a non-English speaking immigrant.

"I'm familiar with the term."

Oh Liam would love that. A Catholic mass. The icing on the retribution cake.

"Of course we'll have a mass," Claire said. "I've already talked to Joe Lansing about it."

Rob Rhino coughed, rattled the pages of the magazine Claire knew he was only pretending to read. She glared.

"Oh okay. We talked about moving Emmet, how that would work—"

"I need to call over there, Grace. I'll talk to Joe Lansing and let you know all the dates and if we need anything else." She hung up.

Rob put his magazine down. "Nice touch, the mass."

"Stop judging me."

He didn't say anything, but she could feel his disapproval.

Claire started to dial the chapel then changed her mind. She took a sip of her now lukewarm chocolate before turning to Rob. "She's sure anxious now."

"Who... what?"

"Grace. She's raring to go forward with this whole thing now."

"Isn't that what you wanted?"

"Well, yes." Claire took another drink. "Just odd, that's all. She was so reluctant at first. Downright nasty."

Rob mumbled something under his breath. Claire couldn't make it out.

"What?"

"Nothing."

"Oh no you don't. Out with it."

Rob picked up his magazine, thumbed through it.

Claire reached across the console, yanked the magazine out of his hands. "Out with it, I said."

"She was faking."

"Huh?"

"She was faking—her reluctance. Bet the farm on it."

"Why would she do that?"

"Manipulate her kids. Make them think she didn't want to do it."

Now that was making *some* sense. "Why?"

Rob rubbed his chin. "Habit more than anything by now, I'd guess. Poor Mom, so victimized, first by Liam, then by you. So bullied."

"To what end? If she was faking her reluctance, that means she wanted to bury everybody together. With Liam. The son who so disappointed her."

Rob laughed. A short harsh sound. "Yeah, the son who humiliated her with his spiritual and marital faux pas. Whose first wife killed herself here in Peyton Place. Who then refused to bail her out when she found out Saint Hubby had a secret porn life and died on film with his pants down or his frock up so to speak."

"All the more reason to be against this whole scheme."

Rob's tone suggested Claire wasn't the brightest bulb on the Christmas tree.

"Maybe you're not the only one who wants revenge."

CHAPTER FIFTY

O ut of the mouths of porn stars.

"Think about it, Claire." Rob picked up his magazine.

So the old shrew'd beaten her at her own game. And on her dime no less.

"You're probably wrong, Rob Rhino." Claire picked her phone up again to resume dialing. "You usually are."

Rob peeked at her over the top of his magazine. "Or I could be right and you have a lot more in common with the old swamp lizard than you think."

Claire grabbed the magazine and swatted him with it. "That's a low blow, Rob Rhino."

Rob leaned down and pushed the lever on the side of the loveseat forward, his chair back resumed its upright position. He got up and shuffled toward the kitchen.

"Think about it, Claire Corrigan."

****

"You're not bothering me a bit. I'm delighted to hear from you," Joe said.

Delighted—the gay man's constant state.

"Grace said she called you?"

"Ohhh... yes." Joe's voice dropped, sounding more Raymond Burr, less Richard Simmons. "She seems quite anxious to get the funeral dirge moving along, if you don't mind me saying."

"Indeed."

"I confirmed the mass, the exhumation, some minor details. I think she was satisfied."

"I'm sorry if she made a pest of herself. She's an odd one."

"I've dealt with worse." Joe chuckled. "Before I forget, you'll want to meet the priest prior to the service so we can set that up now if you'd like."

"I will?"

"Won't you?"

"Oh yes, of course. I guess I will."

"Let's see, we've got about a week left 'til we're ready to go, 'til the service. How about Monday, that's about midway?"

"Sure, fine."

"I'll call you back with a time."

Claire gave him her cell number. She heard him scramble for a pen.

"How did Trustee Week end up?" Claire made conversation.

"Fabulous. Thanks to your gift we raised a lot more money. Totals aren't in yet but I'm sure Lawrence will let you know. He's greedily counting donations and pledges as we speak."

"I'm sure he is. Well, glad I could help."

"By the way, your sister-in-law was prom queen on Trustee Night."

Elizabeth. She'd forgotten all about her and her debut.

"Really? Do tell."

"I think everyone had a marvelous time. You were right." Joe sounded amazed. "I think she'll fit right in. They all loved her. Especially the old-timers. She spent most of the night chatting up the emeritus, or is it emeriti? Whatever they're called. Lawrence gets so exasperated with me, can't keep them straight. A gaggle of old geezers like Elgin Grady." He paused. "That was insensitive of me. So sorry."

Elgin Grady. Bonnie's father. Charming. Bet he was thrilled to see her.

"Oh good heavens," Claire said. "That doesn't bother me a bit. Liam's first marriage is old news."

"Right, of course. I'm sure she knows quite a few of those folks since this is such a small town. Can't swing a cat around here without hitting someone you know, whether you want to or not."

****

Claire's legs felt wet. She kicked off the blanket. Her head hurt. Pill time. She took close to her usual dosage minus a couple the first few days, less every few days after, but Doogie didn't have a sense of humor about the occasional cocktail alongside. That was a no. She closed her eyes, inhaled. Goddammit she needed a drink, a handful of pills.

She could hear Rob puttering in the kitchen. Making dinner she supposed. The renaissance porn star, there was nothing he couldn't do. He'd bring her drugs with her plate, he did every night on time. Claire knew it was time to medicate, wouldn't want to have a seizure or anything. Her skin felt like it crawled, threatened to leap off her body. Didn't Doogie say something about not going cold turkey for fear of seizures? So she wasn't going cold turkey. Felt like it though.

Her phone rang. Andrew. Somebody (she could take her pick who) must've let him know she wasn't at the hotel anymore. He could leave a message. Claire wasn't ready to talk to him. She couldn't yet wrap her addled brain around what had gone down. Or what she needed to do yet. Normally she'd have medicated. Maybe after she got home, she still would.

The ringing stopped but then nothing. No annoying beeping sound to indicate he'd left a message. Fuck him then.

****

"You're such a Jew." Claire slurped the homemade chicken soup with matzo balls Rob Rhino brought her on a tray. "This is superb. I don't even like soup."

Another of his weird secrets—he was a fantastic cook. Every night something more delectable came out of the kitchen. Claire never lifted a finger. As though she could've. Except to ring the dinner bell.

They sat in front of the flat screen with their TV trays, ate dinner, and watched *Wheel of Fortune*, their like-an-old-married-couple ritual they'd developed since Claire moved in.

"My grandma's recipe." Rob picked up his bowl and drank the remnants. "She was the Jew, a real one, not like me—a Jack Jew. Like Liam was a Jack Catholic. We were born to it, but we don't practice." Rob wiped his face with his cloth napkin. "I have a bad taste in my mouth for the religious since Gloria's family. But not for this soup."

"P you idiot. The letter's P," Claire said to the fat woman contestant in the polyester pantsuit on the show. "Good decision. Take the recipes, leave the dogma."

"*Somewhere Over the Rainbow.*" Rob put down his bowl and pushed his tray out of the way.

"What? You can't guess already." Claire took another quick slurp. "Besides there's no P in that."

"Somewhere Over the Rainbow." The fat idiot contestant in the polyester pantsuit cried out. She tried to jump up and down, all two hundred and seventy-five pounds of her.

In an orgasmic frenzy, Vanna turned letters, her skinny neck barely holding her oversized head upright. "Ohhh... looks like Margaret's going home with seventy-five hundred dollars." Pat Sajak smiled, his orange face arranged in its fake for the camera way. Dead from the chin up.

"Smartass." Claire said.

"What can I say? I can spell."

"That sounds like something my son would say." Claire laughed. She hadn't thought anything about Jordan that would bring a smile to her face in days. "He's a smartass too. Plus he thinks the answer to everything is 'Somewhere Over the Rainbow.'"

Claire pushed her tray aside too. Reached down and jerked her lever. Both of them reclined, settled in to let their dinners digest.

"How old is he?"

"Almost thirty." When did that happen? "I'm getting old."

"Married?"

Claire felt her right eye twitch. She looked straight ahead at the TV. Rob turned the volume down. "No. He has a roommate. Steven."

"What does Jordan do?"

"He's a writer. Screenplays mostly."

"Oh that's cool." Rob reached into the ice chest console and pulled out a soda. Claire declined the one he offered her. "Does he live near you?"

"No. San Francisco."

"Queer?"

If Claire'd been drinking soda she'd have choked. "What makes you ask that?" she said. "Just because he lives in San Francisco and isn't married?" She felt the steam rise.

"Queer huh?" Rob took a swig.

"Rob Rhino, of all the—"

"Look at you all hot under the collar again." Rob laughed. "There's nothing wrong with it you know. Who cares?"

"I didn't say there was. *If* he was and that's a big if—"

"Claire... hello? It's me. Let's wake up and smell the K-Y shall we?"

"Goddammit, Rob Rhino... I—"

Rob was laughing so hard tears came out the corner of his eyes. "It's cool. Calm down. I'm sorry." He looked over at her stern face. "Really. I'm sorry."

"You are too much—"

"And you are homophobic."

"I most certainly am not."

"You certainly are too."

Claire's face felt as red hot as it had right before she overdosed. "I am not." She seethed.

"I saw the way you acted around Joe Lansing and Dean Sumner. You don't like gays. If you don't like gays, you're homophobic, Claire."

Like an overripe watermelon hit with a hammer, Claire burst. Everything underneath her rind-like skin spewed out. "I am not... you don't know what you're talking about. I love my son."

Rob jumped out of his chair and rushed over. "Claire, don't. I'm sorry. I'm an asshole. Really. You know I blurt out stupid shit. I shouldn't—"

"No. It's not—you don't understand. I—" Claire cried. Her shoulders shook.

"You're right. I don't. More reason I should keep my big trap shut." Rob tried to rub her arm, then stopped, started again.

"Jordan. He's gay." *There.* She said it and buried her face in her hands.

Rob sat on the hardwood floor at her feet. "That's okay. He sounds like a great guy Claire. He loves you right?"

Claire sobbed harder. She nodded, her head still covered by her palms.

Rob kept talking. "It's no big deal. There's nothing to be ashamed of—"

Claire's head flew up so fast she thought it'd fly off. "I'm not ashamed of my son and I never would be. It's just—" She couldn't speak.

"It's just what?"

"Nothing." She wiped her nose with the back of her hand but not the tears. "You don't have kids. You can't appreciate what it's like."

"Try me."

"It's just—"

"It's just what, Claire? Come on now. It's just what?"

She leaned down, grabbed Rob by both arms. "Do you think I want my son strapped to a barbed wire fence and beaten to death in some bumfuck town like Laramie, Wyoming?"

Rob looked like Vanna just told him he'd run out of vowels.

"What?"

"Matthew Shepard. Ever hear of him? That's what they did to him. They tortured and beat him to death. Because he was gay." Claire could her hear own voice—loud, hysterical. "Tied up, defenseless, no one helped him. That's what happens. Here—in a *civilized* world." Claire cried like she'd never stop. "It was all over the news in the late nineties. Jordan was eighteen, only five years younger than Matthew when they killed him. Do you think I want that for my son?"

Rob started to comfort her. "Oh, Claire—"

"It's not like I didn't know." Claire's washboard chest puffed up as she sucked air. "He's my son for God's sake. I knew before he did. I felt so sorry, scared. He didn't have a father to guide him when he was young. It could've made a difference—"

Rob said, "Claire, that doesn't matter in the least. Jordan was born gay just like you were born straight. He's who he is no matter who guides him or doesn't."

"That's what Liam used to say. But I'd lie awake at night, sick with worry that he wouldn't fit in, he'd be an outcast, lonely. Then the hate crimes, AIDS—" Claire's sobs began again in earnest. "I couldn't sleep or stop thinking about it. I still think about it. The pills helped for a while—"

Rob Rhino put his arms around her. She let him.

After several minutes he whispered, "Jordan is going to be fine. Nothing like that would ever happen to him."

Claire sniffled. "How could you know that?"

Rob held her out away from him so he could see her face, look into her eyes.

"We'll send him condoms and won't let him go to Laramie."

C laire hadn't yet seen Warden Rhino that morning when she noticed a missed call from Jordan on her cell phone screen as well as several from Andrew and Annabelle.

"I'm impressed, Mother, the cell phone is still working."

"I've turned over a new leaf."

"Does the leaf check messages?"

"What are you blabbing about?"

"Your voicemail is full. No one can leave you a message."

Crap. No wonder Andrew wasn't leaving messages. She'd had over thirty of them she'd never bothered to listen to from way back when.

"I'll get around to it."

"Maybe you need someone over there to do your bidding."

"I wasn't going to call you back. I'm already sorry I did."

"Mother, you can't stay pissed forever." Jordan said exasperated. "I screwed up. I have to pay the piper now. I'm taking care of it. That isn't why I called."

Claire couldn't take him to the mat on it now. "I'm all ears."

"So were you going to enlighten me on Liam's girlfriend and the kid or what?"

"I figured Annabelle would tell you in that drama-fest way you love."

"Well, she did. It was fantastic."

Claire expected Jordan to laugh but he didn't.

"And I knew I could count on your heartfelt and sensitive reaction. So everyone got what they expected," Claire said her throat tight.

Annabelle must've left out the part about having her committed.

Jordan didn't reply for a few moments. Claire thought she could hear him light a cigarette. She thought he'd quit smoking. She thought a lot of things.

"I know you might not believe this, Mother, but I feel terrible about the whole thing." Jordan exhaled. "What I feel worst about is you didn't tell anyone. Why didn't you say anything? We could've helped."

Claire started to cry. Jordan the smartass was the suit that fit, that she was used to.

"How could I tell you something like that? I didn't want you to hate Liam, to feel bad about him. Especially since he was dead."

"I wouldn't have."

"What?"

He wouldn't have? She lied. Damn straight she wanted Jordan to hate him.

"Well, I wouldn't have been happy about it. I'm not thrilled about it now."

Claire closed her eyes, tried to picture her son as he spoke.

"Relationships are tough, complicated." Jordan said.

"And? So?"

"I loved him Mother. He was good to me." Jordan's voice got soft. "I think he did the best he could."

The lump in Claire's throat felt unmanageable.

"I'm so sorry about it all. Clearly he didn't make a good choice there. But for now, Mom, I just wanted to let you know I was thinking about you. That's all. And to offer our help."

Claire knew her son. There was something he wasn't saying.

"Jordan, what do you want to say?"

She could take it. Couldn't she? She dried her tears with the bottom of her shirt.

"You need to finish up whatever familial fiasco you're intent on pulling off over there and get home. We're all worried about your health. Annabelle—"

"Jordan, forget about all that for now. What were you going to say before?"

Claire could hear him smoking. "Mother, I just..." Jordan exhaled again. "It's just, well, you know, we're all stumbling through life licking our wounds. Sometimes so much so we can't see we're wounding someone else. I hope you can appreciate that eventually."

No, she couldn't take it after all. What she could take was pills but those were rationed. She let go of the chair and made a tight fist.

"Mother, are you there?" Jordan said.

"Umm... yes."

Best to talk about something else.

"How does Annabelle seem to you?" Claire looked at the sore palm of her hand. Her nails left moon-shaped marks where they'd dug in.

"Hysterical as usual."

Rob Rhino tiptoed in. Claire almost laughed, a stealthy pudgy porn star in screaming green plastic clogs, holding a white envelope against his chest. He paused, on pointe, set the envelope down in front of her, mimed some weird interpretive dance kind of thing, then tiptoed out.

"Mother? Hello?"

"Oh sorry. Right. Have you talked to Annabelle since her surprise visit here?"

"What?" Jordan coughed. "She flew there? To Pennsylvania? What in the—"

"She didn't tell you she talked to Andrew?"

Claire picked up the FedEx envelope, puzzled. Room 244 blared across it in red felt-tip marker. Her hotel room number. She flipped it over. Addressed to her from Conchita. Rob must've picked it up from the hotel.

"Yes, she did." Jordan let out a big puff. "She didn't say much. Come to think of it, I guess I didn't give her much of an opportunity. Well, Steven didn't. He ripped into her about the inappropriateness, lack of ethics, blah, blah. You need to fire—"

In a rush, a random thought bounced to the tip of Claire's tongue. "You said *we* could help. Who's *we*?"

"I misspoke. I'm pretty useless. I should've said Steven's help."

Him.

"Steven? What on earth could he do for me?"

Floral arrangements for the memorial had already been decided.

"Steven is an attorney. Let him help you with this mess with Andrew."

♣

C H A P T E R

FIFTY-TWO

◆

The contents of the envelope hit the smooth shiny antique table top with a whop, a thick wad of correspondence rubber-banded together in a neat packet. Conchita's signature—organized neatness. Claire's mail. She'd forgotten she'd asked Conchita to forward it.

A letter from her great-aunt Charlotte in Milwaukee. A reminder from AAA—her membership expired in thirty days. A condolence card (right on time) from someone she'd never heard of in Florida. Must be another of Liam's business associates. A postcard from Frank's Luxury Auto Service, the forty thousand mile reminder for Liam's Range Rover.

Claire almost doubled over.

She didn't want to remember but too bad so sad. Her sober brain had other ideas.

"Hey, it's Frank. You had an appointment this morning?"

"Oh I... umm... I... what?" Claire almost fell, tangled in her bath towel, sopping hair slapping her cheek. The only reason she answered the phone in the first place was because she thought it was Guillermo.

"You were going to bring Liam's Range Rover in this morning? The brakes." Frank yelled over the mechanic noise in the background, the clatter in Claire's head.

Did he think she was a servant? "Conchita must've—"

"No. Liam said she was off today. You were going to bring it. I offered to send someone to pick it up. He turned me down. Said you guys worked it out on your end?"

Shit. Crap. Forgot. "Yeah... well—"

She rummaged through the nightstand halfway listening to Frank's mechanic lingo. "Those brakes won't hold up, pads are about gone. I told Liam that the last time he was here. You know Liam, never wants to take the time. He'll be out of time if he slams on those——"

"Sorry, Frank. I had a... thing. I'll call you back in a few to reschedule."

"Who was that?" Liam rushed in.

Claire plonked down the receiver.

"Oh... ah... Jordan. He's... he might come to town. Wants to have dinner or something."

"I gotta go. I'm late as usual." He grabbed his car keys, didn't glance in her direction, or even make listening sounds. "I've got that presentation."

Claire would've met her husband's eyes had he been looking at her. She picked up her empty wine glass, held it aloft in a mock toast.

"Good luck with that."

Her trembling fingers felt the raised letters of the printed address on the card like a Braille reader. Somewhere in Rob Rhino's house a phone rang. Like it had the day Liam died. Her eyes closed, slow, deliberate, weighed down.

Claire'd never told Liam she hadn't gotten the brakes fixed.

They'd held out a while longer after the missed repair appointment. Not long enough. She'd never said a thing. Not even when he'd stormed out in a rage that day while she screamed at his back. She'd followed him to the garage, never letting up. The driver's door slammed behind him.

Claire'd wished him dead, knowing it was a definite possibility.

****

"What are you doing?" Rob hit the floor on both knees.

Claire, caught, but not caring, barely glanced in his direction. "Where'd you put 'em all?" All of Rob's period-correct kitchen cabinets hung open. The subzero restaurant size fridge waved open, its contents in chaos. Claire's bony ass stuck out of the last cabinet she searched, under the sink.

"No drugs under there." Rob tried to squeeze into the cabinet with her.

"I know." She pushed him out, sucked herself out too. "It's not my birthday."

"What's going on?" He yanked her by the arms, sat her upright.

"Where'd you put the beer?"

"I threw it out." Rob sat cross-legged across from her on the black and white tiled floor. "You didn't answer me. You've been doing so well." He looked stricken.

Claire lay prone on the cold floor. Must be what it's like in the morgue on a slab.

"Rob Rhino. Give it up. You can't save me." The tears ran down her neck. "I don't want to be saved."

"I want it enough for the both of us. That's enough for now." Rob lay next to her.

"Rob, it's not that simple... it's—"

"It's like they say, as stupid as it sounds. One day, one hour at a time." Rob gripped her hand.

"You don't know me, Rob. I'm not worth saving." Claire took her hand away from his. "I'm not what you think I am." She wrinkled up the corner of her T-shirt with one hand. "Underneath the anger is... something else."

He snatched her hand back. "I know, Claire. I know about Liam."

"What about him?"

"You know. The car. The brakes."

Claire went still. "You can't possibly—"

"You told me. About not getting the brakes fixed." He clutched her hand tight as if he knew she'd try to run. "You got stoned, drunk, forgot about the appointment. Forgot to tell Liam. Then he got in the car, you were so angry, still half pie-eyed—"

"How—" She cried out the words in a rasp. "I never told you."

"You did. That night in your hotel room, the night you'd had dinner with Liam's family, and called me. The first time you almost overdosed. It was just you and me."

"You've known all this time." Not a question.

Quid pro quo, Rob Rhino.

"Gloria?" she prodded. Their hands stayed clasped.

"What about her?"

"What happened to her?"

His breathing stayed even. "Her heroin addiction ruled us. We had nowhere to go but down."

"And?" Claire propped her foot on his calf. They lay still on the cold floor.

"We had her trust fund money so I had to cut that off, discourage the supply. She started whoring herself out for cash." His voice got quieter. "I'd come home, there were men there, off the street, zipping up. She sold our car. Got the clap." Claire could hear him start to cry. "I had to give her the money back. Thought it was the lesser of two evils."

Claire wanted to say something, nothing came to mind.

"With cash there was no stopping her. She'd overdose once a week. Looked like shit, dead woman walking. She'd started crushing pills and snorting them too 'cause she'd fucked her veins up so bad she could never hit one with the needle. When she was too high to do either of those she'd gulp 'em by the handfuls. She was so loaded, such a fucking mess, she couldn't swallow, almost choked to death every time."

Claire's disgraceful memory of Rob's adeptness at finger induced vomiting made her stiffen.

Rob paused, maybe to summon courage, maybe to reconsider his confession. "Gloria was hell bent, headed to the grave. Time was the only question."

"Some people are. Can't save them from themselves."

Lame, but what else could she say? It's what she felt about Gloria, about herself. Without letting go of Rob's hand she closed what little gap there was between them on the floor, her body pressed right next to his for shelter, comfort. To make him keep talking, make him stay.

"That last day, I knew she couldn't last. I couldn't either. I knew she'd never get help. She'd made that clear. I'd grown to hate what she'd become, what I'd become with her." Rob covered his face with the hand that wasn't hanging on to Claire's. "She was so high, weighed next to nothing. Her beauty trashed like a used syringe. She tried to swallow a bunch of pills, started choking. As long as I live, I'll never forget that look on her face, the pleading. She thought I'd put my fingers down her throat like I always did, keep her alive. Only I didn't."

Claire stared at the ceiling, watched the faux turn-of-the-century gaslight fixture.

"I left her there to die like a junkie in her own vomit."

C laire drifted into the back-room office in time to hear Freddie Eddie utter the most disturbing words she'd heard him say since they'd been introduced.

"You know you're my only baby doll."

Rob Rhino sat at one desk, his bifocals perched at the end of his nose, stubby fingers hunting and pecking at the keyboard in front of him. Einstein with a dyed combover. Melissa worked at the desk next to Rob's at a much quicker pace while Freddie Eddie continued a cutesy wootsy convo with some poor sap on the other end of the phone at the desk toward the back.

"Hey you." Rob looked up from his computer screen, his heavy head swaying ever so slightly like a giant bobblehead. "Thought you were napping."

"Stuff to do." She leaned against the doorjamb, manila envelope firmly in hand. Claire couldn't take her eyes off Freddie Eddie. Cupcake? Get outta town.

Rob looked over his glasses.

Melissa piped up. "Is there anything I can help you with?"

The girl had a brain and a halo.

"No, but thank you," Claire said. "Oh wait. Actually there is something. Can I sit at one of these desks to finish going through my mail?"

She could've used the dining room or stayed holed up in her bedroom, but truth be told since their mutual purges Claire'd felt shaken. She wanted to be near Rob. He had that way about him. He made her feel safe, despite his story. Rob was like a quilt in the winter. Without him she felt cold, exposed. Besides, who was she to cast stones? Maybe he should be scared of her.

"Pick any one." Melissa smiled like an angel, motioned around the room.

Claire plopped down at the first empty desk next to Melissa's.

"I'm making a mess of this. Back in the day we used pens and paper." Rob Rhino peered down, his eyes traveled back and forth, searching. "Aha, M, there it is." He hit the key with a loud clack. "God my eyes are worse than yours Claire Corrigan."

"Didn't you learn to type, Doctor?" Claire said.

"Yes. I am typing." Rob's sausage fingers stabbed out a key here and there.

Freddie Eddie hung up after making kissing sounds into the receiver. Claire almost gagged. "Afternoon Claire. Are you feeling better?" Freddie Eddie said his eyes reptilian.

They hadn't exchanged two words since their confrontation her first day in Rob's house. Claire tried to peer into his mouth to see his forked tongue.

"Been gone too long, usually don't stay away from the missus more than a week or two," Freddie Eddie announced to the room.

Away from *who*?

"He gets all moony after a few days." Rob rolled his eyes. "You'd think they were newlyweds."

Did he say missus?

Melissa giggled, kept clacking away, diligent at her work.

"You have a missus? There's a Mrs. Freddie Eddie?" Claire didn't hide her horror.

Apparently not the sensitive type Freddie Eddie let out a loud guffaw and smacked the desk top with the flat of his hand. "Yes, ma'am, there is indeed a Mrs. Freddie Eddie." Rob

Rhino and Melissa cracked up too. "For the past thirty-two years if you can believe it."

She couldn't believe it. Freddie Eddie married for over thirty years. And from what she could tell happily. Even he was better marriage material than Claire.

****

"You never told me Freddie Eddie had a wife."

"Thought I did."

"Ahh... NO."

Rob laughed. "Marie's a kick in the ass."

"I'll bet. Probably kicks his ass every day."

Claire looked around the empty office. The man in question had just waltzed out with the threat he'd see them tomorrow. Right behind Melissa. Rob Rhino and Claire had the place to themselves.

"He's pretty well behaved."

"Doesn't seem that way to me." Claire had a vague memory of Freddie Eddie and a young usherette in the parking lot at Rob's speech.

"Oh that's all show. He's too chicken." Rob laughed.

"Doubt it."

"Marie is... what you'd call... sturdy." Rob looked down through his glasses at Claire with a you know what I'm talkin' about look on his face.

"Freddie Eddie married a fat chick?" Claire howled.

"You're not supposed to say that anymore." He frowned. "She's a great Italian cook."

"Now that's funny."

"I've heard him call her mommy."

"Stop. You're killing me—"

"Oh don't say that." Rob's face crumpled.

Claire stopped, felt bad for her insensitive choice of words. "Oh sorry."

She looked at his pouting face, his drooping jowls, then burst out laughing again.

"Get over yourself, Rob Rhino. *Mommy,* for Chrissake."

****

She took another pass at her mail. After sorting through it earlier and finding the reminder card from Randy she'd stopped. Randy's Luxury Auto Service's postcard rested comfortably in the trash so Claire could buck up and carry on. Rob resumed his hunt and peck. She tried to squint her way through.

"Do I look like I want a Victoria's Secret credit card?" Claire huffed, shooting silent accusations in Rob's direction, tearing up an envelope. "Want to know who Victoria's Secret is? She's a slut."

Rob didn't look up from his keyboard. "Not touching that one with a thirteen inch—" He giggled to himself. "Never mind."

A small party invitation-sized envelope came up next. No return address. Something disagreeable slinked around her skin. She ran her pencil under the glued flap, tearing it open with a quick rip.

"Jesus Christ. I need to use a computer."

C heck your email.
A simple phrase turned ominous. In the decade Claire had known Andrew's wife Meg, she'd never paid a social call. They'd known each other through their husbands, ran into each other at the occasional holiday or cocktail party, the usual.

"Guess she left me a few messages on my cell. They're still on it since I've never checked them. She gave up."

Rob shook his fat finger at her. "Maybe you should get with it, start taking care of business."

Claire balled the engraved stationary in her fist, the MC monogram crumpled. The note had been short. Meg had tried to reach Claire by phone, no luck. She had information Claire might find interesting.

Claire and Rob Rhino sat close to the computer screen.

"Wish I had a drink." Claire keyed in her email address.

"I hear ya." Rob rubbed her back. "Use these." He handed over his bifocals. "Good God woman, get yourself some reading glasses. You're sad with all that squinting."

Meg was only too happy to spill her guts, air their dirty laundry. Like thousands of men before him Andrew emailed, texted, Facebooked, and voicemailed his ass into a sling. Complete with photos. Copies of which Meg was delighted to email to Claire as long as she promised not to have him disbarred until after Meg took him to the cleaners.

Here comes da judge.

They read through email after incriminating email detailing less a romance than an extortion scheme. At least on

Andrew's end. Ellen appeared pretty clueless, at least from her side of the correspondence. Claire almost pitied her. Andrew talked money almost exclusively.

She spends more on drugs.

We need to speed this up. She might not live to trial.

She has no idea your lawyer is me.

They shared Rob's glasses and each read to themselves. Claire could feel herself get tense, her eyes fill. Without taking his eyes off the emails Rob put his arm around her shoulders, pulled her to him. He had her back.

"Oh my god. What the—"

Rob turned back to look at the screen and cackled. "Oh brother."

There was an all too clear photo of Andrew, naked, alone, and pointing at his not quite but probably the best he could do hard-on with a proud semi-smile on his pampered Botoxed face. His gray hair artfully mussed, his flabby body oiled up 'cause it looked *much better* that way.

"Oh... gross. If that's not bad enough he's got man boobs." Claire covered her mouth with one hand. She didn't need the glasses to see what pitiful corner the situation had just turned.

Rob Rhino pointed to Andrew's crotch and talked to the screen over his glasses. "Claire how do you work that zoom thingy? Dude you call that a prick? Please. Stop embarrassing yourself. I could beat that with a—"

Claire elbowed Rob in his gut.

"Stop it."

****

She got up to stretch her legs, to try to absorb some of what she'd read. There seemed to be no end to the emails. She couldn't read anymore.

Rob whistled through his gap. "Christ on a cracker. I've never seen anything like this." He rubbed his eyes.

Claire leaned on a desk. "I can't deal with it now. I need to get this memorial over with. It is what I came here to do remember?"

"Still with that damn revenge scheme." He put his glasses back on, turned back to the screen.

"I think I'm heading upstairs. I've had it for one day." Claire could see the stars out the office window. They'd missed dinner.

"Hey, Claire. Who's Connor?"

CHAPTER

FIFTY-FIVE

———◆———

C laire felt a ripple wave through her, not of fear exactly, something else disturbing, uneasy. She made short work of the space between her and Rob.

"Connor is Liam's brother." She sat back down in her chair, a heavy flop. "What the hell are you looking at?"

Rob stayed focused on his computer. "There's a bunch of emails between him and Andrew."

Claire almost shoved Rob out of his chair to see.

Looks like the adoption might be on again.

Thought that died with Liam.

Ellen will take ten million to ride off into the sunset, leave the baby.

Claire's already challenged vision blurred. She could hear Rob's blood rushing. Or was it her own? Rob's arm around her kept her from falling. She glanced at him to make sure he wouldn't leave even though she knew he wouldn't. He nodded, pulled her closer.

Don't forget, you're not supposed to know she's bald.

Keep her stoned. She might be easier to deal with. Her purse is full of all sorts of shit.

Not sure what's going on with her. Should be easy to control her with all the drugs.

I don't know if I can do this. She was my brother's wife. She doesn't seem so bad.

You want the kid, right?

Claire started to cry.

I don't know where she is. She won't answer my calls. Her voicemail is full. She's not at the hotel. My mother says she's staying with friends.

She doesn't have any friends.

Rob hugged Claire close.

"You sure have bad taste in men."

****

Who knew Jordan would have such *good* taste in men?

Steven turned out to be an actual lawyer in real life. Not too swishy either. He hadn't liked the idea of Claire calling Andrew directly. He wanted to handle it all for her. He wanted to press charges, blah, blah, blah. Claire didn't want to. Steven hadn't liked that either. Whatever Steven learned in law school, he must've missed catching a clue class.

Claire did a shitload of stuff no one liked. He might as well get used to it.

"I hope you've had some time to come to your senses," Andrew said indignant.

"Yes, I have. And I'm the one with a proposition for you."

"*You* have a proposition for *me*? I think you should worry about yourself and not me."

"Of course you do."

This was fun.

"How about this, Andrew? Are you sitting in front of your computer?"

"Yes, actually."

Ron Rhino sat across from her, gave her two thumbs up for courage.

"I'm emailing you a couple things." She had her finger poised over the send key. "You and Ellen go fuck yourselves with her kid. I will pay her... say... zero. Starting now. And I'll consider not bringing you up on extortion charges. You can also refund me all the money I've paid her and you for the past year."

Rob clapped his hands together with no noise. Smiled his big missing tooth, goofball smile.

"That's crazy. Extortion? Refund? I don't know what Meg told you but she's as delusional as you are. And what Ellen's case has to do—"

Claire could feel his distraction over the phone.

"I don't know who you—" His voice sounded farther away. "What the fuck... where in the hell—?"

"Get your emails?"

"Where did you get these?"

Claire wondered if he was as purple-faced as he sounded. She looked at Rob Rhino and mouthed, "We got him."

"Does it matter?" Claire felt like laughing but refrained. "You can sell that kid to anybody you want, but I'm sure as hell not paying for it."

"Claire, it's not like that." Andrew stumbled for excuses. "Liam just tried to right a wrong, his brother couldn't have kids, he—"

"And you can tell my loser brother-in-law I'll see him in hell."

After a couple beats of silence and some heavy breathing Andrew said, "You'll hear from *my* attorney."

Claire smiled. "I doubt it. And before I forget. You're fired."

C laire cleared all thirty-three messages from her cell phone. Listened to them too. Most were from the kids, Conchita, a couple from the travel agent, three from Meg (that poor woman). Claire felt her slate washed a little cleaner. Sure she missed all her drugs, her booze, but one day at a time, one hour or minute. Plus she still had Guillermo's number. The yoke around her neck that had been Andrew, Ellen, and her kid was gone. Maybe Claire could carry on.

She'd taken her daily dose, doled out by Doctor Rhino, watched *Wheel of Fortune* again, (how Rob always got it right with only three letters filled in was a mystery) and nodded off on her side of the tricky loveseat. Rob shook her awake, mumbled it was time to call it a day. She dawdled in front of her bedroom door until he disappeared ahead of her off to bed. Unusual for him to trot off without a backward glance. He liked to helicopter over Claire a lot longer.

She could resist the call of the wild no more. Her Chanel flats moved over the thick Persian runner without a sound. Claire could see light from under his closed door, a van Gogh night out the window ahead. Even the sky looked more picturesque from this house. Without hesitating she knocked.

The door opened wide, startling her.

"Is something wrong?" Rob Rhino said.

Claire looked over and around him ignoring his question to get a good look inside. It wasn't a bedroom. It was, from what she could see, more like an office or a library.

He stepped back, mercifully not undressed. "Come in, come in."

"I... I'm sorry. I'm invading your space... or something."

She tried to think of a reason why she'd be there. Why didn't she think of something before she knocked?

"No, it's fine. Come sit. This is my private office. And bedroom over there." He pointed a dwarf-like finger.

She followed his outstretched arm to the adjoining room off to the side. She walked farther in. The room looked like an affluent history professor's space seen through the eyes of an overpaid designer. The thick rug, the marble mantelpiece over the fireplace, the ornate yet masculine mahogany desk that sat opposite it, and the deep burgundy colored walls lined with bookshelves filled with hardbound books and knickknacks. Nothing tacky. Behind the French vanilla leather wingback desk chair, hung a near life-size painting of a woman with a magnificent head of auburn hair.

Gloria. Had to be.

"This is where I keep my sanity." He waved one arm around the spacious room. "Excuse the mess. I wasn't expecting ladies." He gave a lecherous smirk, led her onward.

Claire felt herself blush but wasn't going to miss out. The giant four poster bed nearly swallowed the small room. What a mess. Towels on the floor, magazines (*Time* and *Newsweek*, no porn), newspapers (*Wall Street Journal, New York Times*, no small-town *Gazette* for him), and empty soda cans. The bed wasn't made and looked like an army slept in it. No clothes. He owned one outfit and he wore it.

"Now this is what I'm talkin' about," Claire said.

"What?" Rob said.

"I expected your whole house to look like this. This I can wrap my brain around."

Rob laughed. "Yeah, I bet you can. I try to keep my mess contained. Having a regular maid helps." Rob glanced around his wreck of a bedroom. "Gloria hated my sloppiness."

Claire reached over and touched Rob's arm. Small comfort.

They stepped back out and Rob led her to one of the other two matching chairs that sat in front of the fireplace.

Rob nodded his head toward the painting. "Wasn't she beautiful?"

It wasn't a widower's fond remembrance. It was fact. Especially for a man with a face only his grandma could love.

Claire got up to get a closer look at the painting. "Looks like a wedding dress."

"Impressive guess. Yeah, I had this painted about five years ago from one of our wedding photos."

Gloria looked like a seventies bride. Cream colored gauzy cotton maxi dress. They were called way back when. She'd have looked like Stevie Nicks if she'd had a tambourine. Her skin skimmed cream perfection. And that hair. Long auburn curls worn loose almost to her waist. Claire reached for her own head. Nope, nothing. She sat back down.

"This is the only likeness of Gloria in the whole house?" she said.

There were no photos of her anywhere. How had Claire not noticed that before? Too busy on the lookout for porn.

Rob fiddled with the armrest rivets. "Yes, it is. I don't think I need too many reminders." He scratched at something on the leather. "Besides, this house is all about the business. She hated it. It's why she started taking drugs. To deal with it."

Rob got up, bent down behind the desk. Claire heard a suction sound and glass shaking around. He came up with two root beers.

"There's a refrigerator back there?"

Rob smiled, nodded. "Under the desk, a mini one. Never know when I might get thirsty."

A loveseat and a desk that did tricks.

"You live here only part of the year, right?" Claire said.

"Yeah. LA the other part." He gulped his root beer. "I hate it there. It's depressing."

"Southern California is great. I live there you know, just a couple hours north of LA," Claire reminded him. "You could visit me when you're there."

Rob laughed, looked surprised. "Seriously? You'd want me to show up at the door?"

Claire bristled. "We're friends, aren't we?"

"Claire Corrigan. What would the neighbors think?"

"Fuck the neighbors."

He brightened. "Can I?"

****

He seemed melancholy.

She looked closer at his paunchy face. Everything drooped more. His hair was greasy, stringy, gray at the roots around his temples and near his bald spot. He'd let himself go far more than usual. Now he looked his seventy years, even in the soft light. His hula girl shirt was stained and wrinkled, jeans torn, his bright green clogs scuffed and dirty. Claire didn't have to inhale too deep to get a good whiff of him. He could've been the homeless man she thought he was at the airport. Why hadn't she noticed? First Gloria's pictures, now Rob's decline. Guess they had to be on fire for Claire to pay attention.

It didn't take a Mensa candidate to figure out what was on his mind.

"We're a pair aren't we Rob Rhino?" Claire ran her finger around the lip of her root beer bottle. "You and what happened with Gloria. Me and what happened with—" She stopped. Still she couldn't say it. Not sober.

Rob shut his eyes, leaned back in his chair.

Claire's tears ran before she could beat them back. "I tell myself I didn't remember it, the brakes. I didn't remember in time. I'd been drunk, stoned. He'd driven it lots of times after, it'd been fine. How could I know it'd be that day? I was so angry when he got in the car. As soon as he drove off... I somehow knew he wouldn't come back. I let him go anyway."

"Claire, it was an accident. Your head doesn't work when you're fucked up." Rob's eyes stayed shut. He didn't lift his head. "You've got to put it behind you. You have to get better. You have a lot to live for—yourself, your family."

"I could say the same to you, Rob Rhino. You need to put Gloria behind you, get well. A lot of people need you."

"Don't worry about me, Claire Corrigan. I'm fine."

"Don't look fine to me."

"Is that why you came in here?" He opened one eye, shimmied a caterpillar brow. "To nurse me?"

"I came in here because I'm nosy." What'd she have to hide? "You're a porn star for Chrissake. I wanted to see in here."

Rob let out a bark-like laugh. "That's priceless, Claire Corrigan, priceless." He smoothed back his rat's nest hair. "You must be disappointed."

"I am. No whips, no chains. Your reputation's ruined." Claire stared him down. "But don't change the subject."

They sat for a few minutes, swigged their root beers, looked at the marble mantle with the expensive bric-a-bracs on it. Her stomach churned, the root beer sat at the bottom of it and bubbled up like lava.

"I'm tired. I'd like to call it good, retire." He leaned his head back again, closed his eyes.

"Well, didn't you plan to eventually?" Claire said surprised at the subject change.

"Plan? There's no porn plan." Rob opened his eyes a slit to see her. "It's not an old man's business. I'm not supposed to still be in it."

"Is anyone older than Hugh Hefner? He's still in." Claire remembered Jordan telling her about the pictures of Rob and Hef at the Mansion online.

"Only guys like Hefner and Guccione, God rest him, hang around past their prime, and Jesus, Flynt. Who wants to end up like Larry? They're pathetic. But they were never on screen. I'm the worst." Rob picked his head up off the back of the chair and sat up straight to emphasize his point. "I'm sick of talking about my cock. At my age it's pitiful."

"You're probably not going to get too much sympathy."

Rob slumped back again. "No, probably not." He fiddled with his squirrely moustache. "Who knew it'd turn out like this? Like you said now I'm a brand. A corporation."

"Heads of corporations retire."

"Gotta walk away sometime." Rob shut his eyes again. Tears seeped down his withered cheeks. "I don't want to keep it going anymore. It was all for nothing, didn't mean a fucking thing." He spun his big head in her direction. "It didn't turn out the way I thought it would."

Claire reached across the divide between their chairs and put her hand on his.

****

She stayed long enough to finish her root beer.

"You're meeting with the priest tomorrow?" Rob said.

She nodded, stood up to leave.

"Freddie Eddie's gonna take us."

"Us? I can drive myself. My rental is just sitting there."

"You're still weak as a kitten." Rob stood up too. "I'm going with you. Father McKinley from St. Theresa's is a friend of mine—"

"Let me guess. He's really a porn star."

"Now that's funny."

Rob stood poised for battle. A battle Claire knew she'd lose.

"I want to go early, check out the crypt site," she said. "See if it's all kosher."

Claire stopped in front of the bookcases by the door and squinted to read some of the titles. She expected history books but was surprised to see books with titles like *How to Win Friends and Influence People*. She took a better look—*Seven Habits of Highly Effective People, Men Are from Mars, Women Are from Venus, The Secret,* and *I'm OK, You're OK*. There were more, but she stopped.

"You've got the self-help market cornered," she said.

"It's never too late to make improvements," Rob said.

Claire got closer to see better. There were several books on the topic of manic depression, anxiety, and schizophrenia. She glanced at Rob Rhino from the corner of her eye.

"I got those from the rehab center. They come in handy for my volunteer work over there," he said too fast.

"Do you mind if I skim through a couple these?" she said.

"Help yourself." Rob Rhino laughed at his own lame joke.

Claire stood. She didn't want to go back to her room yet. His kicked-dog gloom made her want to stay. He said he kept his sanity there in his private rooms. It seemed to Claire it's where he kept his sorrow, the weight of his guilt. As soon as he crossed the threshold it came at him like a blowtorch.

She thought about offering to sit with him, stay and talk longer, but didn't know how. Reaching out, offering real comfort wasn't her thing. She didn't have the faintest idea what could ease his suffering, or her own for that matter. A pat on the hand was about the only item on her empathy menu. The words stayed in her mouth.

"Okay then. Good night," she said finally.

She took a couple steps with the books in her hands, stopped and turned. He was still standing in the doorway. She went back, dropped the books, embraced him, and didn't wrinkle her nose at his pungent aroma. He put his arms around her. She could feel the heaviness of his belly pushed against her, his sweat through his hula girl shirt. His mouth brushed her neck. He could've kissed it if he'd wanted to. Her breath quickened, she pressed into him.

"Claire Corrigan, are you trying to seduce me?"

Ten insults flew to her lips, but she kept them there. All the blood left her face only to race back. She held him at arms-length, blurted accidental truth.

"What if I am?"

He didn't smile. He looked as serious as Claire'd ever seen him. "You'd only break my heart." He kissed his fingertips then touched her cheek. "Good night, Claire Corrigan."

****

A long day stretched into a long night. Claire grabbed her pillow so she could pull the coverlet down, a piece of paper that had been stuffed underneath it fluttered to the ground. With a quick glance, she could see it was a copy of a newspaper article. The bold headline hit her brain with a pop. Her hand jerked with a life of its own to the faded bruises on her throat.

80s Adult Film Star Found Dead
By Gerald Hill

PENNSYLVANIA - Elaine Chester, better known to fans of Adult Entertainment as Lana Chalmers was found dead yesterday. Local authorities say her body was discovered behind a local adult movie and gift store, Alex's Adult World Gift Emporium and Warehouse, by a warehouse employee. Lana had appeared at Alex's with former costar reality TV star Rob Rhino to sign autographs. No official cause of death has been released pending a full investigation.

The warehouse employee, who has not been identified, said he found Lana "propped against the building, in a sitting position, partially clothed, with bruises around her jaw and neck." Rob Rhino, her costar in the cult classic *The Postman Always Screws Twice* said, "Lana struggled with drugs. I thought she was doing better. She had a lot to live for—herself, her family. We are all saddened by this terrible loss."

———— ◆ ————

"So this is what five million gets you?"

Claire turned to Freddie Eddie, surprised he spoke to her. She only nodded.

Claire looked at the now sodded ground and the orange-flagged stakes that marked off the mausoleum site. The outbuildings were gone and the parcel, other than its lack of dead people, looked like the rest of the cemetery; flawless creepiness.

This won't end well.

Claire couldn't stop thinking about Freddie Eddie's words, the article he must've put under her pillow. Who else would've? Certainly not Rob.

"... will be out here?" Rob Rhino said.

"Huh?" Claire said.

"I asked when the mausoleum would be out here."

"Today or tomorrow. It's a prefab so—"

"A prefab? Like a...like a mobile home?" Freddie Eddie said forehead wrinkled.

"Just like that."

She and Freddie Eddie sat on one of the new wrought iron and concrete benches placed under one of the new, yet miraculously mature (even Mother Nature had her price) shade trees near the Corrigan family's final resting place. Rob Rhino stretched out on the lawn next to them.

"Quite a coincidence all of this," Freddie Eddie said.

Claire did a double take. Yeah, two dead women. Was he going to bring it up in front of Rob?

"Old Father Pat, your father-in-law." Freddie Eddie sucked on a toothpick he must've brought with him.

"*That* coincidence. Right," Claire said.

"Beats all, doesn't it?" Rob said from below.

Claire let out a heavy sigh, was about to go on a woe is me tirade about Grace's shortcomings, the family ill will, when the sounds of snoring wafted up from Rob Rhino. She looked down. She'd forgotten how near narcoleptic he was. Certainly he wouldn't take Dramamine for such a short car ride.

"He's gone downhill quick this time," Freddie Eddie said. "Just found out about that meeting in LA and *wham* it's like a one-way ticket to psychoville. He sleeps a lot, doesn't shower, looks like shit. Rob's a different man as soon as he hears LA. Gloria died there." He let it sit.

"I noticed," Claire said.

She wanted to ask him about the girl, the article, what he knew about Gloria, but didn't want to risk Rob overhearing them. She glanced down at Rob sleeping like a well-hung baby on the grass at her feet.

"She must be on his mind a lot, especially here," she said.

"She's always on his mind, I think."

Freddie Eddie leaned down and stared at his friend and client of so many years, his hair and clothes a rumpled dirty mess. "Rob loves an underdog. Always has. But he can't handle it when they don't come out from under." His stare made her squirmy.

Claire felt herself blush. "My husband's first wife committed suicide. My mother's lost her mind." Freddie Eddie kept staring. "Some people aren't made for disappointment."

He nodded, the sun glinting off his nose jewelry.

****

"How far is it?" Rob called out.

Claire hollered back without stopping or turning around. "Are you going to make it?"

"I don't remember it being this far. I'm draggin'."

Like a whippet, Freddie Eddie darted back and forth between Claire and Rob yipping.

"Come on, Rob. You're bottom heavy." Freddie Eddie cackled as he zigged and zagged his way up the walk.

Claire could see the chapel ahead. She stopped by a shade tree, glanced at her watch. She'd worked up a bit of a sweat on the walk, her head felt slick, she swiped at it with one hand.

"Look at this name." She pointed to a headstone. "Charles Darwin. No way."

Claire looked back at Rob for confirmation. He shuffled to catch up.

"Different Darwin," Rob said.

Freddie Eddie kept walking toward the chapel slower while Rob and Claire dallied. The cemetery grounds were fairly empty since Trustee Week was long over. A small group of tourists mingled near the chapel doors. Claire was about to crack wise about the town and Darwin's waiting room when she suddenly didn't. Someone said something she couldn't make out from behind, like an echo her joke stopped cold. Claire turned, tried to see who said it.

A small wrinkled man, his head shrunken and bald, jerked in their direction. His rickety movements almost comical, zombie like. He seemed old as Methuselah or fresh out of a grave. The walking dead welcome wagon. His outstretched hand held out something too small to be a fruit basket.

"Why can't you leave well enough alone?" His ancient voice a jagged rasp. "Let my daughter rest in peace." He never stopped moving, not quick but moving.

"Did he say daughter?" Claire was pretty sure he did.

"Let my daughter rest in peace." Crazy old man, the broken record kept coming. "Let my daughter rest in peace."

Rob smiled a funny crooked cavernous grin, obviously at a loss for words because he wasn't saying any. Freddie Eddie came toward them from one side, or she thought he did. Rob dashed in front of her, his back facing her, fast for a fat man. His arms spread out, waved like Batman's cape. The heel of his clog smashed the toe of her Chanel flat.

Claire jumped at the crack.

First one, then another, and one more. Sharp, quick, brutal.

Later she'd say it happened just like in the movies.

Batman's cape folded. Rob dropped to the ground.

Claire blinked. The place in front of her taken up by Rob Rhino just seconds before emptied. She didn't get it at first even with the all the blood. Rob's mouth hung open a little, his weird smile still plastered on his face. Claire stared at the gap where his tooth should've been. Freddie Eddie kneeled to one side of Rob Rhino, hands pressed to Rob's gushing chest, Rob's hula girls and palm trees soaked red.

Was someone screaming?

Most of Claire's senses had stopped working. She'd gone deaf and dumb.

She dropped to her knees almost on top of him, her cherry red Hermes bag still gripped in one hand. He smelled like sweat, grass, and something new, rancid and metallic. She played possum. A small crowd gathered. Only moving her eyes Claire spied the old man through the tourist's legs, lying soles up, a gun flung there like it was no big deal, blood sprayed on the walk and something else fleshy. A few more legs, clad in dark blue, hovered around the old man's body.

Rob Rhino's chest gaped open, overflowing.

He'd be so mad. His favorite shirt, maybe his only one, ruined. Claire opened her mouth, but no sound came out. She could see Freddie Eddie's mouth moving, his eyes like pinballs. He patted her down like he was looking for something hidden. The two blue men hunkered down next to her, their lips flapped. She couldn't figure it out.

Claire thought she still lived but couldn't be sure.

Joe Lansing shoved his way in with the priest who made the sign of the cross over Rob. Claire wanted to grab the gun, shoot him. She thought she saw Evelyn Wallace's funny blue hair weaving through. Hours or seconds went by, she didn't know which. She watched Rob's blood spread, drip, run onto the sod. Claire sat drenched in it. Two paramedics pushing a stretcher made their way through.

Heads shook, faces grimaced. One of the paramedics said something to Freddie Eddie, squeezed his arm. He pressed his eyelids shut with the fingers of one hand and nodded in response to something they'd said to him. Claire could see him crying. They were ready to put Rob on the stretcher.

She snapped to, dropped her bag and scrambled on her knees toward his body.

"Don't," she said finding her voice.

They looked surprised, not sure where she'd come from. This hairless blood-covered woman.

Claire smoothed Rob's ratty hair, pulled the bottom of his shirt down to hide his exposed belly. They'd closed his eyes. She gently leaned down, lay on his wet bloody body like she had all the time in the world. The gathering stepped back a respectful distance to observe the oddball pair. The bald woman, the dead porn star, locked in a macabre embrace.

He felt warm. His shirt drenched, the smell of blood sweet, sickening, like raw meat. She didn't care. Claire scooped him into both arms, held him close. She pressed her ear hard to his chest, looking for familiar refuge in the sound of his heartbeat.

She couldn't hear a thing.

****

The on-call nurse walked by her with a stack of folded up something or other.

"Where's Freddie Eddie?" Claire's skin felt scalded, the top of her scalp seared. "Where did they take Rob?"

"Someone will be in to talk to you in a minute," the nurse said.

After they'd scraped the bodies up they'd made her and Freddie Eddie go to the hospital. She heard someone say they thought she was in shock. Is that what this was? She'd heard they brought both Rob and the shooter here. Claire and Freddie rode in separate police cars. She hadn't seen him since she'd arrived.

She put her face in her hands.

Freddie Eddie walked in.

"Oh thank God. Freddie Eddie." Claire almost collapsed with relief. "Where have you been? What've they done with Rob?" She could feel the nervous breakdown making its way in. "What in the name of..." She couldn't finish her sentence. She broke down.

He tilted his head in Claire's direction and spoke to the hovering nurse. "Her doctor's name is Levinson. She's been at this hospital before, not too long ago. She's in recovery and I think he needs to know she's here and what happened. Thanks, honey."

Freddie Eddie reached into his pocket and pulled out a blue pill. Claire swallowed it dry like the old days. So like Rob to make sure Freddie Eddie had her covered. Just in case.

Claire sobbed. She hadn't thought of a pill. She couldn't remember when she'd last taken one. They must be right. She was in shock. Freddie Eddie pulled a chair up next to the exam table she sat on. She'd been in this room before but didn't remember it. She'd had a stomach full of Xanax then, instead of like now, her hands and face covered in the dried blood of Rob Rhino.

This time the on-call doctor gave her a clean bill of health. No wounds. The blood was Rob's. The bullets lodged in his chest, no passing through. The shooter turned the gun on himself immediately after.

The been-there-done-that murder suicide.

Claire'd taken off her bloody shirt and still wore the open-in-the-back gown. Her hands, arms, and face bore Rob Rhino's dried blood. Freddie Eddie looked like a combat survivor.

Claire could feel the heaviness of their grief in the room.

"You were right Freddie Eddie."

"About what kid?"

Claire could hear the ancient man's voice, old as dirt, and would forever, bouncing off the walls of her skull.

Let my daughter rest in peace.

"About Gloria's dad. Rob told me you were afraid he'd do this, get revenge." Claire tore a hole in her paper gown with her red stained finger.

Freddie Eddie turned his chair so he was facing Claire. "The shooter wasn't Gloria's dad."

"What? He said *my daughter*—"

"I know."

Claire felt dizzy, nauseous, her mind pushing away the information.

"What are you saying?"

"He was talking to you, Claire. The shooter was Bonnie's dad."

"The shooter's name was—"

"Elgin Grady," Claire said more to herself.

"Umm... yes," the police officer continued.

"Go on, officer." Freddie Eddie still had Claire's hand. He squeezed.

"His wife Marta is here. She identified the body." The policeman rocked back on his heels. "She came out to the cemetery but too late. She tried to talk him out of this... his folly before he left home. She didn't think he'd do it. Said she didn't know he had a gun. Apparently their daughter Bonnie was married to your now deceased husband Liam Corrigan?"

Claire nodded.

"Mrs. Grady says she committed suicide after their divorce. Her father Elgin blamed your husband for her death."

"So I've heard," Claire said. "But that was over twenty years ago. I didn't even meet Liam until she'd been dead several years. I wasn't the reason they divorced. So why would he want to shoot me?"

The silver-haired officer took a small pad of paper out of his shirt pocket.

"Marta Grady told us you're here to bury your husband. In the university cemetery. You've made a multimillion dollar donation, bought a family crypt. Put Mr. Corrigan's sister on the board of trustees. Is that correct?"

He'd read down the list of the crimes committed by Claire as if these heinous infractions were punishable by lethal injection.

"So what? She can do all of those things if she wants to." Freddie Eddie stiffened, all of a sudden her defender.

"She can." *If she wanted to cause trouble* the not so subtle undertone. "Marta Grady said they heard it all over town, in the papers, on TV." He consulted his notes again. "The sister cornered Elgin at some function. Marta said he wasn't the most stable guy anymore. It pushed him over, he lost it. He didn't want your husband or any more of his family anywhere near his daughter."

The policeman put his pad back in his shirt pocket, crossed his arms in what looked to Claire like silent agreement. "She said Elgin didn't think it was right. Your husband's family getting pats on the back for good works when his daughter killed herself."

"How the hell did Elgin Grady know Claire was going to be at the cemetery today and what she looked like?" Freddie Eddie got out of the chair.

"Well... for one thing..." The officer licked his too full lips. "She's got a distinct look, don't you think?"

"I'm bald Freddie Eddie. Hard not pick me out of a crowd."

"Okay, I'll give you that, but how did he know where you were?"

The policeman consulted his trusty notes.

"Elizabeth Corrigan, your husband's sister, told him at Trustee Night."

****

Claire and Freddie Eddie were free to leave the hospital but didn't.

The police said they'd continue their investigation, keep them posted. Since Elgin took himself out only Elizabeth was the missing link. Marta Grady was an old lady in her nineties. Miraculous she'd driven herself to the cemetery. No wonder she didn't get there in time. She'd probably started out three days prior. No one would look at her too seriously as any kind of accomplice.

Claire felt like she'd been hit with a stun gun. Freddie Eddie sat back down in the cheap rickety chair. Claire's lips quivered.

"I can't believe it. It's my fault," Claire said tears falling.

"Claire—" Freddie Eddie didn't look at her.

"It is."

Claire and her schemes. She swung her legs back and forth on the edge of the table.

"You don't know."

Freddie Eddie got up and hopped up on the table next to her. "I *do* know why you're here. This might come as a shock but not everything is about you."

Claire cried, the waterworks running faster than her nose. "Well, this is."

"Claire—" Freddie Eddie smoothed back his heavily gelled hair with one hand. "Everyone does what they want. Rob was no exception."

Claire clamped her eyes down like lids. "If it weren't for me he'd still be alive."

Freddie Eddie reached over and turned Claire's face toward his by her chin. "You don't get it, because you don't want to. You're not ready, I guess. Rob walked in front of that bullet because he wanted to."

Tears ran down her cheeks and onto Freddie Eddie's hand.

"I told you, he loved the underdog. More than anything he wanted to save you and himself." Freddie Eddie wiped her face with a tender swipe. "So he did it the only way he knew how."

****

Claire stared at him through the glass, laid out on the steel gurney, covered to his double chin with a white sheet.

Cleaned up a little. She knew it was him, his wild hair still recognizable. It was Rob Rhino only different. He looked made of something other than skin and bones. The way the dead do. She'd gone to view her father when he'd died. He looked similar. A body without life, the color of paste, the features familiar yet strange. Liam had been mangled and burnt beyond recognition, identified by dental records.

The fluorescent lighting in the hospital basement morgue (why are they always in the basement?) cast a greenish tinge. Even the living didn't look it. Claire pressed both palms and her nose against the glass as if Rob could feel her there if she did.

Freddie Eddie stood next to her, his hand on her back. Claire felt breathless, overwhelmed. Freddie Eddie's hand felt like steel against her spine. If it hadn't been there she'd have fallen. Her eyes spilled over. Hard to believe she'd only known Rob Rhino for such a short time.

She'd wanted to see him before they left, to remember him. Most of her time with Rob had been spent in a narcotic daze, on the desperate edge of an overdose. Her mind a puddle, distracted by her pill obsession and rage. She stared at Rob's pockmarked face and stroked the glass.

If she'd known the end of the road would come so soon she'd have wanted to be more conscious for the journey.

She never wanted Rob Rhino in her life, didn't realize he wormed his way in. She guessed she didn't care how or why. She stood back away from the window. Her gut wrenched at the thought of the dead porn star behind Alex's warehouse. Claire had no way of knowing what really happened to Gloria. She couldn't bear to think of those things while her only real friend lay with two bullets in his chest, dead on a table behind glass in a basement.

Maybe she should've done everything different. Or nothing at all.

"What next?" Claire said.

Freddie Eddie looked almost as dead. "Well, I need to gather my wits. I told the police I'd need time to find his next of kin, so they agreed to not release his name to the press until I give them the go ahead. Not sure how much time I've got. I'm calling in favors. They'll keep it quiet for me as long as they can."

"Next of kin? I thought there was no next of kin?"

"There isn't. But I don't want the press swarming around right now. And neither do you." Freddie Eddie led her to the only two metal chairs in the stark hallway.

"I talked to Joe Lansing too. This isn't great for them either, so I'll get with their PR guy and decide the best way to handle it."

Claire rubbed both temples with her hands. "This is all a nightmare."

"Do you still want to go through with your memorial?"

"You better believe it." Claire set her teeth, ground her molars. "It's what I came here for. I won't let Elgin Grady win."

"When is it?"

Claire thought, counted. "Thursday."

"In the meantime I'll make Rob's arrangements. I told them he was Jewish so we can get a quick burial."

Jack Jew.

"He's not though," Claire said. "He's not any religion."

"No, he's not." Freddie Eddie closed his almost black eyes, his voice terse. "But I don't want anyone posting anything disgusting on the internet. I want him off that table, out of the morgue, and cremated, so we can give the man a decent burial."

He nodded his head toward a nondescript guy in a uniform sitting in the corner of the room with Rob behind the glass. "I've got twenty-four-hour security."

Claire felt her face fold in. The internet. She hadn't thought of that.

"Please, Freddie Eddie, let me help you. I insist on paying."

"I'm afraid there's nothing to pay for. I'm going take his ashes home with me." Freddie Eddie kept staring at Rob. "Rob let Gloria's parents stash her remains who-knows-where so I'm gonna take Rob home with me. Rob doesn't meet the guidelines for burial at the university so—"

Freddie Eddie really didn't know about the switch. She started to tell him but didn't feel good about betraying Rob's confidence. She'd done enough damage for one day.

"Rob hated Los Angeles."

"I don't live in Los Angeles. I live in Connecticut." Freddie Eddie gave a weak smile. "Beautiful place. He loved it there."

One of the long tube light bulbs above their heads flickered, popped, and burnt out. Claire lifted her head. She remembered when she'd first met Rob, the day she almost ran him over, drove him to Alex's Warehouse and asked his name.

"There it is," he'd said pointing up to the marquee lit up with sparkling neon.

She'd looked up and there it shone. In lights.

The Last Day for Rob Rhino.

Claire squeezed her eyes shut and covered her mouth, dried blood still under her nails.

Freddie Eddie prodded her upward by the elbow of her blood-covered shirt. "Let's go home, kid."

CHAPTER SIXTY

"I can't believe Elizabeth had a role in this. I can't." Grace's voice shook. "However misguided. What with all the swanning around she's been doing lately—"

"Grace, what do you know about Elizabeth and this mess?"

"Well, the police questioned her. She said she struck up a friendship with Elgin. She felt bad about how Liam treated Bonnie, of course we all did. Said he told her he was upset about everything he'd been hearing. Elizabeth said she told him that if he could meet you he'd know you meant well."

"So Elizabeth's story is she told him I was going to the chapel today just so he could come meet me, to talk to me?" Claire glanced over at Freddie Eddie who looked almost asleep on Rob's side of the recliner. "And she was kind enough to offer a description of me?"

"Yes. That's what she assures us and the police. She had no idea he went with a gun or bad intentions."

"It wouldn't have made sense to call me and ask me about it?"

"Now why would she have done that?"

"Never mind."

"Well, the police are satisfied with Elizabeth's explanation." Grace said. "As am I."

"I'm sure you are."

"This isn't going to postpone the memorial or anything, is it?"

On that they were in agreement.

"Absolutely not."

"Good," Grace said obnoxious with relief. "Have they identified the poor man Elgin killed yet?"

Don't worry about me, I'm fine.

"Not that I've heard. They're still trying to find his family as far as I know. Probably a tourist."

****

Claire padded up the stairs, phone in hand, leaving Freddie Eddie asleep in the loveseat. She'd called Jordan against her better judgment. She wasn't sure when the shooting would make the national news so she thought it was better he hear it from her. She still wasn't speaking with Annabelle. In due time. She was just a spoiled kid, Claire knew. But they'd have a lot to talk about when Claire got home.

She wanted to head to the nearest alleyway to see if she could find some nice man in a trench coat with some pills in the inside pockets. She'd love a drink. She thought of Rob's bleeding body on the ground, his life running out around her loafers. Her hands started to shake.

She'd talked to Joe Lansing, who made the kind offer to bring dinner over, which she declined. He assured her the memorial arrangements were set without the face-to-face with the priest. He'd received the photo of Liam from Conchita. They'd have that in a frame at the service. All Claire needed to do was bring his ashes to the chapel.

Claire headed for her room but paused. At the end of the hall Rob Rhino's sanctuary offered silent solace. She felt Rob's presence in her chest, behind her knees. She stumbled, catching herself on a tufted chair. For a moment she thought she'd throw up. She knelt, tried to squelch her panic underneath Gloria's serene gaze. After a few minutes she stood and looked at the painting of the woman whose unseemly death had wreaked so much havoc.

"So this is it? The man cave?" Freddie Eddie said startling her.

"You've never been in here?"

"Claire, straight men don't hang out in other straight men's bedrooms." Freddie Eddie wandered the room. "Where's the bed?"

Claire pointed to the bedroom. Freddie walked over, peeked in, turned on the light. "Good night nurse. What a mess. That's more like it."

"Right?" Claire laughed. "That's what I told him."

Claire sat in the same leather chair she'd sat in the night before. Freddie Eddie took Rob's.

"So you've been in here, have you?" Freddie Eddie smiled and winked.

"Oh for God's sake. The man's not even cold—"

"Don't get your dander up." He ran his hands along the smooth surface of the supple leather armchair. "Stranger things have happened." Freddie Eddie shrugged and laughed.

Claire felt herself turning crimson, remembering the close calls. Freddie Eddie laughed harder.

****

"Cheers." They clinked their root beer bottles together.

Freddie Eddie drank almost the whole bottle in one throw, he'd been sufficiently impressed by Rob's hidden desk fridge. Claire took a much smaller sip of her root beer along with the pill Freddie Eddie gave her. She didn't know what she'd do when she went home. On her own.

"What really happened to Gloria?"

Freddie Eddie balanced the almost empty bottle on the edge of chair's arm. "I only know what he told me. She died of an accidental overdose. I knew she was a junkie, knew he tried to save her." He scratched the side of his nose with one long finger. "Next thing I know he's calling, crying. She's dead."

"Were you around?"

"No. She'd already been cremated by the time I got back." Freddie Eddie got up, fetched another root beer. "I'd been out of town with Marie when it happened. It was after that he started with the charity stuff. You know he's a donor. A big one. He gives a couple million dollars away every year anonymously."

Claire swallowed hard. "And the other one, the porn star? You think he had something to do with that?"

Freddie Eddie lowered himself back down in the chair, let his air out. "I do."

"Was she an addict?"

"Yes. When the dust settled the investigators chalked her death up to *accidental overdose* too."

"What about the bruises?" Claire fingered her own.

"Never any suspects, no motive."

"Rob wasn't suspected?"

"Are you kidding?" Freddie Eddie crossed his polyester bell bottom-covered legs at the ankles. "He was beloved around here. No way."

"Why would you suspect him? Could be coincidence."

"I don't believe in coincidences."

Claire had said that herself, to Rob Rhino.

Freddie Eddie continued. "And she wasn't the only girl who ended up dead."

Claire grabbed both arms of the chair, her root beer bottle headed toward the rug. Freddie Eddie swooped to catch it.

"What do you mean?" she said.

"She was just the only one they found," Freddie Eddie said.

"How could that be?

"Pat the janitor was Rob's good friend for a reason."

Claire knew if she opened her mouth she'd weep.

"Everybody loved Rob. My wife is inconsolable," Freddie Eddie said. "He wanted the best for the worst. When it didn't happen he went off the deep end." He stared into the empty fireplace. "Like a magnet he'd suck right up to 'em. The worse off they were the harder he'd stick. He'd get real involved. Sometimes his help worked. One recovering addict married a doctor, one a day trader. But sometimes it didn't."

"Mercy," Claire said.

"What?"

"He thought killing them was merciful."

****

It felt weird to sleep in Rob's house without him in it. Freddie Eddie promised not to leave so he slept down the hall in one of the other bedrooms. Claire pulled off her jeans and lay on top of the beautiful canopied bed in just her Michael Kors top. She thought about taking it off when she saw Liam in his usual spot.

The thing about dead husbands—you always knew where they were. One of the perks.

That and all the money they leave you. She reached over and pulled off the top of the urn. There he was, up in smoke, tied in a neat little baggie.

She remembered how terrible she'd felt the day he'd died. She'd been so stunned, felt so guilty. She found out you can't die of shame because she hadn't. Her rage possessed her and never left. Then all her hair fell out, then the worsening anxiety, the never-ending quest for pills. More rage, the plotting, her quest for revenge.

So different than how she felt about losing Rob Rhino.

Claire slammed the urn lid down, leaned back against the headboard. She felt an overwhelming sadness at his absence. Her heart ached knowing she'd given so little to him, yet he'd given everything for her.

Claire realized when Liam died, she felt bad only for herself, for what she'd wished, done, found out, omitted.

I don't know what you feel for me, Claire, but it isn't love.

Liam's words kept coming back to her.

Claire'd been tapering off her drugs and this was the thanks she got. Reality bites. Claire brought her legs up and rested her forehead on her knees. Liam took care of her, protected her. His money ensured it for her lifetime. She'd taken care of his child, his home, did her part.

But love?

No. She didn't have it in her then. Maybe she didn't have it in her now. But she wanted to try to find some.

If she could've known Rob Rhino first.

Claire took her last pill of the day, got undressed and crawled under the coverlet. A few more days and her quest would come to its satisfactory conclusion. She'd get with Freddie Eddie to see when Rob's name would be released to the public, when his cremation would take place. The death details, a nasty business.

The two most important men in her life were dead. Soon they'd both rest in peace. Well, not Liam. He'd rest but not necessarily in peace. Rob would. She hoped.

Rest. In. Peace.

She turned out the light. Her eyes adjusted to the darkness after half an hour. Her mind rumbled.

Shit.

She got out of bed, pulled on her jeans, padded down the stairs in her bare feet.

"Freddie Eddie wake up. Get a shovel."

SIXTY-ONE

"Oh my god. I'm so glad you're all right. If anything had happened to you I'd have died." Elizabeth threw her arms around Claire's neck, yelled in her ear.

She'd have died?

Claire stood with her arms straight at her sides at the front of the chapel.

The surviving members of the Corrigan family paraded up the center aisle. Elizabeth led the brigade. She'd seen Claire first and like a goony bird attempting flight she squawked to her, wings spread, beak flapping.

"Elizabeth, this is a church. Keep it down."

Grace, the madonna herself, didn't greet Claire. She took her place in the first pew on the right in front of the easel holding her husband's framed photo. Liam's urn stood on the left. In opposition for eternity.

Connor, eyes downcast, veered into a front row pew, silent, somber. Claire had to admire his nerve. Deborah was a no-show.

"I got it all straightened out with the police." Elizabeth grasped her throat with a hairy knuckled hand. "Why, I had no idea—"

Father McKinley saved Elizabeth from the bitch slap Claire itched to give her.

Joe Lansing and Dean Sumner fussed over her. Joe handed out programs. They both sat in the pew designated for Claire in front of Liam's photo.

Father McKinley took his place underneath the stained-glass window as the stirring sounds of some church type music filled the stone room. Claire peeked over at the other side of the church. Elizabeth's eyes were closed tight, her hands together in a steeple.

Who was the bitter wretch kidding?

Grace looked smug. She could hardly hide her satisfied smile. Claire held her program tight.

Hag.

"Grant them eternal rest, O Lord, and let perpetual light shine upon them…" Father McKinley droned.

Claire snuck a glance at Joe Lansing. She'd miss him when she left. He'd been good to her.

All the Corrigans were pulling down the kneelers. Oh no. The kneeling. How many times would they have to do that? It's a funeral for God's sake. Not aerobics class.

****

"Claire, I—" He must've followed Claire to her car after the chapel service.

Claire turned only half surprised to see him. "Connor."

"I know I should leave you alone. I don't have the right."

He looked haggard, old. A lot like Claire. She guessed he wasn't sleeping. The rage she expected to feel for him didn't materialize. Something short of pity seeped in.

"Whatever you have to say—it doesn't matter, Connor."

He hung his head. "As inadequate as it is I just wanted to say I'm sorry."

"I know." She took his hand. "I don't think I care about it. I'll go home and you'll still be here with them. I win."

He met her eyes, the saddest man. "We were so desperate." A single tear rolled. "We lost sight of right and wrong."

Claire got it. Desperation she understood.

Her mind rolled on. "You don't intend to go through with this family crypt, never did. Am I right?"

His head still hung low. "Yes, you're right. Our son is at Creekside where we'll be eventually."

"You just strung me along."

Claire's hand on the handle of her bag turned white.

"I didn't know what I was doing." He put his head up. "I just wanted to keep an eye on you, keep the drugs—" He cried in earnest. "God I'm so ashamed."

She wondered if Liam would have looked like this had he ever cried.

"Well, the crypt is there, feel free. This is a beautiful place."

Connor swiped at his wet face with an impatient hand. "No, we'll pass." He glanced over his shoulder at his mother and sister loitering outside the chapel. "Liam wasn't the only one who didn't want to spend eternity with my family."

Claire almost smiled. "Go home to your wife, Connor."

He shoved his hands in his pants pockets, tripped back toward the chapel.

"Connor?"

He looked over his shoulder.

"When did you and Liam start speaking to each other again?"

"We never stopped."

****

"Still no idea about the dead guy?" William the buffoon said.

"Not as far as I know." Claire lied. "I heard the whole sordid story on the news this morning and they're still saying they're looking for a next of kin. He had no driver's license, no ID."

She looked out across the lot at the crime scene tape. Her legs wobbled.

"Well, it's only been a few days," Grace said in her *Law and Order* tone.

"Are you coming with us?" Grace had flagged Claire down before she could drive off. The Corrigan clan, minus Connor and Deborah, was headed for the crypt. Claire opted out. She'd gone to look it over with Joe before the service. Her deed done, she was ready to go home.

Claire started the car. "You guys go ahead. Emmet's on the left. The stone guy still has to do the engraving. They're going to plant flowers, a couple more trees. Everything was such a rush job, we're lucky everybody's in."

SIXTY-TWO

Claire squinted at her boarding pass. She reached into her Prada bag, pulled out Rob Rhino's bifocals. They worked like a charm. They were too wide for her head but she didn't care. They were perfect enough.

O'Hare buzzed. She searched the terminal floor for a hobo-like man knowing she wouldn't find one. At least not the right one. Her eyes clouded. A low ringing cleared her head. She pulled her phone out of her bag, took off the glasses.

"Hello?"

"I don't believe it. Your phone is still working?"

"Hello to you too Jordan."

"How far are you?"

"Chicago."

"Thank God. Civilization." Sounded like Jordan was driving. "No one's tried to shoot you or anything?"

"Not so far, but I'm only halfway."

Someone else was calling. Claire held her phone away from her ear. Pennsylvania area code. It could wait. She'd just left for Chrissake. Number looked familiar, hard to tell without the glasses. Maybe Joe Lansing or Freddie Eddie.

"Okay, well, just checking."

"So since I have you on the phone, I ah... well, I—"

"You're cutting out."

No she was chickening out.

"I thought I might come up. To San Fran, to see your new place." Claire twitched. "I mean, when it's a good time for you... and... for Steven. Annabelle could come too after we've talked some things through. She says she has a new boyfriend and a job. God help us."

No sound.

Still nothing.

"Jordan? Can you hear me?"

"Yeah. Sure," he said in his what the hell tone. "Mother, you know Steven lives here. With me. This is our house together. We sleep in the same—"

"I know. So what?"

"So what? Who is this?"

"Very funny."

The connection went quiet again. Then Jordan said, "We'd love it, Mother. You'll love the house. You'll want to decorate."

Claire didn't want to cry in the airport again. "I'm sure I will."

She told him the dates she preferred. He didn't think there'd be a problem. She didn't mention his arrest.

"I thought I'd stay a few days before I go to... well... before I go to rehab."

"What?"

"I'm going to rehab. Sixty days. There's supposed to be a good one up there."

She'd go first. Think that over, Jordan.

She could hear him cover the mouthpiece, say something muffled. "Mother, that's... that's wonderful. I mean it really."

"Yeah, okay whatever." Claire tried to clean a bifocal lens one-handed.

The same someone from Pennsylvania called again. Pants on fire? She ignored it.

"Anything from Andrew?"

"Steven was going to wait 'til you landed but it looks like they're going to accept your generous offer of nothing down, zero later and go away quietly. He's already sent you a hefty refund. It's over. I think he realizes it's only because of Meg you're not bringing down the house."

Claire plopped the glasses down, let the tears run. She didn't care who stared. They stared anyway. Crying or not she was still bald.

"He's not going to call me "Mom" is he?"

"Who?"

"Steven."

Jordan laughed. "We were thinking more like Mommy Dearest."

****

Claire rounded the corner of the terminal walkway headed for the bookstore. Rob Rhino's face on the TV monitors hanging from the ceiling stopped her in her tracks. His murder wasn't under wraps anymore. She read the running captions at the bottom of the screen.

"Reality TV and Seventies Adult Film Star Rob Rhino Killed in Bizarre Murder Suicide."

Old footage and photos accompanied the story. They interviewed Freddie Eddie. A photo of Liam and Bonnie ran across the screen. Good God. And one of Claire. With hair. She felt sick. Her phone rang. She answered without taking her eyes off the monitor.

"Claire?" Freddie Eddie's voice, beleaguered.

"Did you just try to call me?"

"No."

Must've been Joe.

Freddie Eddie sounded hesitant. "Have you seen the news?"

"I'm looking at it right now. In the airport."

"I didn't think it was going to air until tonight."

"Where did they get the pictures?"

"Who knows?"

Claire found a row of chairs. "Well, it was bound to come out. I'm shocked you held it at bay for as long as you did."

"Yeah, it should fizzle out quick. He was famous but he wasn't Brad Pitt. You'll get some calls initially but direct them to me. They're going to be looking for a woman with hair."

An upside to bald. Finally.

Her phone did that thing it did when someone tried to call through. Again. She held it out, same number. Give it a rest.

"What a scandal."

"I'll say."

****

Claire prepared for landing.

The guy sitting next to her seemed perfectly normal. Cretin. He'd even helped her shove her carry-on into the overhead. Like a gentleman. He probably thought she wouldn't survive the plane ride. She'd caught him stealing furtive glances at her head the whole way.

She pushed her tray back up, rearranged her purse, put her seat into its original position. Her stomach lurched, she felt anxious, panicked. Times like these she missed taking a bunch of pills with a drink or two. She took fewer now, her intake ratcheted down some. But she missed the lull she got with an alcohol buzz. With no one to monitor her she could've had a heyday on the plane. But she didn't.

The plane taxied and came to its shriek of a stop. Claire jumped into the aisle. She felt ready to start her life. It was good to be home. She leaned over and peered out the small commuter plane window. Overcast. As usual. Beach towns were always socked in. The plane door opened. It was time.

Claire bounded down the steps onto the tarmac. Her Tods loafer no more than hit the pavement when her phone rang. Jesus. Probably that same number. She'd never answered or called it back. No wonder she never plugged the damn thing in. She fished it out of her purse, narrowed her eyes, held her arm out to bring the number into focus. Nope. Hometown call.

"Hello?"

"Hola."

Christ, not this.

"Conchita. I'm on the tarmac, I'll be home in half an hour. What is it?"

"Oh si. I forgot you were coming in this afternoon. I never know what you're doing on the weekends." Conchita never worked weekends. "Well, you'll never believe it. Grace Corrigan called."

"Oh she can call California then? What pray tell did she want?" As if Claire didn't know.

"She was so mad it was hard to tell. Said she called your cell, but you wouldn't answer. Anyway sounds like there's been some mistake. At least I told her it must be one."

Claire stopped walking. "Oh? Mistake?"

"Si. They engraved the wrong name on Liam's stone. In the crypt."

"What name?"

"It's weird. I had to write it down."

"Conchita what—"

"Rob Rhino."

Claire looked out across the tarmac and smiled.

"Claire? Did you hear what I said?"

"Yes I heard."

"It's a mistake no?"

"No. No mistake."

"Who's Rob Rhino?"

How long do you have?

"He was my friend. My very good friend."

"Excuse me." The guy she'd sat next to on the plane tapped her on the shoulder.

"I'll call you back Conchita. Turn on your TV."

He'd rolled her Louis Vuitton across the pavement.

"I think this is yours? You forgot it in the overhead." He handed over her carry-on.

The one with Liam in it.

"Oh thank you. Yes, it is."

****

She hit the trunk button on her key fob. It opened almost without a sound. The baggage guy (or whatever they called themselves these days) schlepped her suitcase along with her carry-on. She'd had to ship a lot of her stuff back via FedEx so she traveled home pretty light. She gave him a twenty and slid behind the wheel of her red Mercedes CLS 550 sedan, ran her palm over the coffee-with-cream colored supple leather. Ahhh... to the manor born. Not. But she'd warmed up to it quick.

As she pulled out a yellow taxi veered to the left and nearly hit the minivan coming around the corner. The driver laid on the horn and yelled obscenities out his window. They hadn't learned to drive in her absence. Serene as a monk Claire headed toward home and thought about the switch.

It was easy.

Probably a lot easier than when Rob did it with Gloria's ashes.

He'd been right though. *You can't get through this life without good friends.* Joe Lansing turned out to be a good friend. He pulled the switch. Freddie Eddie took Rob's cremated remains to the chapel right before the memorial service. Joe dumped out Liam's into a brand-new urn and put Rob's in Liam's old one and there you had it.

Digging Gloria up was a little trickier.

It had been dark after all. But Freddie Eddie did all the labor, Claire supervised with a flashlight. Gloria's urn was right where Rob said it was. At least that had been true. No laws were broken. Rob was interred in Liam's spot with Gloria his beloved wife. In the only place he felt at peace in the cemetery, where he belonged.

That he happened to be next to Emmet Corrigan, aka Pat the Janitor, his partner in porn and crime... well, coincidences do happen once in a while, despite Freddie Eddie's assurances to the contrary. And Claire took Liam home where *he* belonged. Near the kids he loved, and who loved him, and the wife who liked him just okay.

Claire pulled over, dug out Rob's glasses, and did a quick search through her missed calls.

"Grace? It's Claire. Were you looking for me?"

Let's go to the mat once and for all.

"If you think you're going to get away with this you've got another thing coming," Grace said in a rabid dog snarl. "I know exactly what you did and why."

"That makes two of us." Claire felt a calm settle over her. "Game over, Grace. You wanted to get back at Liam for not bailing you out, for leaving the church, for Bonnie, for everything. And you wanted to get back at Emmet for his porn. All on my dime. So don't cry foul."

"Well, what if I did? What's it to you?" Grace yelled louder than Claire thought an old lady could. "I never bought your sob story, your peacemaking. Whatever you came here to do it wasn't to make peace."

Claire thought about that for a few seconds.

"You're right. But I did anyway."

Claire hung up. She'd had enough of Liam's mother. They both spoke the truth though. Claire hadn't gone to make peace but she'd found some. Along with forgiveness. Enough, anyway. Claire pulled back into traffic, horns blaring around her like a presidential motorcade.

Her phone rang.

Her good friend Joe.

"I was just thinking about you," she said.

"Just saw the news and heard from your lovely mother-in-law. As soon as it hit the airwaves my phone rang. Such a treat," Joe chuckled.

"She might get carpal tunnel with all the calls she's making."

"She's livid. Naturally. Wants us to move Emmet. She called Rob the most hideous names. Some I'd never heard," Joe made clucking sounds. "From a God-fearing woman no less."

"I'm not surprised, but she'd better not move him an inch."

"I told her it's a bit late with everything and everyone set in stone, so to speak." Joe laughed at his own cleverness.

"I'm not paying this time. I hope she's got a lot of money to foot the bill."

"I told her I suspected that'd be the case. She hung up on me."

Claire felt much too pleased. "Oh well."

"I don't think there's much danger of her moving him anyway even if she could afford it," Joe said. "No love lost for the dear departed mister if you know what I mean."

Claire mulled that over. "I think you're right. In the end she doesn't care. I think she hated that poor man."

"My, my," Joe said.

Claire could imagine Joe kicked back in his chair, his Brooks Brothers clad legs crossed, propped up on his desk.

"That was quite a story you told me about Rob and your father-in-law. The naughty priest. One for the record books. No wonder the old battleaxe is so peeved. Brothers in porn together for eternity behind the marble walls of a crypt. The gift that keeps on giving."

"She had it coming."

Revenge. It's the Lord's work. Claire was happy to do it.

"Did Freddie Eddie tell you they had a little service out there this morning?" Joe said.

"No. Last time I talked to him I was running for my plane."

"Well, as he said himself, it was quite a gig," Joe laughed. "We gave the big guy and his missus a lovely sendoff."

"Who's *we*?" Claire missed them all already.

"Well, there was a crowd I can tell you. I didn't catch all the names, but I do remember two gifted blonde girls named after an ice cream and a very large man named Alex," Joe said. "We bought some gorgeous arrangements, planted a lovely shrub. Freddie Eddie led everyone in a rousing rendition of 'He Stopped Loving Her Today.' I've never heard a more hideous tune for a funeral. Glorious. Lawrence and I cried like babies."

Freddie Eddie warbles George Jones.

"You know his catalog really suffered after he and Tammy called it quits." Claire's tears hit her lap.

"What?"

"Nothing. Wish I could've been there."

"Bad timing for you."

"That's okay. Everything worked out just fine."

"Things have a way of working out the way they're supposed to." Joe sounded weepy. "Rob was a good man."

Who knew what sort any man was?

Rob Rhino might've been the most fucked-up knight in shining armor on record. But he'd been hers. He'd ridden in on his thirteen-inch stallion and saved her.

"I'll miss him every day of my life," she said.

"I hate to point this out, Claire," Joe paused. "I feel bad about the whole thing. I mean besides losing Rob, not to mention your husband, you went to so much trouble, donated all that money. Only one Corrigan is buried there and it isn't Liam."

Claire drove smiling into the long driveway leading to her Mediterranean-style estate. She hung her arm out the car window, felt the southern California sun warm her skin. She pushed in the security code and counted herself lucky.

"Best five million dollars I ever spent."

~~ **The End** ~~

Read on for a preview from:

The Invisible Heiress

Dark, disturbing, deliciously inappropriate.

THANK YOU!

Thank you for reading my book. If you enjoyed it, please take a moment to leave me a four or five-star review; I would be very grateful. It doesn't need to be more than a couple of words, and it makes a huge difference.

CONNECT WITH ME

Email: authorkodonnell@gmail.com
Facebook: facebook.com/kodonnellauthor
Web: http://www.authorkathleenodonnell.com
Twitter: twitter.com/authorkodonnell
Instagram: instagram.com/kathleenthewriter
Goodreads: goodreads.com/author/show/7200820
Pinterest: pinterest.com/authorkodonnell

PREVIEW: THE INVISIBLE HEIRESS

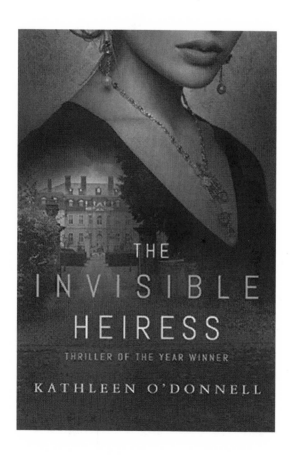

Chapter One

Preston

I don't know which scene satisfied me most—my posh parents waiting in the concrete-walled visitors' room or me deposited in front of them by a uniformed guard.

They sat across from me at the Formica-topped table. My father's face was tight, eyes damp. Seeing him distressed kicked a dent in my smug demeanor, so I stopped looking at him, my eyes ping ponged toward my mother. Despite the sordid circumstances, she shone, her beauty ferocious, perhaps highlighted even more by the dour surroundings. Thick hair still a perfect shade of bombshell blonde, skin pale but flawless despite time's march, the blue of her eyes a perpetual shock.

So entranced I forgot to insult her.

Almost.

"My incarceration poses a real problem for you. Doesn't it, Mother? Harrison Blair doesn't sully herself with the downtrodden."

She shifted backward then forward quick.

"*You're* the problem, Preston. Downtrodden? That's how you think of yourself? You—"

"Harrison, Preston," Dad said. "Please. Let's start right. Preston, your mother and I haven't seen you in so long. Though God knows I've tried. Let's all make a real effort."

He paused, probably to steel himself for objections in stereo. None came.

Dad continued. "You're not incarcerated. You're hospitalized. Your new therapist what's her name." He squeezed his eyes shut like her name had been tattooed inside his lids. "Um, she, Isabel, says you've made some headway, participating in therapy now."

"Might as well," I said.

"That's the spirit. Won't be long until you're back home. You're doing so well considering how difficult, well you're done with that part of the, uh, the rehabilitation."

"You mean the sweating, shaking, puking, padded room part?" I said.

"You're sober. That's all I meant."

My mother's eyes popped like a kidnapper just yanked the hood off her head.

"Sober?" she said. "Doesn't that term apply to alcoholics? Surely they have another term for homicidal, drunken pill add—"

"She's clean, Harrison. That's all that matters."

Dad kept yanking on his tie. I thought he might hang himself with it right before our eyes.

"*All that matters?* Is that your idea of a joke, Todd?"

"Nice dye job, Dad. Only you'd believe those stupid commercials. So natural no one will—"

"*Darling*, stop," he said to Mother. "Of course sobriety's not all but it's a start. I think, *we* think enough time has passed. We should jumpstart our family therapy."

"*We* who?" I said.

The guard took a step forward, disapproving of my elevated tone. My father waved him back.

"Not *Mother*, I'm sure."

"Well, Isabel thought—"

"Just because I'm in the cuckoo's nest doesn't mean I don't have rights," I said. "Isabel shouldn't talk to you at all about me. I'm an adult. She's *my* shrink. Confidentiality too big a word?"

"Shrinks. Therapy," Mother said. "In my day you poured yourself a scotch and got on with it."

"You don't pour yourself anything. You hire that out," I said.

"Family therapy's part of the deal," Dad said. "The judge insisted—"

"*You* own the judge. *We* don't *have* to do anything. Remind him, Mother."

"You should kiss Judge Seward's robed ass," she said, hissing like a stabbed tire. "You'd be someone's bitch if not for his mercy."

"You mean, if not for *your money*. Don't pretend you did shit for me. You did everything for yourself, Mother, to stop the gossip. That's what you do."

With both fists, Dad twisted the tie he'd finally managed to take off.

"Preston, we hoped something good could come out of—"

"Todd, the only good that could possibly come out of this mess is if Preston stays *hospitalized* for the rest of her natural life."

"Harrison, please. We agreed—"

"*You* agreed. With no one but yourself."

"Hate to break up the party but I'm ready to go back to my room," I said more to the guard than my parents.

"Wait, Preston," Dad said, peering around the room, looking for his spine. "It doesn't feel like it now, but here's a chance for you and Mom to, I don't know what, start again, improve your relationship, even a little. That's what we all want, isn't it?"

"Steady on, Dad. The devil comes dressed as everything you want."

I let the guard take my arm, turned in time to see Mom lean her head back enough to dab at the scar under the collar of her ivory silk blouse, a scarlet line cut across her throat, not quite ear to ear, a vicious permanent necklace.

~~~End Preview~~~

Like *The Invisible Heiress?*

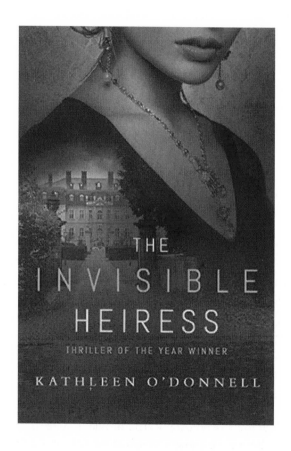

Read it now!

ABOUT THE AUTHOR

Kathleen O'Donnell is a wife, mom, grandmother and a recovering blogger. She currently lives in Nevada with her husband. She is a two time Book of the Year finalist for her debut novel The Last Day for Rob Rhino. You can find short stories and blog posts on her website: www. authorkathleenodonnell.com

CONTENTS

Made in the USA
Middletown, DE
11 October 2020